NO ONE WAS SUPPOSED TO DIE:

An Addictive Page-Turning Thriller

PENNY CROWN FILES
BOOK 1

VICKI HINZE

No One Was Supposed to Die:
An Addicting Page-Turning Thriller
Penny Crown Files, Book 1
Text Copyright © 2024 by Vicki Hinze
All rights reserved.

This is a work of fiction. Names, characters, organizations, places, events, and incidents are either products of the author's imagination or are used fictitiously. Otherwise, any resemblance to actual persons, living or dead, is purely coincidental.

No part of this book may be reproduced in any form or by any electronic or mechanical means, including information storage and retrieval systems, without express written permission from the author, except for the use of brief quotations in a book review.

NO AI TRAINING: Without in any way limiting the author's [and publisher's] exclusive rights under copyright, any use of these publications to "train" generative artificial intelligence (AI) technologies to generate text is expressly prohibited. The author reserves all rights to license uses of these works for generative AI training and development of machine learning language models.

Published by Magnolia Leaf Press, United States of America.

ISBN (Paperback): 978-1-939016-44-7
ISBN (Digital): 978-1-939016-43-0
Cover design by VK Hinze
Cover image: ©JackyBrown/YayImages.com

This book is dedicated to
Kathy Carmichael

*This one is yours.
When I first spoke to you about this story,
your excitement and enthusiasm was
all I had hoped for and much more.
Sorry it's taken so long to
actually get the book written, yet
thrilled and grateful you're here to read it!
Thank you for all the years of friendship,
steadfast support, and patience.
You're an amazing human being, Kathy,
and it is an absolute privilege
to be your friend.
Until we next meet at the rock!*

*Love,
Vicki*

ONE

Alderburg, Lovenia
March 11th

The Chief Councilor stood alone on the tarmac. Acrid smelling fires burning low on the horizon snuffed out one by one, the team reclaiming the protective cover of darkness. Collateral damage from the fierce firefight surrounding the plane had been cleared, leaving the ground free of evidence. Once the remnants of smoke dissipated, it would appear as if the intense battle had never been fought. The distant staccato beats of automatic weapons being fired had ceased, replaced now by spates of exchanges occurring away from the airstrip, far beyond his line of sight.

"Nautical dawn, fifteen minutes," he whispered the warning into his lip mic, watching the ambulances being loaded with human remains from inside the aircraft.

Two of the three ambulances departed without sirens or flashing lights. A team of trusted cleaners streamed down the stairs like ants, their arms filled with debris they tossed into a dump truck, then jumped into the back of their own canvas-topped transport. Both the truck and the transport departed. Traveling without headlights, darkness quickly swallowed them.

Minutes later, a streak of movement caught his eye—the sound of rushing feet, approaching him. Dressed in all black tactical gear, the officer joined him. His hand rested on the grip of his gun, but he didn't draw it. He was expected.

"Sir," the officer said, slightly winded.

"Report, Captain." The Chief Councilor continued his visual sweep, his senses open to any sign their actions had been detected by lingering hostile forces.

"The plane has been cleared, sir. All evidence has been removed and the truck carrying it has arrived for incineration. Completion ETA is seven minutes. Verification is pending. As soon as the last ambulance leaves, the plane will be ready to depart."

Seven minutes. "Civil dawn is in ten minutes." The Chief Councilor worked to keep his voice calm and steady and met with partial success. "Are we going to make it?"

"Yes, sir. The plane has passed inspection and the pilot has boarded. His preflight check is complete."

The Chief Councilor nodded, satisfied the covert operation, Phantom I, was progressing without exposure. That was not only essential. It was critical. "The package?"

The captain passed over a parcel the size of a large mailer. Something so small and yet it irrevocably impacted the future of so many. Chief Councilor tucked it inside his coat and lifted his face to the bitter cold wind. No one appeared at the plane's rear window. Not yet.

The remaining ambulance received the final body bag. Tiny, carried with reverence by one man, not two. *The child...* The Chief Councilor swallowed a knot of tears from his throat, blinked to clear his blurred vision. *Horrendous sacrifice. Horrendous...*

Finally, the attendant slammed the vehicle's rear door and the ambulance departed. He riveted his gaze back to the plane's rear window, waiting, watching, anticipating the signal that all was as it should be. Every nerve in his body sizzled, hyper-alert and threatening to fray. It was the same for all the team. And if they knew the truth, it would be the state of every citizen in Lovenia. Fortunately, most had no idea, and he prayed it would stay that way until after phase II of the mission activated and was executed successfully. Otherwise, the men who fought valiantly here tonight would meet with certain death. There was no other penalty for what would then be deemed treason.

"Sir, was the diversion inside the gates successful?"

The staging, the entire Phantom mission, relied heavily on the fog of war. "Yes," he told the captain. "Six witnesses attested to seeing the bodies firsthand, including me."

"And the coronation of the new king?"

"Is now in progress. The public coronation will be held at his pleasure." Likely once he felt confident his throne was secure. The Chief Councilor's stomach lurched, hollow and empty. The transfer of power. An era ending...

"The last obstacle has cleared, then." The officer exhaled a stuttered breath. "There's every reason to hope for survival."

"Provided this plane gets off the ground." Why wasn't he at the window? Of all roles assumed in this mission, his was by far the most important. If he failed, they all failed. What was taking so long?

The captain paused, tapped a fingertip to his ear, then relayed an update. "Incineration is complete, sir."

The Chief Councilor nodded, glad to hear it verified but not daring to glance away from the window.

The familiar face he awaited suddenly appeared. *Kasper.* He lifted a hand in farewell.

From the ground, the Chief Councilor returned the wave, uncertain if Kasper would see it. *Thank you, God. Thank you.*

"He's there, sir. He's there!" The captain made the sign of the Cross.

"Yes." Tension coiled tighter in the Chief Councilor's body, and he willed the plane to go, prayed for a swift and safe departure. That, not the coronation, was the last obstacle. It would define the success or failure of all that had happened tonight. It would determine who lived and who died.

3

In the annals of history, it would forever define his homeland, his country's future. The monarchy's future.

The plane moved, taxiing from the tarmac, and then lining up for departure. The two men waited silently, breathlessly, watching the 727 roll then sweep down the runway, gather speed, lift off, and fly.

Moments that seemed like lifetimes passed. The plane's lights dimmed, weakened to distant specks, then finally disappeared into the threatening dawn.

"Sir, if that plane doesn't find its way safely…"

The Chief Councilor locked gazes with the officer. "We're all dead." He turned and left the airstrip.

Walking from the terminal to the parking lot, he ordered the tower chief to eliminate the flight from his log, and before he slid into the seat of his car, he received the final verification.

"Sir, Phantom has left our airspace and escorts have engaged. Phase I is complete. Going dark."

The allies had engaged. It was up to them now. With a sigh of relief, the Chief Councilor removed his earpiece and lip mic then squeezed his eyes shut. *Dark.*

Enormous risks had been taken, unparalleled sacrifices had been made, and the night's covert work ordered by His Majesty was done. The secret plans were active, the protections in place. All that could be done to preserve his legacy had been done.

The king is dead. Long live the king.
Until the dead heir is grown…

The long silent wait had begun.

TWO

**United States of America
Kerra, Georgia**

Sixteen years later...

Penny Crown blotted the coffee drip from her black skirt with a tissue. At least, no stain would show. Standing near the media center's hallway door facing the stage, she watched Lucas and Alana interact with reporters and journalists at the tenth press conference they had requested the couple attend in the past two weeks to talk about the international swim meet being hosted next week at Miller University in Kerra, Georgia. It had been an incredibly busy May, and Penny silently rejoiced today was the 29th and this soon would be over.

No one could have predicted such intense interest, and were it the meet alone, the media wouldn't have been intrigued beyond a quick mention. But Lucas, the swim team captain, was tall, blond, and charming, and his fiancé Alana, a team competitor, was a beautiful woman with rich red hair and twinkling green eyes. Together, they made a striking couple, wearing their hearts on their sleeves for all to see and experience.

Early on, Lucas and Alana speaking of their engagement had captivated audiences and started a buzz. Revealing that the demands of the competition required them to delay their engagement celebration fueled it. When the media coverage went national, the couple shared their engagement party was scheduled for the Friday night before the swim meet opened on Monday, and the wedding attendants were all members of the swim team. That captured the nation, and people everywhere got caught up in their romance.

Americans love nothing more than a love story, especially with their sports. The media requests erupted, and social media expanded the frenzy to cyberspace. Now, the couple received congratulations, questions, and marital-bliss advice from all around the world.

As swim team mom, Penny had agreed to escort the couple to these media events—for her daughter, Lisa, also a swim team member, and for Lucas. Though he was four years older than Lisa's seventeen, Lucas and Lisa had been close friends since her first birthday. Penny had developed a tender spot for him right away, and after Lucas's mother had passed away when he was twelve, Penny had felt those bonds strengthen. His father, Kyle Hoff, flatly refused to get within a mile of any media or any camera. After the dogging Penny had experienced, with reporters nipping at her heels non-stop —including an incident where two reporters outed her while she was on a stakeout, destroying her chances of gathering evidence against an unfaithful husband whose wife, Penny's client, sorely needed it—Penny understood Kyle's refusal. But Lucas needed someone in his corner present.

Trying to support herself and Lisa with her fledging investigations business, Penny could ill afford to spare the time, but when asked, sometimes you must make time for those who matter, regardless of the cost. As a widow who knew there would be occasions when Lisa needed her father and he couldn't be there, Penny hoped someone would step up and fill in for him. She prayed for it.

Believing someone would appear for Lisa when needed allowed Penny to sleep at night. How could she refuse Lucas's request for mothering, knowing her daughter would one day be making similar fathering requests?

Some might be able to refuse him anyway. Penny couldn't. Besides, she tilted her head and watched him—*Relaxed. Conversational. Utterly adorable*—she loved seeing Lucas happy. For such a long time after his mother's death, he wore the sadness of grief. It gave Penny hope to see life on the other side of grief. It existed. Lucas found it. She would, too. One day, she would find life on the other side of Mark Crown. One day…

Her phone rang.

Recognizing Lisa's ringtone, Penny stepped out the door and into a quiet hallway then answered. "Hello."

"Mom. Oh, Mom, you're not going to believe it!"

Lisa sounded breathless, excited, elated. Penny's lips curved into a smile. "What it is, honey?"

"I got it. I…got…it!"

From the awe in her voice, she'd conquered something significant to her, yet confusion flooded Penny. "What did you get?"

"Accepted to Oxford *and* to U.G.!" Lisa squealed.

Penny jerked the phone away from her ear. *University of Georgia.* That had been Penny's choice, more for financial reasons than school preference. Lisa had longed for Oxford forever. How in the world would Penny pay for Oxford? Crown Investigations was growing but still in its infancy.

Not now, Penny. Worry later. Celebrate now.

Tamping her concerns, she laughed. "That's wonderful news."

"It's amazing. I can't believe it," Lisa said, then rattled on for a full three minutes.

Penny didn't want to cut her off, but she really did need to get back inside to monitor what was happening. "This is terrific, honey."

"Yeah. Now I just have to decide if I want to take on loans for Oxford or take the U.G. scholarship."

So, Oxford hadn't offered a scholarship at all. Penny's worry returned and doubled. *Maybe a mortgage on the house?* "What are you thinking?"

"I haven't decided yet. I'd love to get through college without loans, but for Oxford… I don't know. I've always wanted Oxford, Mom."

Penny's heart tugged. If Mark were still alive, they'd have easily managed Oxford. But without him…? "I know."

"I'm debating."

And worrying about money. A shaft of resentment streaked through Penny. She nixed it. Everyone worried about something, and pity parties and could-have-been regrets never resolved anything. "Well, isn't it wonderful that you have a choice? I'm so proud of you, Lisa." Penny's mouth went suddenly dry. How she wished Mark could have been here to share this. He would have loved seeing Lisa so happy. "I have to run, honey. The press…"

"No problem. We'll talk more when you get home. Don't tell Lucas. I want to do it myself. John William and I are having lunch to celebrate."

John William. Penny's old boss, art mentor and dear friend. And he already had gotten the news. "Perfect," Penny said. John William had always been there for Lisa and Penny, and he would be until his last breath. Alone himself, he had claimed them as his family years ago. "Love you."

Lisa hung up.

Certainty bit Penny. Her daughter was too excited not to share her news, but she was still miffed about their disagreement that morning. Otherwise, she would have called Penny with the news first and she would have responded with an *I love you, too.*

You're smothering me to death, Mom.

Smothered. Still baffled by that declaration, Penny sighed. How could expressing an interest in her daughter's life be smothering her? Weren't mothers supposed to be interested in their kids? Apparently, not that interested because her grief counselor, Dr. Elizabeth Mason, agreed with Lisa. *Do more for yourself, Penny. Something just for you. Don't live vicariously through Lisa. And don't observe life, participate in it.*

Penny resisted an urge to sigh again. Deeper. Since Mark's

murder, she and Lisa had disagreed far too often. The shock of Mark's death had numbed them both for a time. When the numbness wore off, the disagreements began. There'd been a brief respite from them right after Penny had discovered Mark's killer and he'd been arrested, but the reprieve hadn't lasted long. Right or wrong, fair or not, Lisa felt Penny smothered her and she deeply resented it.

That discovery still horrified Penny. Honestly, it annoyed her, too, though she kept that reaction to herself. Lisa was all Penny had left of Mark, the most important thing in her world. How could Penny not want to do all she could do to support her? She had been totally invested in her happiness, success, and well-being long before Lisa's first breath.

Rites of passage. Dr. Mason's voice echoed through Penny's mind.

Yeah, well. Moms have them, too. The issue that had been a brick wall between them certainly wouldn't be resolved right now. Penny took in a steadying breath, dropped her phone back into her handbag, then opened the media center's door.

Laughter greeted her.

A quick scan of the thirty or so reporters seated in front of the stage proved Lucas had charmed the media. Again. He definitely had a knack for it.

Penny ducked inside and listened.

"Family tradition is for the groom to give the pendant to the bride on their wedding day," he said, responding to a question Penny had missed.

Whose family tradition was it? His or hers? Unsure, Penny listened closely.

"So, Alana, why are you wearing it now?" A familiar female reporter wearing red stopped and gasped. "You haven't eloped!"

"No," Alana said. "The wedding is still the Saturday following the swim meet." She glanced at Lucas, who nodded, then went on. "So much goes into preparing for an international meet. Miller University has been amazing, but the logistics alone, coordinating all the teams, are a nightmare. They just make it look easy." Alana smiled and lifted her shoulder in a dainty shrug. "Lucas knew I was disappointed about delaying our engagement party and so I got the pendant early." She pivoted to smile just for Lucas. "He was being thoughtful, and, well, being Lucas."

He dipped his chin and smiled back at Alana, clearly head over heels in love with her. "Every man who has ever loved a woman knows exactly why," he said. "I want her to be happy—and I want to stay out of the proverbial doghouse."

Laughter echoed off the walls, mingling with a buzz of mumbled agreements. A plethora of camera flashes aimed at the couple had Penny averting her eyes. Gauging by expressions, there wasn't a person in the room who disagreed with Lucas. Not a woman who didn't want that thoughtfulness aimed in her direction or a man who wouldn't move mountains to avoid landing in the doghouse. Mark would have been among them. He couldn't stand Penny being angry with him. *Another winner, Lucas.* He won over the women without alienating the men. Maybe he should have majored in diplomatic relations instead of public administration. *You've definitely got a gift.*

Before nightfall, these photos would be plastered across the globe.

THREE

Alderburg, Lovenia
May 30th @ 0945

The long, silent wait was over.

Seated at his office desk, the former Chief Councilor, demoted to Councilor immediately after the coronation of King Berthold sixteen years ago, studied the photograph of the smiling couple, focusing on her pendant. His mouth burned dry. *Kasper had received the message.*

He swiveled his chair and pulled the trashcan closer to the window, then burned the photograph, letting the ash fall into the can. This was far too significant to risk mere shredding. Smoke lifted and swirled, got drawn by the draft and sucked out the window.

When the last ember turned gray, he cranked the window closed and stared out onto the forest, feeling the burden of history and a spark of hope for the future that filled him with equal parts of excitement and dread.

Finally, Phase II of the Phantom mission had begun.

Soon, old sins would be exposed, new sins committed, and lives irrevocably changed—

A tap sounded at his office door. A stern, "Sir?" followed it, muffled by the heavy wood. The door creaked open.

Recognizing the voice, Councilor turned toward the door and saw Dirk ducking in his head. Dark hair, darker eyes, thick and toned, he projected who he was, an enforcer. "I'm here, Dirk." Hoping this appearance signaled what it should, Councilor added, "Come in."

Dirk strode into the room, his presence commanding. "I regret disturbing you, Sir." His high forehead wrinkled; his entire body tensed. "I've been instructed to inform you His Majesty has reversed your decision. Our swim team will be participating at the international meet in America."

Councilor's objection had been a gamble, but apparently a successful one. "Was a reason cited?" Still predictable, and considering the photograph, perfect timing.

"No, sir." Dirk crossed his arms, pulled himself up to his full six-foot height and lifted his arrogant chin. "But one isn't required, or is it?"

"Of course not." Councilor softened his expression. "We serve at his pleasure."

"I'm glad to hear you say that," Dirk stepped closer to the desk, "because his pleasure is that you accompany the contingent to America."

"Me?" Councilor feigned surprise. "Whatever for? It's a swim meet, not a policy summit."

"His majesty didn't say, but I suspect, in case your diplomatic status becomes helpful in some small way."

Dirk couldn't resist the barb and expected him to challenge. He could; Dirk also had diplomatic status and travelled extensively doing whatever it was he actually did. So far as the council knew, the man executed orders. No explanation beyond that had ever been offered. Enforcer could mean anything, of course. Deliberately vague. But Councilor hadn't survived these sixteen years on the council by disagreeing, especially after the hostilities of the Phantom Operation and being demoted, as expected, from Chief Councilor to Councilor. With Phantom Phase II finally active, this certainly was no time to start. "Very well. When do we depart?"

"Tonight. Be at the airport at eight o'clock."

"Tonight?" That did surprise him. "The swim meet doesn't start until Monday...or am I mistaken?"

"Monday is correct. The team needs a few days to adjust. Time, weather conditions." He lifted a shoulder. "It's hot and humid there."

Councilor nodded. "So, the hosts are prepared to receive us early?"

"We'll be at a private estate until Sunday. The coach required accommodations equipped for training the team."

"Ah, acclimation is a valid concern. Will you be dispatched as well?"

"I will, to ensure the team's safety. Their government has warned us of escalated risks. Terrorism is an issue there, you know. We've been assured they've taken precautions and currently have no credible threats but, naturally, having our own security resources available is prudent."

"I see." Councilor rocked back in his seat. That disclosure removed any doubt. The powers that be had seen the photograph of the couple and the pendant. Dirk would be embedded with the team to assess the threat. Unfortunate, but an interaction had been inevitable. The question never had been *if* but *when*. Later would have been preferable, but the Phantom II crew had prepared, and a contingency plan had been drafted. "Very well then. I'll be ready."

"I'll pass that along." Dirk dropped his crossed arms to his sides. His thick muscles stretched the sleeves of his black shirt tight. "Now, if you'll excuse me, we both have a lot to do to prepare to depart."

"Of course." Councilor nodded, watched Dirk leave, and close the office door.

Councilor waited a long moment, then hastily cleared his desk, and lifted his phone. This conversation, he wanted recorded.

His assistant, Hathaway, answered. "Yes, sir."

"At His Majesty's request, I'm accompanying the swim team to America for an international swim meet. I'll be away nearly two weeks. Clear my calendar and let me know if anything arises that can't wait until I return."

"What date will that be?"

"I'm not sure. Ask Dirk. He has details."

"Of course." His assistant, Hathaway, cleared his throat. "Are you departing now, sir?"

"This evening, but I'm leaving the office straightaway to pack."

"Very good, sir. Have a safe trip."

"Thank you, Hathaway." He, too, knew the significance of this journey. Bent and nearly eighty, Hathaway should have retired years ago, but he remained resolved to continue his work until the final phase of the Phantom mission was complete. Considering how few on the council could be trusted, Councilor relied heavily on his assistant. Thoughtful, Councilor hung up the phone, then left the office.

Half an hour later, he arrived across town and stood in a warehouse storage area he had rented under a fictitious name nearly seventeen years ago. Certain he hadn't been followed and that his mobile phone had been properly disabled for tracking, he moved through the building to a long counter and signed in.

A gray-bearded man with more wrinkles than face ambled over. "Help you?"

"Cubicle 1277, please."

"Got your key?" the man asked. "It's a walk, and no sense making it if you ain't got your key. I don't open cubicles."

"I have my key."

The man nodded, then began moving through the partitions. An empty diplomatic pouch tucked under his arm, Councilor followed, the layout reminding him of large wooden crates placed side by side in long rows.

Listing, possibly due to a bad right knee, the man progressed through the plywood maze and stopped. "This here is it."

Seeing 1277 written in a black marker on the wood, Councilor nodded. "Thank you."

Dismissed, his escort issued a reminder. "Don't forget to stop by the desk and sign out." He didn't wait for a response, just headed back through the maze.

Councilor watched and waited until the ambler disappeared from sight. From the outside, his cubicle looked like every other one in the long row. Raw plywood, no windows, a single door. But on the inside, his was vastly different. Steel reinforced walls, ceiling, and floor. And nothing visible to the naked eye inside except a five-foot high vault. To open, the vault required two keys, a combination, and biometric iris and left thumbprint recognition, all performed in the proper sequence. Any attempt to open the vault without each requirement performed in appropriate order would result in an explosion that would take down the warehouse. Perhaps the one beside it as well.

Councilor began the ritual, held his breath, and completed it. The door opened. Inside he reached for the painting, an 11 x 14 framed, and then to the shelf below it for its specially designed diplomatic pouch. Thanks to his instructions, taking the pouch along would be easy to explain and a non-issue.

He fitted the painting into the pouch, placed the empty pouch into the vault, repeated the ritual in reverse to close the vault door, then backed away and steadied himself. When he stepped outside the cubicle, he would again be under surveillance, and he must appear normal and unaffected. One slip on his part, and the entire Phantom mission could unravel.

Years of sacrifices by the Phantom crew would be wasted and, to a man, they would all be executed. Knowing the tight-fist and intolerant mindset of those in power determined to retain power and squelch even a hint of discontent, the crews' families too would be murdered.

That could not happen on his watch.

Councilor straightened his shoulders, tucked the pouch under his arm and then opened the outer door and stepped into the empty hallway. Fluidly, he shut then locked the door behind him. If the powers that be should connect the dots and elect to examine the cubicle, they'd find nothing. If by some miracle they managed to open the vault without exploding the building—zero odds, but if they should—they would find an empty pouch and nothing more.

He hoped to live to see the Phantom mission completed, but he only had to live long enough to deliver the painting. If he could survive to do that, he'd die a satisfied man who had upheld his oath and fulfilled his promise. His loyalty and devotion would eternally remain intact.

Unfortunately, that essential delivery posed high risks and, success or failure, lethal consequences. For him and many others, including a nation of subjects.

It would unleash a tempest.

Unleash the beast.

And currently that beast wore the stolen crown…

FOUR

Kerra, Georgia
June 2nd @ 2000

Over two hundred people had signed the guestbook at Lucas and Alana's engagement party. Many had written their good wishes, including several members of the press. Penny Crown stood at the peach-draped table and entered her own hopes for the couple and their marriage. She glanced from the book to their favorite engagement photo framed in gold and placed beside the arrangement of peach roses and leafy greenery. They looked so happy; Lucas with his arm around Alana's shoulder, hers tucked under his arm with her head bent to the cay in his neck. Penny had felt that way once. Joyful and full of hopes and dreams of a bright future. Stirred memories of Mark tempted her to fall into them, to—

"Are you done, Mom?" Lisa claimed Penny's attention.

She glanced over at her daughter. Tonight, there was nothing on display of the child Lisa had been. She stood two-inches taller than Penny, five-seven in bare feet, and was dressed in a subdued pastel green dress. Mark would have looked at her and winked, called her his princess, and his pride in the woman she'd become would be evident in every way. Penny swallowed hard.

"There you two are." John William Archer joined them, not a silver hair out of place or an unintentional crease in his impeccable navy suit. "I've spent half an hour searching through this gaggle of people for you."

Penny smiled. The near recluse, who enjoyed being alone in his museum with his artifacts more than with people, had arrived not ten minutes ago; she'd watched him enter. "Sorry. I was just signing the guest book."

Lisa planted a kiss to John William's cheek. He flushed—he always flushed—and Lisa laughed as she always laughed. "Nice suit."

Had Lisa ever seen John William, a sixtyish meticulous dresser, not in a suit, including at backyard picnics? Since high school, Penny never recalled a time, which made her smile. One of his little idiosyncrasies. They were common in geniuses, and John William was the poster boy for geniuses when it came to anything about art, antiquities, and historical documents.

Lisa and John William danced, and Penny meandered through the crowded tables to an area where the Coach had Lucas and Alana and what would be their wedding attendants gathered, posing for pictures. From the camera flashes and laughter, the media had again engaged.

She visually panned the crowd, saw far too many stranger's faces, and moved closer to watch the photos being taken. Lucas spotted her and motioned. "Come, Mrs. Crown."

The crowd parted and Penny stepped toward him. "Do you need something?"

Lucas smiled. "We want a photo of the three of us—you, Alana, and me. Would that be all right?"

He didn't feel smothered by her mothering. "Of course." Alana stood on Lucas's right and Penny moved to his left. The camera-flashes blinded her.

"Dip your chin and blink fast," Alana whispered. "It helps."

Penny glanced over at her. Tall and slender, her hair up in an elegant sweep, her diaphanous peach dress softly draping her body, Alana was a vision. The perfect blend of strength and beauty and grace. Penny smiled. "Thanks."

The pendant dangling from Alana's neck caught Penny's eye. She'd never seen it closeup. Stone arches backlit in a forest, a Weimaraner standing guard, and two red stones—rubies or garnets, though they didn't really look like either—in an oval-shaped pendant trimmed in gold. Something pricked at her memory. Familiar. She'd seen that pendant before. Where?

"Mom?" Lisa stepped to her side. "John William says he's leaving in ten minutes. If you want your dance with him, now is the time."

"The dance after his is mine," Lucas told her.

"I look forward to it, Lucas." Penny smiled then joined John William on the dance floor.

"Even for you, my dear girl, I cannot abide this infernal chaos much longer."

"You really do need to get out more, John William." Penny stepped into his arms. "Aren't you the one who insisted I go to the dances at school? That I participate in the spirit rallies? You made me do all kinds of group activities."

"I encouraged you," he insisted. "I did not make you. I doubt anyone has ever made you do anything you did not want to do."

"You shamed me into it," she insisted. "Be honest."

He sniffed. "I admit that a small amount of shaming was involved, but my intentions were for the most honorable of reasons."

Penny followed his steps smoothly and looked over at him. "What were they?"

His stern expression softened and the look in his eyes turned paternal, tender. "I did not want you to be like me."

A near recluse. Her heart squeezed and her eyes burned. "You're one of the best, kindest men I've ever known in my life." She'd known it the first time she'd seen him, when at sixteen she'd walked into his art museum and asked if he had anything she could do. He'd hired her to dust. She'd recognized the trust he had placed in her, permitting her to touch his art. Later, on learning of his love for it and that it was all he had in life, she fully grasped the value of his gift of trust to her, and she'd worked hard to assure he never regretted it. "It would be the highest honor to be like you. The highest."

A soft smile curved his lip. "Spoken like the true daughter of my heart."

The music stopped. Lucas appeared. "My turn."

John William nodded and stepped away. Lucas swept Penny into his arms. "I just wanted to thank you for helping us plan all this."

"My pleasure," Penny smiled. "You both seem to be having a good time."

"We are." He shrugged. "You've given up a lot to help us. I mean, you can't do much of your own work if you're with us all the time."

True. She was getting as much done as possible around her other commitments, but that hadn't left much time for anything else. "Your engagement is a once in a lifetime thing. Seeing you and Alana happy and doing what I can to help you means a lot to me, Lucas."

He went serious. "You've always done everything I've ever asked you to do. From school costumes when I was little, to answering questions about women and resolving squabbles with friends. You've been there for me like a mom would be." He shrugged a shoulder, his expression tender. "I was just one of Lisa's friends, but after my mom died, you made sure I never felt lost." The skin between his brows wrinkled. "Why did you do that?"

Penny adjusted her step to avoid an elbow in the back by an enthusiastic couple dancing near them. "At first, because you and Lisa were friends. But then when your mom got sick—"

His expression sobered. "You promised her you'd watch over me like a second mother, didn't you?"

He called the question, but he already knew the answer; the truth burned in his eyes. "I did," Penny said. "But even if I hadn't promised, I would have watched over you."

Lucas tilted his head. "Why?"

"Because you are the son of my heart, and you needed me." Clearly, not an answer he expected. Penny let out a low laugh.

"I've often felt like a son to you, but I couldn't make myself ask. I think I was afraid of your answer."

"You knew my answer, Lucas. You've always known."

"I guess I did, but I didn't want to be wrong."

He feared more grief. Understanding that too well, Penny glanced at Lisa, chatting with Alana. "Your mother would be proud of the man you've become. And so am I."

"Thank you." He squeezed her hand, then brushed her cheek with a butterfly kiss. "I'm grateful, Mrs. Crown. You're the best." He flashed her a smile then returned to Alana and Lisa.

Penny watched him a long moment, her heart full. At least she'd done something right with him. Now if she could find her way with Lisa. Why did everything with her seem so much harder?

"It was very kind of you to mention his mother, Mrs. Crown."

Penny turned to see Lucas's father, Kyle Hoff, standing behind her. Short gray hair, full beard, thick black-framed glasses he always seemed to hide behind. For as well as she knew Lucas, his father remained mysterious and aloof. Not with Lucas. But with everyone else, including Penny.

Gazing at the guests, he halted, then looked right at her. "I too want to thank you for all you've done for my late wife and my son."

His wife, Grace, had been gone many years. How odd that he wouldn't say a word until now. But maybe it wasn't odd. His only son was about to be married. He'd devoted his life to Lucas and now he faced an empty nest and a major transition in his own life. Those significant changes made people emotional. "It's been a privilege to help in small ways."

"After she became ill, my wife told Lucas he could trust you with anything. And Lisa has been a good friend to Lucas her entire life. I don't know how well he would have coped without either of you or Mr. Crown."

"That's been mutual." Lucas had been a rock for Lisa when Mark died. In quiet and unassuming ways. Long after friends and others returned to their own lives, he continued to show them support. He and John William.

"Please accept my gratitude for helping him and Alana plan this event," Mr. Hoff said. "I would have made a mess of things."

"You're welcome, but I did very little. Alana knew exactly what she wanted."

"She's a good woman." A flicker of uncertainty and then regret washed across his face. It was gone so quickly, Penny wondered. Had she imagined it? "Alana loves your son." Guests were departing. Penny motioned to Lisa. "A parent can hope or ask for little more."

His gaze again wandered. "Ah, the exodus has begun." He turned to Penny. "I don't wish to offend you in any way, but I would like to compensate you for all the time you've spent assisting—"

"No need," Penny interrupted. "I've been compensated."

"Really?" He retreated behind his glasses and the guarded look returned to his eyes.

"Mmm, yes." She placed her glass on a passing waiter's tray. "Very well, actually."

"Lucas didn't mention this to me." Mr. Hoff appeared perplexed.

"Paid in full."

"May I ask by whom?"

"Lucas." Penny smiled. "A lovely dance and a kiss on the cheek."

Mr. Hoff treated her to a rare smile that transformed his face. "Spoken like a true second mother."

Lisa joined them. "Everyone's going, Mom. We need to get to the valet or we'll be waiting an hour for the car."

"Good night, Mr. Hoff."

"Good night, Mrs. Crown." Thoughtful, he nodded toward her and then Lisa.

A slow shiver crept up Penny's spine. Kyle Hoff never had been anything but polite. So why did talking with him set every nerve in her body on alert? And why did her instincts scream he was a man with a lot to hide?

NO ONE WAS SUPPOSED TO DIE:

"Lucas." Alana stopped short on the crowded sidewalk outside the hotel. "I forgot my wrap." She turned to go back inside, confident it would be where she'd left it at the engagement party.

"No, you stay in line," he said, reversing his steps. "I'll get it."

Penny and Lisa stood on the walk surrounded by the thick crowd. The valets delivered car upon car, working furiously, and guests weren't lingering at getting in and pulling away as quickly as possible. Everyone seemed eager to end a long day and pleasant night.

"It'll be at least another twenty minutes before we get to the front of the line," Lisa whispered. "I'm tempted to walk down the block and hail a taxi."

"You can if you like, but I need my car first thing in the morning." Penny glimpsed at Alana, standing at the front of the line.

A strange man with a high forehead and dark hair approached her and said something. Her hand went to her neck. She no longer wore the pendant. Had she lost it?

Large and muscular, he seemed doubtful and annoyed. Now, Alana did, too. Why were they arguing?

A black sedan pulled to the curb. The driver stayed inside. It wasn't Lucas or Alana's car. The man grabbed Alana's upper arm and jerked her. Terror flashed across her face, galvanized Penny. "Hey, stop that!" Penny shouted. "Let go of her right now!"

The man dropped any pretense, shoved Alana into the backseat of the sedan. Penny screamed. "Somebody stop him. Stop that car!"

People gasped and gawked, but none moved. Trapped in the crush, Penny couldn't shove her way to the car; she could barely move. She raised her phone above the heads of the crowd, videoed the man diving into the backseat and slamming the door. She aimed for the license plate, praying she'd captured it, and watched helplessly as the car pulled away.

People on the sidewalk began to scatter. A guest with the press began taking photographs.

Lisa tugged at Penny's arm. "Mom, what are you doing? What's wrong with you?"

"Call 911."

Lisa faced her mother. "Why?"

"Do as I ask, Lisa," Penny shouted. "Dial the phone and hand it to me!"

Minutes later, Lucas came back outside, carrying Alana's wrap. He scanned the crowd, looking for her and spotted Penny. She waved him over.

"Where's Alana?" he asked.

Penny looked him right in the eye and spoke distinctly. "Lisa's on the phone with the police now. They're on the way here. Lucas, it breaks my heart to tell you this."

"Tell me what, Mrs. Crown?" He frowned. "What is wrong?"

"Alana has been kidnapped."

FIVE

June 3rd @ 0115

The crowd had dwindled significantly. Detective Jay Voigt crossed the street and headed Penny's way. He was too far away to recognize his face, but there was no mistaking his gait or the ill-fitting suit that looked as if he'd worn or slept in it for a couple days. Typical Jay. Just this side of fifty and slovenly, but his detective skills always had been finely honed and superb. Mark had known Jay well, and more importantly, he'd trusted Jay.

Relieved he had the case, Penny took a couple deep breaths. Adrenaline still blasted through her. She had to get it to ease down.

"Penny." Jay extended a hand. "Good to see you, though I wish for better circumstances."

"Thanks, Jay."

"You're my point of contact, so I take it you know Alana."

Penny nodded. "A man pulled her into a black sedan. I couldn't get to her to stop him, but I got photos." She lifted her phone and displayed a shot of the abductor, one of the vehicle, and the best one of the tag. "Sorry it's blurred. I was unsteady, stretching to get above the crowd."

"Kudos on your quick thinking," Jay said. "People don't typically think of photos until it's too late to take them." He studied the photographs on her phone. "These are great. The guys should be able to work with the tag."

"What about the abductor?" she asked. "It's pretty grainy."

"They'll try." Jay's dark eyes praised her. "Well done, Penny." He motioned to the photos.

"I worked with Mark a long time, and with my father before him. He was an FBI agent and a bit paranoid."

"Now, I hear, you're a private investigator in your own right." Jay guided her aside. "You've earned it. Impressive job solving Mark's case."

"Necessity breeds invention." Realizing that sounded critical of the police's efforts to solve the murder of one of their own, she added, "I'm not bound by the same restrictions and protocols you guys are. In his case, that helped."

"I'm glad, and I'm very glad your investigation didn't get you killed."

"To find the truth, risks had to be taken."

"I understand." Admiration had him nodding. "So, who are the players in this case?"

"I didn't recognize the abductor." She gave him a brief description. "With all the people around, I was in a crush and a fair distance away. I couldn't get a crystal-clear look at him, but nothing I did see triggered any memory. He was a stranger to me. None of the others I asked recognized his photo."

"How many did you ask?"

"All of them I could find." Penny couldn't stave off a sigh. "Those here, and via text with those I knew who had already departed."

"Any idea why this stranger would kidnap her?"

"Not yet."

Jay rubbed his chin, rustling a stubble of beard. "Perhaps due to all the press she and Lucas have been receiving?"

"Maybe." Penny frowned. "That does often attract some who are less than stable."

"But...?"

"It's probably nothing, but Lucas gave Alana a pendant that I've seen somewhere, at some time, though I can't recall where. Anyway, this abductor was surprised, I think, that she wasn't wearing it tonight. It was just a feeling, you know, but they were arguing, and she kept tapping herself where it would have rested." Penny demonstrated, fingertips to upper chest.

"What's special about this pendant?"

"It's been passed through generations by Lucas's family. Groom to bride on their wedding day. Lucas broke the pattern giving it to Alana early because of the wedding delays due to the swim meet." Penny shrugged. "The pendant may not be related at all, though she was wearing it earlier tonight at the engagement party."

"But not when she was abducted?" Jay asked.

"No." Penny verified it. "Like I said, I got this feeling, watching them argue. I'm positive she didn't have it on when she was abducted."

Jay nodded. "Thanks, Penny. Stick around, okay? You and Lisa. I'm going to go talk with Lucas and—who is the man sitting with him?"

Penny glanced over. Poor lamb was beside himself. "That's Lucas's father, Kyle Hoff." She swallowed hard. "I'll introduce you, if you like."

"That could be helpful. First, would you send me the photos?" He gave her an email address. When he received them, he forwarded them on to someone. "We need to get word out on the vehicle as soon as possible."

Lisa stood talking to two other swim team members. One was crying. Lisa had that set in her jaw she'd had since the cradle when she was furious. She rarely had seemed scared, but often had appeared angry. Penny suspected that was a trait she'd inherited from Mark. He had been the same way.

"Ready?" Jay asked.

Penny nodded, and they approached Lucas and Kyle. They were sitting on a bench to the right of the main entrance. Lucas sat hunched over, his head clasped in his hands. Penny touched his shoulder and offered a few words of comfort, then introduced him and his father to Jay Voigt, vouching for him as an excellent detective and a friend of Mark's. That endorsement carried weight with Lucas. He'd always respected, admired, and trusted Mark. Those feelings had been mutual.

Jay told Lucas that officers were already looking for the vehicle and abductor. He asked questions and scribbled down detailed answers in a pocket-sized notebook. Kyle silently watched but offered nothing to the responses, which Penny supposed was normal. Lucas knew Alana best.

Penny listened to him give background information on his fiancé, and openly answer everything he was asked. Unfortunately, after extensive questioning, Lucas didn't appear to know anything he hadn't heard from others here about the abductor or any reason anyone would abduct Alana.

Jay sent Penny a curious look about Kyle. His silence wasn't typical for a parent. Honestly, it made Penny oddly uncomfortable, too. But this was typical behavior for Kyle Hoff.

Concluding his initial questioning, Jay asked Lucas and his father to stay put for a few more minutes, then he backed up a couple steps and phoned someone. Penny couldn't hear the conversation, but Jay finished his call and then questioned all those guests an officer had held over because they'd been physically closest to Alana and the abductor when he'd jerked her into the vehicle.

"It happened so fast," one woman said. "The car sped off before we could do anything."

"Sit here, Mrs. Crown." Lucas scooted to the end of the bench and Penny sat down between Lucas and his father.

"Try to stay calm," she told Lucas. "Jay Voigt is very good at his job. You can bet they're doing all they can to find Alana."

About forty minutes later, Jay returned. "Thank you for waiting. I'm sorry it took so long." He pivoted, his shoe scraping against the concrete. "Lucas, may I ask why Alana's parents aren't here?"

"We told everyone they couldn't get back in time." Visibly shaking now, he went on. "They've been in Europe for nearly a year on business, and they're at a critical juncture in negotiations on a major project, but they'll be back for the wedding." Lucas flushed.

Lucas was lying. By omission, but lying, and he hadn't said a word about Alana's parents to Penny.

"You said that's what you told people," Jay said. "What is the truth? Did they disapprove of the wedding?"

"No. No, nothing like that." Lucas shot Penny an apologetic look. "They died in a freak avalanche in Sweden last winter." He shifted to look at Penny. "I'm sorry I didn't tell you. Alana was naturally very upset, and she feared talking about it with everything else would be too much. They were close, and she just wanted time to grieve in her own way."

"I understand," Penny said, noting Kyle hadn't been surprised by the news. "Grief is a personal thing, and everyone must cope with it in the way that works best for them." Surely that always included grieving without the press.

"Thank you. Alana appreciates your understanding, too. It's meant a lot to her, the way you've stepped in to help us with all this media and the party and everything."

Penny nodded.

Apparently satisfied with Lucas's explanation, Jay closed his notebook and shoved it into his suit pocket. "You can all go home now. We'll keep you advised of any developments."

Penny stood up. So did Lucas and Kyle.

"I'm going to search for Alana." Lucas swiped a hand through his hair.

"Don't. I have officers doing that." Jay focused on Lucas. "You need to go home. A team of agents will be arriving shortly to prepare."

"Prepare for what?" Kyle asked.

Jay softened his tone. "In case the kidnapper calls."

Except for Lisa, Kyle had never been a fan of having outsiders in his home, but he uttered not a word. Simply nodded.

"We will be waiting," Lucas said.

He'd agreed to go home. Penny hadn't been at all sure he would. Relieved, she and Jay watched Lucas and Kyle depart.

"His father seems a bit of an odd duck," Jay whispered.

"He's a good man, and acting perfectly normal—for him." Penny met Jay's gaze. "Kyle has always been a little bit of an odd duck, but Lucas and he are extremely close, and he loves the man to distraction."

"That tells you he's a good man?"

"It does." Penny nodded to add weight to her claim. "Lucas is discerning."

"Discerning?"

"Wise beyond his years and his judgment is rock solid."

SIX

June 3rd @ 0300

Shortly after 3:00 a.m. Penny settled into bed, comforted by the soft glow of a nightlight she'd begun using after Mark's death. She'd needed something to break the all-consuming darkness where the hours dragged by and the clock ticking in the hallway triggered memories that descended on her like tempest floods.

Tonight, memories of Mark stepped aside and worries about Alana and what could be happening to her moved front and center. Guilt seeped into Penny and settled. How had she not picked up on Alana's parents' deaths? How had she not gotten to Alana and stopped the abductor?

No matter how many times she replayed events in her mind, the bottom line was she had failed to protect Alana. If only she had been able to break through the crowd and get to Alana before he shoved her into the sedan.

A thought even more horrible snaked into Penny. What if the abductor wasn't a fame-seeker? What if Alana wasn't his only target? He could be after more team members—maybe after Lisa or Lucas.

Penny's heart beat hard and fast. Even deep breathing and the calming scent of lavender on her pillowslip didn't calm her. If she ever wanted to get to sleep, she had to go check on Lisa.

Resolved, Penny tossed back the covers and got out of bed. When she left her bedroom, seeing Lisa seated at the kitchen's breakfast bar surprised her. "You okay?"

"Is anyone?" Lisa brushed her hair back from her face, then slid a glance at Penny. "Sorry, Mom. I've been wracking my brain on who that goon was that snatched Alana."

Penny poured herself half-a-glass of milk and slid onto a barstool across from Lisa. "Did you come up with anyone?"

"No." Lisa muttered her frustration. "Neither has anyone else."

She'd been talking or texting with a group of friends.

"She had no enemies. Everyone loves Alana."

Penny had to tread carefully. "What about those jealous of her?" Alana was bright and beautiful and talented, and she'd captured the heart of the campus darling. Her family had been well off, so presumably now Alana was…

"Half the school is jealous of her. She's got it all. But there's no one who would or could pull off kidnapping her." Lisa folded her elbow on the granite countertop and dropped her chin into her upturned hand. "Though she has been tense lately."

"Do you know what was troubling her?" Penny sipped from her glass. No doubt losing her parents contributed, especially with the wedding coming. They had to be on her mind. Their absence, that is, at this significant event in her life.

"I asked. She said it was nothing. Just meeting herself coming and going," Lisa said. "Between practice, classes, the media events and the wedding, she was running all the time." Lisa sent her mom a reprimanding glance. "She did say her mother insisted on going all out on the wedding. It's not what Alana wanted." Lisa lowered her gaze. "I guess after her parents died, she felt she had to go all out for her mother."

She probably did. Penny could empathize with that. "I'm sorry to hear that about the wedding, but I do understand it." Penny paused then added, "As for the rest, it has been a crazy couple of weeks."

"Without the meet and extra practices, it would have been crazy. With them, it's been insane."

"I don't want to add to the upset, but do any of you think that the rest of the team or anyone else on it specifically could be at risk?"

"We've talked about it," she said. "No one has noticed anyone odd hanging around anywhere or anything. Our best guess is it's some nutjob who's seen her on TV or something."

"It might be." Penny said and meant it, but she couldn't get that man's face out of her mind. The way he kept glaring at Alana's chest. He seemed angry and bitter, as if he knew she was lying to him.

"When they were arguing, did you notice how Alana kept hitting her chest with her hand?" Lisa asked. "There was nothing there. One of my friends said that's common body language when you're stunned—to do that." Lisa tapped her chest with her hand. "She didn't think anything of it, but it seemed strange to me."

"They were arguing," Penny said. "Did anyone hear about what?"

"Nothing they could make out. Just raised voices. But none of them were that close."

"Alana wasn't wearing the pendant when she was abducted. But she had it on earlier. Do you know what happened to it?"

"Not a clue." Lisa thought a second. "If anyone knows, it'd be Lucas. In his family, that pendant is a really big deal." Lisa sighed and stood up. "I'm going to bed. Practice is going to come early."

"What time is it?" Penny really should be at the practice. The kids would still be rattled. Did she dare to hope Alana would be found and returned safely by then?

Waiting, worrying, hoping reminded her so much of what had happened with Mark. She didn't know if she had it in her to go through that trauma again so soon.

"Ten. The coach sent out an email to not be late, regardless of tonight's events. He's worried about Alana's abduction, but he's also worried about the impact of it on the meet."

Fragile or not, Penny had to go for the kids. "I suppose so." A week and it would be two years since Mark died, but it seemed like yesterday... especially tonight.

"Try to rest, Mom." Lisa studied her with a softness not seen in her eyes for a long time. "You look tired."

"Headed to bed in just a minute." Penny nodded. "Sweet dreams."

Lisa left the kitchen and walked down the hallway. When her bedroom door softly closed, Penny moved to her laptop and fired off an email to the coach to keep an eye out tomorrow. There was nothing to say that the other team members could be in jeopardy, but there was no evidence they weren't, either. Until they found out why Alana had been abducted, they must consider everyone at risk.

Worried about Alana and about Lucas, Penny fought to resist the urge to phone him for any update or just to see how he was doing. It was the middle of the night, and if by some miracle he had dozed off, she didn't want to wake him. His father was there. He would talk to Lucas, offer what comfort he could.

Kyle had lost his wife, Grace, just as Penny had lost Mark—though to illness, not murder. He understood the pain of loss and the worry of uncertainty. Penny's uncertainty had been all-consuming, wondering if Mark was dead or alive and then wondering who had killed him. Needing the answer to that question and understanding the slow progress by police hamstrung in legalities, policies, and procedures had driven Penny to seek the killer on her own. She had been terrified the entire time but determined. With hard evidence, she'd revealed his killer and lived to report it. She'd seen him arrested and convicted. That too had been a miracle.

Penny prayed for another miracle, that Alana would return safely and unharmed. Poor Lucas had grieved the loss of his mother so hard. He just couldn't have to face the loss of Alana. He was so young to have to deal with that kind of merciless trauma at all, much less twice.

Too agitated to sleep, Penny lifted a copy of *The Atlanta Journal* she'd kept for the photos of Lucas and Alana. In it, she spotted a photo of Alana wearing the pendant. Again, that familiar feeling seeped into Penny. Where had she seen it?

Moving back to the laptop, she ran a quick Internet search that yielded nothing on the unique piece of jewelry. She checked the photos snapped at the abduction. Alana definitely didn't have the pendant on in those photos. She had worn it during the party. So where had it gone?

Penny rubbed at her temple. Could the pendant have been the reason Alana had been abducted? Being a family heirloom made that doubtful in Lucas's case, but Penny needed to know more about that pendant. And where it was now. If only she could recall where she'd seen it. Was her mind tricking her into believing she'd seen it when perhaps she'd seen something similar? She considered that possibility but didn't think so. Why was the piece so familiar to her? It was odd and an antique...

John William. She resolved to go to his art museum first thing in the morning, before the practice. John William had forgotten more about art, antiquities, and historical documents than most curators ever knew. If anyone could help her find more information on that pendant, it would be him.

SEVEN

June 3rd @ 0830

Penny checked her watch to see if she should use the residence or museum entrance. Eight-thirty. John William would already be in the museum. She walked over the stone walkway then tapped on the heavy wooden door of the Kerra Museum and Cultural Center, certain before he answered John William would view her on the security monitor.

The door swung wide. "Good morning, Penny. What an unexpected pleasure."

He didn't know about Alana. If he had known, he would be peppering her with questions and not offering Penny a cheerful good morning. "Good morning. I'm sorry to bother you so early, John William," she said, following him through the elaborate entry into his office. His stone-gray suit jacket hung on the back of his chair. He wore a light grey sweater to ward off the chill always present in the museum. "Are you well?" Seeing him not in his suit wasn't just odd, it only happened when he was ill, and no one else was around to see him.

"I'm fine. Just slow moving this morning." He ushered her to a seat in his office and poured her a cup of tea, then refreshed his own cup. "The blame for that exhaustion sits squarely on the shoulders of your daughter."

"Lisa? I'm so sorry. What did she do?" Penny sat down in her favorite antique chair across the desk.

"Absolutely nothing wrong." He ruffled his gray hair. "I am still excited from our celebratory lunch. Before she decides between University of Georgia and Oxford, I want to speak to you about her education."

He was tiptoeing with Penny. Going all the way back to the beginning, the only time John William tiptoed was when he had already decided on something and was unsure of Penny's reaction. He'd been that way since she was sixteen and boldly walked in off the street and asked him for a job. "She hasn't yet decided."

"The girl has longed for Oxford her whole life," John William said, lifting his teacup. "I guess we might as well discuss this now." He set his cup on its saucer. "Bluntly put, I intend to pay her tuition and expenses."

Penny hadn't seen that coming. "I can't let you do that, John William."

He set his jaw. "I do not see why not. I have always considered Lisa my granddaughter, and you, my daughter. You two are the only family I have left now that Mark has passed. If I want to send Lisa to Oxford or to university, I do not see one valid reason I cannot, provided that going is her choice."

"It's a very generous offer, and means more than I can say, but I can't let you do it," Penny said, pressing her hand atop his blue-veined one. "Everyone wants something from you. It's always been that way. We love you because you're you, not for what you can do for us. I can't be like they are toward you, John William. I won't. You're too important to me."

His skin wrinkled and blue eyes softened. "I love you, too, my dear girl. Lisa, also, of course." He paused, sipped from his cup. "May I just remind you that you have always been at my beck and call to help me. Mark and Lisa have, too. Am I not allowed to be helpful to you or to her?"

"You do help us in all kinds of ways. Especially since Mark's passing."

"No, Penny." He looked her right in the eye. "I either am or am not a member of your family. If I am, then I should be free to assist where I wish or see it is needed. If I am not, then I need to know it."

"Of course, you are family. You always have been. You know that."

"Very good." He nodded that it was settled. "We will speak of this again, after Lisa makes her decision. If she wants Oxford enough to go into debt for it, then I will handle it." He paused, then looked her right in the eyes. "You must understand, my dear. I fully intend to do this. I asked your permission as a courtesy."

"But John William—"

"No, Penny." He lifted a staying hand. "I could never mistake the love you and Lisa show me for being used. We must let Lisa decide what she wants, and then go from there."

Tears threatened Penny. "I'm...overwhelmed."

"It shall pass." He refilled her teacup. "So what has you upset enough to be here so early this morning?"

"I'm surprised you haven't yet heard," she said. Reaching across the table, she clasped his hand, aware her own was trembling. "It's about Alana." She let him see the worry in her eyes. "She was abducted after the engagement party last night."

His gray eyebrows shot up on his forehead. "Abducted!"

Penny nodded.

"Why?" He looked befuddled.

"We don't know yet." Penny steeled herself, then went on to brief John William about the incident.

"How dreadful." His forehead wrinkled. "How is Lucas taking this?"

"I spoke to him on my way here this morning. He's struggling, of course. The police are with him in case the abductor attempts to make contact."

John William frowned. "Who is handling the case?"

"Jay Voigt."

"That eases my mind a bit. He's a good man. Mark had enormous respect for Jay."

"Yes, he did."

"It was mutual, I am sure."

"I agree."

"I take it they have not heard anything, or you would have said."

"I would have. The vehicle hasn't been located, though they're looking for it, and there's been no word yet from the abductor."

"We must pray that this resolves quickly, and Alana will return to our Lucas unscathed."

"Definitely. He's upset at being stuck at home with the police when he feels he should be searching for her."

"Of course. But he must stay put in case the abductor makes contact."

"Exactly." Grateful for that, for Lucas's sake, Penny sipped from her teacup. If she wasn't mistaken, it was an 18th century Meissen from Germany. Porcelain. The idea of Lucas confronting the abductors terrified Penny.

"So, you came here to tell me this about Alana?"

Penny swallowed a sip of tea. "Actually, no. I thought you would already know. But my reason is related." She went on to tell John William about the pendant, the tradition of it in Lucas's family, and then about Lucas giving it to Alana early and why. Lastly, she told him the pendant seemed familiar to her. She was convinced she'd seen it somewhere, at some time, but couldn't recall where. "Most likely, my familiarity would be through you, so I hope you can recall."

"Tell me what you do know about it."

She described the pendant to him in detail and showed him a photograph that didn't do it justice. "It's much more delicate and gorgeous than in the photo."

He stiffened in his chair. "I would like to consult a fellow expert before commenting." His face was uncommonly expressionless. "I will get back with you as soon as I am confident of the facts."

"Thank you, John William." She smiled at him. He knew something.

"Of course, my dear." He glanced at the gold clock on his desk. "Do you not see Dr. Mason this morning?"

"Normally, I do." Grief therapy sessions were helping, but Penny had considered skipping out today. "I think I'm needed more at the swim practice. The kids are in a lather about Alana."

"Reasonable reaction, but no. You must go see Dr. Mason. You will be in a better place to help the children if you are more settled. I know you, Penny Crown, and I know you must have been wickedly upset since this abduction. It affects Lucas, so of course you would be. Anyone would, much less his surrogate mother. I will give him a call straightaway."

"Practice is at ten."

"You have plenty of time then, especially if you leave now." John William stood and circled his desk, wrapped a fatherly arm around her shoulder. "Be strong, my dear. And cautious."

Penny hugged him back. "I will." She smiled. "About the pendant…"

"Not a word until after I have consulted Nicholas. I will phone you."

"Thank you." He did recognize the pendant; Penny was certain of it. But until he was convinced beyond any doubt, John William wouldn't utter a word. He'd always been cautious with his credibility and his reputation, and he'd always consulted Nicholas Ryan when there was an oddity that needed verification or confirmation. Penny had never met Nicholas, but John William trusted him implicitly and he guarded his mysterious source in ways that aroused curiosity —not that John William fed or even addressed it. He never had. Penny wondered why, but just as John William trusted Nicholas, Penny trusted John William. No doubt, he had his reasons…

"Now, you go straight to Dr. Mason's office. Promise me." John William gave her a stern look.

"Oh, all right. I'm going." Penny flushed guiltily. She had decided to skip it, but he knew her too well. "I promise."

EIGHT

June 3rd @ 0900

Penny parked at Dr. Liz Mason's office, hoping she wasn't running behind in her schedule this morning. She was young and studious, and if a patient needed a few more minutes, which could be an hour, Dr. Mason provided it. That there were other patients waiting didn't weigh much in her thinking. The saving grace about that was if you needed more time, she'd provide it for you, too. But today, Penny didn't have the time to spare. She needed to be at practice for the kids.

Penny walked into the fashionable office, which was too modern and minimal for her tastes, and greeted the receptionist. "Hi, Sam."

He nodded, not glancing up from the papers in a folder on his desk. "Take a seat, Mrs. Crown. Dr. Mason will be with you in a minute."

A minute. She must be on schedule today. If not, Penny would just cut the session short. She sat down in a white sling chair and closed her eyes. She'd flooded them with drops this morning, but they still felt dry and gritty. John William recognizing the pendant did settle her. He wanted to talk to Nicholas, but only to verify.

Penny had seen that look in John William's eyes too often over the years to not recognize it.

An image of the pendant appeared in her mind's eye. She didn't push to clarify it, just focused deeply, ignoring the ringing phone and Sam's answering it. The pendant was on a page. In a glossy magazine. Not as she'd seen it on a chain around Alana's neck. An old magazine…

Suddenly, the answer she'd sought most of the night came to her. She nearly gasped. The pendant had been in an old issue of Apollo, the oldest and most respected international art magazine. She'd studied it in one of her art history classes at university. Professor Nettleton's class!

Penny had a copy of it with her university materials. It was in a plastic box and stored in the guest room closet.

She snatched up her handbag and faced Sam. "I need to reschedule."

"But you're already here."

"I'm aware of that, Sam, but I must go. It's regarding Alana's abduction."

He nodded. "I hated to hear about that. Everyone is so upset. Go!" He waved her out. "I'll square this with Dr. Mason. We'll see you next Saturday, Mrs. Crown. Good luck finding Alana."

"Thanks, Sam." Penny rushed out the door and to her SUV, eager to get home.

In the guest room, Penny searched through the stack of plastic boxes until she found the one labeled "Professor Nettleton: Art History" and then tugged the box free of the stack. She opened it and scanned through the half dozen magazines until she found the old issue of Apollo she recalled, removed it from the box, and then sat down on the edge of the bed.

Flipping through the worn pages, she spotted the photo of the pendant. There was an article below it on the page. Her heart beating fast, Penny began to read aloud:

"King Alexander of Lovenia, a small country near Germany, designed the pendant for his bride, Kerra."

Kerra. Same name as their town. Interesting. Penny read on, skimming the whole of the article. Alexander's popularity was so great he'd achieved rock-star status within the borders of his country that spilled over into neighboring ones. The press fawned over every detail of his wedding gift to his bride. The pendant incorporated his family crest and two nearly identical red stones, which weren't identified in the article. Garnets? Rubies? They didn't look quite like either. Setting that aside, she kept reading. His castle was called Red Richter and located in Alderburg, Lovenia. At the time, many dubbed Alexander the Fairytale King.

Penny stared at the wall. How had Lucas's family gotten the pendant? That made no sense to Penny, unless… Was it a replica? Possible, she supposed. Kyle Hoff had immigrated to Georgia, but she had no idea from what homeland. Lucas had been at most five, too young to recall anything, not that the topic had ever come up or any questions had been asked. Lisa was still in diapers then, at most a little over a year old. Lucas had doted on her, enchanted by her every move. His heritage was irrelevant, and their immigration was forgotten.

Unsure if Alana's pendant was the original or more likely a replica of King Alexander's pendant, Penny understood John William's reluctance to discuss it before learning more. He could find her information helpful, or at least interesting, though a magazine article wouldn't satisfy his demands as irrefutable proof or even a trusted source. Still, the magazine was respected, and the article was something.

She grabbed the magazine, and on her way to the front door, her handbag. The clock on the stove proved time would be tight getting to practice by ten, but this was important. It could help Alana. How Penny knew that, she couldn't say, but she did know it.

Down to the marrow of her bones.

NINE

June 3ʳᵈ @ 0949

Penny pulled into the Miller University parking lot nearest the pool and cut her engine. She'd tried to stop by the museum to share the magazine and its disclosures with John William, but the museum wasn't yet open, and he didn't answer the door. He didn't answer his phone either, though that was common. He'd get busy and put everything on ignore to avoid interruptions.

She lifted her handbag and walked into the practice session just as the coach was winding down on his comments to the team. He'd gathered them close to make announcements and this morning, no doubt, to warn them to all be vigilant and aware of those around them. Situational awareness was critical in the best of times, but essential until they determined what Alana's abduction was all about.

Penny took a seat on the bleacher facing the pool and set down her handbag. The coach wound down and the trial runs began. Penny watched and waited.

Two girls approached her first. Then a third. They were nervous and tense about the abduction, and Penny did her best to calm them and get them to focus on the matter at hand. Alana would insist on that, and so would Lucas.

It was as if that statement opened the floodgates and many of the competitors dropped by for a few words throughout the session. At its end, the coach came over.

"Mrs. Crown, thanks for coming this morning," he said. "I tried reassuring them, but I'm better at chewing them out for not performing to their ability."

"Glad to be here, Coach." It took a strong man to admit his strengths and weaknesses. Penny liked that about him.

The kids began departing and Penny stayed put on the bench. Finally, Lisa joined her.

"Hi, Mom."

"Hi. You did well this morning."

"Thanks. Honestly, I was beat before I started."

"No sleep at all?"

"Not really. I couldn't wind down knowing Lucas was worried sick." She lifted a hand. "When I think of what could be happening to her... I can't seem to stop." Lisa shook, covered herself with her crossed arms. "We're all worried and scared."

"That's wise, not weak, Lisa." Penny immediately went on, afraid her comment wouldn't be taken as intended and a battle would ensue. "I noticed Lucas wasn't here this morning."

"He couldn't come. The cops say he must be there if the kidnapper calls."

"Of course." Penny gazed at the now still pool water. "Did anyone say anything helpful this morning?"

"No. It's so frustrating. I feel as if I'm letting Lucas down. He's losing it over this, you know? And no one knows anything." Lisa covered her mouth with her fingertips.

"So, what are you trying not to tell me?" Penny lifted her fingertips to cover her own mouth. Lisa had done that since the cradle.

"Some are saying the kidnapper not calling yet is really bad news for Alana." Lisa shook that off like water. "I didn't like it."

What Lisa didn't like was that she agreed with them. "I wouldn't have liked it either." Penny touched a hand to Lisa's shoulder. "Sorry."

"Me, too. Lucas would be even more devastated if he heard that."

He would. "Let's don't borrow trouble. Enough finds us on its own."

Lisa nodded. "I'm really worried about him, Mom. About Alana, too."

"I know. It's hard to see someone you love in this kind of pain." Penny tilted her head. "Especially when you know exactly how it feels." And worse when your experience led to a horrible conclusion.

"Yeah." Lisa blinked hard. "Some of the team is going for lunch, but I'm too tired to eat. I'm going home."

"Hot date with a pillow, hmm?" Penny half-smiled.

"Exactly." Lisa stood up. "You coming home?"

"In a while. I need to check on John William first."

"See ya." Lisa walked out and headed toward the parking lot.

Penny watched her go. Her daughter was feeling vulnerable and wanted her close. The mother in her understood that, but she also understood how seriously Lisa opposed coddling. If she was going to be living away from home on her own at college soon, she needed to know she could handle events in her life. She couldn't leave the nest feeling incapable of coping.

Penny gathered her things and left to try again to catch up with John William.

Though the museum was closed today, John William answered the door. "Penny. I am glad you are back."

Penny walked in and he closed the door behind her. "I tried to bring this to you earlier, but you weren't here."

"I went to Café Vere to hear the latest scuttlebutt. It was a wasted effort, I fear. Very frustrating and concerning. No one has heard anything new on Alana, yet it is all anyone can talk about."

"I have no news either, but at Dr. Mason's office, I remembered where I saw the pendant," Penny said. "It was in this magazine." She passed the old Apollo issue to him.

"And here I thought you had returned to grant me your blessing about Lisa and college." His expression softened. "Being here for you and Lisa is my reason to keep going, Penny. Otherwise, I would be asking myself why bother? I have only the two of you to share my joys."

She clasped his arm. "I understand." After losing Mark, she often felt the same way about him, Lisa and Lucas. "Let me think about it, okay? I always saw her education as my responsibility."

"As have I as mine," he said softly. "Otherwise, as I said, why bother?"

"You bother because you love and are loved." Penny pressed a tender kiss to his cheek. "Were you able to reach Nicholas?"

"Not yet, but I left a message. He will respond as soon as he is able."

"Wonderful." She looked at the magazine he held. "There likely isn't anything in there you don't already know, but just in case… There's a photograph of the pendant and a small article about its history."

"King Alexander of Lovenia."

She nodded, not at all surprised.

"I am looking for a connection to Alana but haven't found one."

"It's Lucas's family tradition. He gifted the pendant to her."

"I'm aware. But there is no Lucas in Alexander's family tree, hence no record of how he got it."

Penny nodded. "It has to be expensive, being a consignment with all that gold and those two red stones. I'm wondering if it isn't a replica."

"That's possible, but there is another possibility."

"What?"

"The pendant and the family fortune disappeared the night the Richter family was murdered in a coup. To this day, who was behind the coup remains a mystery. This is the first sighting of the pendant since then—if it is the original pendant and not a replica." John

William worried his lower lip. "That could be problematic for the current king."

"Who is?"

"Berthold Richter Franke. He was the half-brother of Alexander. They shared a mother. The Queen Mother, Adelphia Richter, was widowed young and remarried Fredrich Franke to secure her throne. They are the parents of Berthold."

"And the Richter family fortune?"

"On being coronated, the new king discovered the royal treasury had been emptied. The Richter fortune has never been recovered."

"But how did Kyle Hoff and Lucas get the pendant?" They certainly hadn't lived as if they had a fortune buried somewhere. Penny thought it through. "Did Kyle and his wife immigrate from Lovenia?"

"I don't know." John William cocked his head. "How long have they been here?"

"I can't say exactly. Lucas started kindergarten here, so he was four or five. But they might have lived elsewhere in the States before moving to Kerra."

"The original or a replica, the pendant was being worn by Alana. The press pushed that story globally."

"Which means whoever was responsible for the original theft could come after Alana, Lucas, or Kyle—likely all of them."

"Precisely my thought," John William said. "Follow the pendant and hopefully find the fortune."

"I still don't see the link between King Alexander and Kyle or Lucas." Penny frowned, thought, and recalled John William's exact words. "You said Alexander's family was murdered. King Alexander and Queen Kerra and—their children?"

"Yes. Their daughter, Princess Briget. She was about two years old then. Their son and heir, Prince Stefan, who was nearly five, and the Queen Mother." John William paused, then added, "All were verified dead by the then Chief Councilor."

"I need to talk with Kyle Hoff," Penny said. "Warn him and Lucas."

"He is Lucas's father. If Kyle gave him the pendant or replica of it, he already knows."

"They need protection."

"Stop, Penny. You cannot protect them from this." John William's fear for Penny reared its head.

"I have to try," Penny insisted. "You know what Lucas means to me, and to Lisa." Penny moved toward the door.

"To me as well." John William snagged her arm. "My dear girl, be warned. You cannot fix all problems for all people."

"I'm not trying to, but if something happened and I didn't warn them, try to help them, I'd never forgive myself."

"I suspect Lucas's pendant is a replica, though I cannot be certain without proper examination. Yet it is most logical, Penny. The original pendant is priceless. How would Kyle Hoff come upon it?"

"I don't know…yet," she admitted. "It well might be a replica, but more significant to me at the moment, is whether someone believed it to be real enough to abduct Alana for it."

John William barely suppressed a sigh. "In which case, your getting involved in the situation could make your greatest fear a reality." His agitation spilled over into his voice. "Listen to me, Penny. Whoever is doing this—the original thief, the new king, or someone else entirely—will kill you for that fortune."

"And if I don't help, they'll maybe kill Alana and Lucas and his father—and maybe Lisa because she's close to them." Penny headed toward the door. "Look, I heard you, and I promise I understand the risks, but if I stand by and do nothing, I'm dead already. I must try to help them."

"I strenuously disagree, my dear. You are Lisa's sole parent."

Penny refused to cower. Of course, she'd considered that. She halted, hand on the doorknob. "What if it were Lisa?" She looked back at him. "Would you get involved then?"

He stilled, sighed, his rigid shoulders slumped. "I will of course help you—and pray we can keep you alive."

"Thank you, John William." Penny left the museum glad he was on her side, and resentful that there were sides to be on. She fished in her handbag for her phone and retrieved it. Walking down the stone walk over to a gazebo in the grassy roundabout, she phoned Kyle Hoff.

"Hello." He answered sounding nervous and exhausted.

"Mr. Hoff, it's Penny Crown. I'm sorry to intrude, but I must speak with you right away. Would it be possible for you to meet me at Café Vere?"

"Now?"

"As soon as possible." Her gaze drifted to a mother pushing a pram down the sidewalk. Normally she would have offered to come to him, but with agents in the house… If she stood any chance of him answering her questions, their conversation must be private.

"Very well. I can be there at four o'clock."

"Thank you." Relief washed through her. At least that hurdle had been cleared. "I'll be waiting."

Jun 3 @ 1600

Café Vere was nearly empty this time of day. Penny walked beyond the heavy wooden doors, smelling citrus and berry pastries, fresh biscuits, and sizzling bacon. She glanced at the rich European décor on the subtle gold walls and in the tables and chairs, upholstered in a soft burnt orange. She'd always loved the feeling in this café. Calm, warm and welcoming, and pretty but not stuffy in any way.

She spotted Kyle Hoff sitting in the shadows at the back table against the wall and walked over. "Thank you for coming," she said, then slid onto a seat.

"You're being very mysterious, Mrs. Crown." Soft light from the fixture above the table behind her reflected off his thick, black-framed glasses. "Have you learned something about Alana?"

"I'm afraid not."

A waitress walked over to take their order. *"Café au lait*, please," Penny said.

Kyle masked a strange look at her then ordered *un café*.

"I know my drink is typically ordered only for breakfast," Penny said. "And yours is for other times during the day, but the steamed milk appeals to me. It's easier on the stomach."

"No need to explain," Mr. Hoff assured her. "Though I will say I admire your straightforward manner of speaking. When worried, acid pours, doesn't it?"

She tilted her head, a demure smile on her lips. "It does for me, I'm sorry to say."

He folded his hands on the tabletop. "So why have you asked me here?"

"I am concerned about Lucas," she said. "Because of the pendant."

"The pendant?" Kyle Hoff looked confused. "I'm sorry. I don't understand."

Was that confusion sincere or pretense? Penny suspected it was pretense, but she wasn't familiar enough with him to be certain. The man always had been distant and secretive. "Could you tell me about the pendant, please? I have reason to believe it's important."

"Important to whom beyond Lucas and Alana and me?" Mr. Hoff challenged.

"I'm not sure yet, but perhaps to Alana's abductors, which in my opinion, puts Lucas in jeopardy."

"My grandfather passed the pendant to my father, then he to me, and I passed it to Lucas. How could that possibly be of concern to anyone else?"

Kyle Hoff was lying to her. Her instincts screamed it. Anger seeped deep into her, and she had to work to keep it buried. "I'm talking with you, Mr. Hoff, because Alana is in extreme danger, and I have valid concerns that Lucas could be in danger as well. I want to protect him—both of them—as best I am able, and you're telling me a fictional tale that doesn't hold up to the facts I know to be facts."

"Excuse me?" He looked surprised. "What facts?"

"The pendant was designed by King Alexander of Lovenia when he married Queen Kerra. It didn't exist when your grandfather was alive." She paused to let that sink in. "Now do you want to revise your explanation?"

"I do not." He calmly sipped from his cup.

"Fine." How could he intentionally expose Lucas to jeopardy? "Tell Lucas if he needs me to just call. Anytime, day or night." She fished bills from her wallet and left them on the table. "I don't know why you are protecting something or someone over your son or Alana. I do know that they need someone looking out for them. I intend to do that—I had hoped, with you. But with or without you, I will give them my best."

Kyle Hoff's phone signaled a text. He quickly read it. "I have to go."

"News on Alana?" Penny asked.

"No," he said. "Another matter." He stood up. "I do appreciate your concern for Alana and especially your concern for Lucas."

Penny didn't flinch. She held his hard gaze. "If that were so, Mr. Hoff, you would tell me the truth."

He paused and dropped his voice. "There is much you do not understand, Mrs. Crown, and I am not free to explain."

He couldn't tell her. That was blatantly clear. "Do you know why Alana was abducted?"

"That I cannot tell you."

"Can't, or won't?"

Regret burned with resolve in his eyes. "In this case, I fear, there is little difference." He turned on his heel and left Café Vere.

Penny watched him go, baffled. There was much she didn't understand. That was fact. But why was Kyle Hoff not free to explain?

TEN

June 4th @ 1500

Penny checked in with a desolate Lucas, who reported there still had been no contact from the abductors, then spent the morning catching up on work and emailing updates to clients on their divorce cases. She really didn't like this part of her job. Being a party to surveillance and information gathering that helped breakup families rather than protecting them or building something constructive grated at her. The cases she had worked with Mark and studied with her father had been far more interesting. But just about every private investigator started building their reputations and client lists working on difficult divorces. Frankly, the sooner she could move beyond them, the better.

Lisa ducked into her office. "Mom, it's after three and the opening ceremony starts at four."

"I need a few more minutes here, and then I'll be right there."

"I'm going on over," Lisa said. "The team is still really upset and the longer there's no word on Alana, the worse it gets."

Odd comment. Reeked of being Lisa's backhanded way of asking Penny to get to the ceremony early. But if it wasn't... Penny didn't need another run-in with Lisa right now. She opted for a neutral response. "Understandable."

Lisa grabbed her gear bag. "If you could get there a few minutes early, I think it would help. You have a way of calming people down."

"Thank you, Lisa." Those were the kindest words she had spoken to her mother in months. "I'll get there as soon as I can."

Lisa nodded and left the office. Moments later the front door opened and closed. Alana's abduction had shaken Lisa more than she cared to admit. That had to be the cause of her turnaround toward Penny. She'd done that when Penny had solved Mark's murder, too. But it hadn't lasted, and her acidic tone soon returned, along with her complaints of being smothered.

Penny finished up, cleared her desk, dressed in red and gray, Miller University's school colors, and then drove to the campus. She talked with a lot of the competitors who were dressed in street attire, which meant they needed to get a move on to change into their swim gear. "You don't want to miss the opening ceremony."

That sent them streaming to the locker room.

Accustomed to the strong stench of chlorine in the pool, Penny looked around at the clusters of people. Competitors, coaching staff, and men in suits accompanying the teams. Security likely, traveling with the others. Penny didn't envy them in their suits in this scorching heat and off-the-charts humidity.

Soon, the university President stepped up on stage and to the podium. He welcomed everyone to Miller University, made a few announcements, and wished all the teams luck. Then he introduced Lucas.

Poor lamb looked a bit ragged. Worried. Tired. As if he hadn't slept the last two nights. Penny's heart hurt, knowing he probably hadn't.

An older man stepped to Penny's side. Focused firmly on Lucas, he didn't glance her way.

Some parent near the podium shouted. "What is the latest on Alana?"

A hush fell, and Lucas adjusted the microphone. "I have no new information that the police have not already publicly disclosed."

A plethora of questions from the crowd bombarded him. He answered a few, then lifted a hand. "Please, while I appreciate your concern about Alana, this ceremony is about the swim meet. Those gathered here for it have trained hard for a very long time, and they've traveled from distant countries to participate. That's where our focus must be—on them and on the meet."

"Remarkable," the European man beside her said. "He's a natural leader."

Penny smiled. "I would agree."

"Has he always been this way?"

"Ever since I've known him."

"Which has been how long?" The graying man in his fifties smiled, open and friendly. He had beautiful teeth and smooth, sun-reddened skin.

"Since he was about five." Penny smiled back and extended her hand. "I'm Penny Crown, and you are…?"

"Gregor, though most at home call me Councilor." He looked from Lucas back to Penny. "I've seen the media coverage and heard all about Lucas and Alana. What a compelling story. And the pendant. People are enchanted. It's been extraordinary."

"It has." Was that admiration or pride in his eyes when he looked at Lucas? "I think it's actually Lucas and Alana's love story that's attracted so much attention."

"You're probably right. The pendant perpetuates that, I think."

"How?"

"It is unusual. It's history and tradition add a touch of a fairytale ending quality, I think. Especially in a time when divorce is so prevalent, people want to experience a lasting love that keeps couples together. Even if that experience is second-hand."

She hadn't thought of it in those terms, but it did appeal on that level as well as on family traditions. "You could be right, Gregor."

"Tragic that she's been abducted." Sincerity rang in his voice and shone in his eyes. "I do so hope everyone gets that fairytale ending. Millions are emotionally invested."

"They are." Penny's phone rang. She looked to see who was calling. Jay Voigt. "I must take this call. Please, excuse me."

"Of course, Mrs. Crown."

She stepped to the edge of the crowd and then off to herself. "Hello, Jay. Please, let this be good news."

"I wish it were, Penny, but there's still been no contact."

Disappointment and fear flooded her. "I'm sorry to hear that."

"The vehicle has disappeared off the planet as well."

"Really sorry to hear that, too." She sighed. "So, what can I do?"

"Can you be at the station in the morning at 9:30? A sketch artist will be coming in to work on the abductor. I think it could help if you'd work with him."

"I'll be there."

"Thanks. See you then."

Penny hung up, stowed her phone, then watched the rest of the ceremony. She scanned the crowd for Gregor but didn't see him where he had been. A shame. She would have liked to talk more with him. She'd like to know what sparked pride and admiration for Lucas in his eyes.

ELEVEN

♛

June 5th @ 0930

Penny spotted Jay Voigt waiting for her near the police station's main entrance. "Good morning."

He fell into step beside her. "Good morning." Same suit, still rumpled, but he had put on a clean shirt. His tie hung loose at his neck. "I didn't know if you'd be okay coming to the station." His voice etched with recrimination. "I should have suggested the sketch artist come to you."

"It's fine." She hadn't been back to the station often, but she couldn't start eliminating places in Kerra that spurred memories of Mark or she'd be as reclusive as John William. "Life goes on," she said a little wistfully. "Sometimes like a floating cloud and sometimes like an anchor. All you can do is keep moving with it."

"Isn't that the truth?" Jay swiped at his chin. "Artist is in from Atlanta today. He's in the conference room."

She remembered the way perfectly well, but only people accompanied by authorized personnel were allowed beyond the main desk. She followed Jay through the open area of workstations and around the corner, then down the short hallway to the conference room. She hadn't dared to let her gaze wander to Mark's old office.

Inside the conference room, Jay introduced her to Michael Provid, a young man with an angular face and dark hair and eyes. He didn't smile or offer his hand, so she nodded and took a seat at the table.

"I'll leave you two to it," Jay said, then walked out and closed the conference room door.

"Ready?" Provid asked.

Penny nodded.

Half an hour later, she examined the sketch. "It's close but still a little off." She pulled out her phone for the third time. He'd refused to look at it the first two times. "I presume since you've finished, you can view the photo now."

He reluctantly nodded.

She pulled up the blurred photo of the abductor and passed her phone to Provid. "His muscles are more pronounced. See what I mean?"

"I do."

"Thicken his jaw a little. His is a sharp angle."

Provid took back the sketch and made some adjustments. "There. How's that?"

Where they would have been twenty minutes ago, if he hadn't been stubborn. "Much better."

Provid stood up. "Thank you, Mrs. Crown. I'll get Detective Voigt to escort you out."

Penny reached for her handbag and started to stand.

Jay appeared at the doorway and then entered the room. "Please stay for a minute, Penny."

"Of course." She settled back down into her chair.

Jay took the seat Provid had earlier occupied. "I've been to Alana's apartment," he said and then frowned. "It's been trashed."

Penny's throat went thick. "Did you find anything?"

"Not really." Jay sighed. "But whoever tossed the place was definitely looking for something specific. You have any idea what that might have been?"

"I've mentioned it before, and nothing's happened to eliminate it from my thinking. I have nothing solid, just instinct, but I keep going back to the pendant." Penny frowned and leaned forward. "The abductor and she argued, and he kept focusing on her neck. She kept swiping her upper chest, where the pendant would have been."

"Why is that significant? Wait…, you said, would have been?"

Penny nodded. "As we concluded the night of the abduction, Alana had been wearing the pendant at the engagement party. But she wasn't wearing it when she was abducted."

Jay agreed. "Yes, of course. I also noted it missing in the photographs. Lucas has it. He plans to give it to her to keep on their wedding day—because of the tradition."

Relieved it had been located, Penny asked, "So were the abductors after the pendant then?"

"No idea," he admitted. "Was it valuable?"

Didn't she wish she knew. "I'm not sure. If it's real, it's priceless. If it's a replica, not so much."

"I didn't realize…" He rubbed at his chin. "Which do you think it is?"

"I'm working on that." She laced her hands atop the table. "The original was lost long ago in a coup in a European country near Germany called Lovenia." She went on to share what she knew of the story. He had clearly dismissed the pendant as significant to his case. Hopefully, this would have him reconsidering.

"So, the pendant could be either real or a replica, but it seems unlikely Lucas would have a priceless heirloom." Jay looked at Penny. "That's what you're saying."

"Unlikely, but not yet proven impossible. I'll let you know when I know."

"Thanks, Penny."

"Sure." She stood and retrieved her things. "Does Lucas know about Alana's apartment?"

"Yes," Jay said, empathy streaking through his voice. "I told him this morning."

Jay's tone signaled Lucas had not taken the news well.

Penny pulled into the driveway at home and parked, eager to get inside and drag herself to bed for a nap. She hadn't slept last night, and sorely needed a few hours respite before she could tackle her to-do list for today.

Unfortunately, it was a long one. Two clients needed updates due to recent activity by feckless spouses. Those were never easy. Lord, she'd be happy when this segment of her business was built, and she could move away from messy divorces and suspicious spouses. Maybe she should focus on corporate cases? Down the road, when her finances were more stable, she would definitely shift her efforts to anything but divorces. For now, she was grateful for the work. Grateful it paid the bills and kept them fed.

With a sigh, she left the car and entered the house. Coming home had been so much easier when Mark was alive.

"Where have you been?" Just inside the entryway, Lisa stood hands on hips, scowling.

Penny wanted to weep. Her daughter was in a mood. "At the police department working with the sketch artist on Alana's abductor." Penny dropped her handbag on the entry table. "Didn't you get my note?"

"Obviously I didn't, or I wouldn't have asked where you've been. I had the final fitting on my bride's maid dress this morning."

That explained the makeup. "How did it go?"

"Fine."

Weariness settled in Penny's bones and turned to exhaustion. "Lisa, it's clear you're upset. Can you spare us both and just get to why? I'm worn to a frazzle." The last thing either of them needed was more drama or theatrics.

That seemed to deepen her anger. "John William offered to help me with Oxford, and you didn't even bother to tell me."

"I don't know who told you that, but it isn't set in stone yet. He's considering it. That's all."

"You should have told me."

"Who did?" Penny challenged her.

"That's not important. What is important is that you have got to stop this."

"Stop what?"

"Interfering in my life."

"Excuse me?" Penny had had enough. More than enough.

Lisa recognized it and calmed her tone. "Mom, I am not a kid anymore. I make my own choices now." She blew out a deep breath. "Look, I know you love me and you're trying your best. I know it's hard without dad. But would you please get a life and let me live mine?"

"What?"

Lisa lifted a hand in her direction. "You suck all the oxygen out of the room. I can't breathe around you anymore."

"Fine. I'll spare you the burden of having to try. Maybe later it'll be easier on us both." Penny made her way to her bedroom and firmly shut the door.

She was too upset to continue that conversation. Upset at them arguing. Upset that Mark had died. Upset that ever since, every single thing was so hard. She was sick to death of working only divorce cases, of people obsessed with getting dirt on spouses they supposedly loved. No trust. Granted, sometimes trust wasn't warranted, and that upset her most of all. She would give anything to have her spouse back. To have the life they'd built, and she'd loved.

She stripped off her shoes and flung herself onto her bed. She'd loved her life, and now... now it was a struggle to get out of bed in the morning and to put one foot in front of the other. And she was sick of wondering if her life had ended when Mark died, or when she'd found his killer, and she was just too hardheaded to accept it.

She curled her knees to her chest, squeezed her eyes shut and clutched at her pillow. Lisa didn't need or want her anymore. Penny had done what Dr. Mason suggested. She'd taken a fistful of art courses and become a private investigator, but neither had helped.

With Mark, Penny had purpose. She had faith that whatever they faced together, they could conquer. Move mountains. Alone, she was mired in muck. Stuck in a strange dark hallway and no matter how hard she tried, she couldn't find her way out. It wasn't that she couldn't exist without him. She didn't want to. She loved him, their marriage, their family, their life. And a thief posing as a confidential informant who had trashed his own life, betrayed and shot Mark to death and stole everything treasured from him, her, and Lisa.

Her throat thick, Penny curled tighter into a fetal position. Everyone thought she was so strong and capable, and she could handle whatever came her way. But she didn't feel strong anymore. She felt weary and worn and empty. She felt lost. Angry and helpless and lost. And now Lucas was in this same position with Alana missing, and Penny's attempts to find her without hampering Jay's investigation seemed so futile. Only God knew what was happening to her. Thoughts of that had to be driving Lucas insane.

Hand pressed over her mouth to silence her sobs, Penny let the tears flow.

TWELVE

June 5th @ 1300

Penny and Lucas sat poolside, watching Lisa compete. Since the argument, she and Lisa still hadn't spoken. Actually, Lisa had already left for the meet by the time Penny awakened from her nap and pulled herself together. It hurt Penny's heart to admit it, but she'd been relieved Lisa already had gone. She didn't often allow herself the luxury of breaking down about the unwelcome changes in her life, but when she did, she paid for it, feeling overwhelmed and as fragile as one recovering from a bender. Add Lucas and Alana's situation to it, and Penny was even worse. While on a more even keel after napping, she hadn't yet fully recovered. But other duties called. Duties to the swim team, to Lucas and Lisa, and welcome or not, to Alana.

"You okay, Mrs. Crown?" Lucas asked softly so those seated near them in the bleachers wouldn't overhear.

"I should be asking you that." She smiled. There'd been no update from Jay Voigt, and no ransom demand. Nearly three days into an abduction, that was always a bad sign. She glanced over at

Lucas. Tense and stressed, but who wouldn't be? She placed a hand on his arm. "Are you sure you are up to this?"

He patted her hand on his arm. "I have no choice." He looked from Lisa in the pool to Penny. "Dad is there to take any call, and the police set any incoming to forward to my mobile." Lucas rolled his shoulders. "The team needs me here, so I am here." He flashed her the hint of a smile. "Alana would agree with that."

Though only Kyle Hoff knew why, he agreed, or Lucas wouldn't be here. For Lucas, his presence was about duty and responsibility. This morning, he didn't wear either any more lightly than she, but his priorities, like hers, were on others. Penny patted his arm. "I understand."

"I know." His smile was genuine this time.

Penny returned it, then paused talking to watch Lisa's race.

She didn't do her best, but came in third. Penny stood and applauded and then sat back down.

"She won't be happy with her performance."

"Third in an international competition is nothing to sneeze at," Penny said.

"It isn't," Lucas said, "but she won't be happy."

He was right. "She won't." Lisa would be in a foul mood. Penny staved off a sigh laced with regret. "Regrettable."

"I'll do what I can," he said, then stood.

"Thanks, Lucas."

He left the bleachers and across the pool Penny spotted Gregor, the man who earlier spoke to Penny of Lucas with pride or admiration. Again now, he focused on Lucas, following him with his eyes as Lucas descended the bleachers and made his way to the locker room. What drew his attention?

Suspicious, Penny glanced at others in the stands. They too followed Lucas's movements. She chided herself for spinning nefarious motives in Gregor. It was just Lucas's magnetism, she supposed. He had that effect on many people. No doubt some were watching him closely to see how he was handling Alana's abduction. Honestly, Penny thought, he was doing better than she had done when Mark had gone missing. But he had the bliss of not knowing the stats on getting no word from the abductors after two days. Typically, they made contact much sooner, and the longer time stretched out, the more likely the outcome for Alana would not be good.

Penny's stomach clutched. She smoothed a hand over it and whispered a silent prayer for a miracle. That Alana would somehow return safe and sound.

At two o'clock, Penny reported to the concession stand for duty until three. Interacting with parents, grandparents, and total strangers who were laughing and excited about the competitions helped lift her spirits.

Lucas dropped by to say he'd spoken to Lisa, and to warn Penny she was very disappointed in herself. "I tried, Mrs. Crown."

"Thanks, Lucas." Lisa had always been competitive, and, like most others, she hated losing. To her, third place might as well have been last. Mark had been the same way. *First or not at all*, he used to say. Penny wished, not for the first time, he'd been more flexible on that—for his sake and their daughter's.

"She promised she'd give you space until she got herself together." Lucas lifted a hand. "I've got to get ready for my race."

"Good luck and thank you."

With a nod, he headed off to warm up.

She served a gaggle of college students bottled water and two servings of nachos.

"Penny?"

Recognizing Jay Voigt's voice and sensing the hesitancy in his tone, she turned and looked at him. The grim expression on his face, the sadness in his eyes, said it all. Penny licked at her lips, commanded her heart to slow its thudding beat, and braced herself, then asked the question she really didn't want answered. "Where did you find her?"

Relief and regret filled his eyes. "Riverside Park." He drew in a sharp breath. "I'm so sorry."

Alana. Alana was dead. Penny couldn't find her voice. She nodded.

"I'm on my way there now, but I wanted you to know." Jay shuffled. "We need to tell Lucas. Mr. Hoff thought you'd want to be with him when he finds out."

"Yes." She blinked hard and fast. "He's in the pool about to race. Five minutes and he'll be done." She swiped her trembling hands down her jeans. "We can tell him then."

Penny got a familiar face to cover for her at the concession stand, then joined Jay. They watched Lucas compete and win. She applauded but there was no joy in her. Even for him, she couldn't fake it.

Lucas picked up on it. Came out of the pool and straight to her. "What's wrong?"

"Let's go to the locker room," Penny said softly.

In the way of things, people around them sensed something bad had happened. From the corner of her eye, Penny spotted Gregor. All the light had left his face, and he sobered, serious and frowning.

In the locker room, Penny guided Lucas to a bench. "Sit down."

"I'll stand." His body rigid enough to snap, he insisted, looking from Penny to Jay and back again. "It's Alana, right?"

"Sit down, honey." Penny guided him onto the bench and sat down beside him. "It is Alana." Tears welled in Penny's eyes. "They've found her body in Riverside Park."

Lucas's expression shifted to stunned. He clasped his hands on his knees, blew out a deep breath, then looked at Jay. "What happened to her?"

"She was shot," he said simply. "I'm so sorry, Lucas."

He shook hard. "Was she assaulted?"

"I'll know more after I've been there. I'm on my way now. I just wanted to tell you before word gets out and you heard it from someone else."

"You go with him." Pain etching every inch of his face, Lucas turned to Penny. "You go with him."

Penny looked to Jay who nodded. "I will, and I'll come to you at home right after. Okay?"

He nodded. "I need to get home. My father will be. . .upset."

Everyone was upset and would be, Penny feared, for a long time.

Jay stepped forward. "There's an officer waiting to drive you home."

"I have my car."

"We'll bring it to you," Penny interjected. "I don't want you driving right now."

"It's probably best." Lucas lowered his head and stared at the floor.

Neither Penny nor Jay rushed him. He needed a few minutes to absorb the shock.

A tear slipped to Penny's cheek. How many years would he need to accept Alana's death and recover?

"We'll bring it to you," Penny interjected. "I don't want you driving right now."

"It's probably best." Lucas lowered his head and stared at the floor.

Neither Penny nor Jay rushed him. He needed a few minutes to absorb the shock.

A tear slipped to Penny's cheek. How many years would he need to accept Alana's death and recover?

THIRTEEN

June 5th @ 1500

Penny and Jay tromped through the lush green grass toward the crime scene tape surrounding the forked-oak tree where many Kerra couples first kissed. Ironic that she'd be left there, at the most popular place in the whole town for that iconic moment in couples' lives. Was it done by a local? By some strangers who knew the tradition started long ago with the first mayor?

Maybe, but unlikely. Penny knew the drill. On suspects, start with those closest to the victim and work your way out in an expanding circle. Still, there were a lot of strangers in town. A jealous competitor from a distant land?

"The medical examiner is here," Jay said, still walking toward the tree. "You sure you're okay with this?"

"I'm fine." Penny lied. She was not okay. But she owed it to Alana to do this, and to Lucas.

Jay didn't call her on the lie. Just walked on and closed the gap between them and the officers.

One in uniform stepped forward. "Det. Voigt."

Jay paused. "You find the body?"

"No, sir. But I was first on scene. Two walkers found her," he nodded toward two senior women standing outside the yellow tape stretched between trees. "They called it in."

"Anyone else around at the time?"

"No, sir. The park was empty. Everyone was at the swim meet, I guess."

It had been crowded. "Are those women locals?" Penny didn't recognize either of them, and there were a lot of strangers in town.

"Yes, ma'am," the officer said. "Retirees. They walk together every morning."

"Anything else?" Jay glanced to the examiner, who was on his knees on the ground beside Alana's body.

"Not yet, sir."

"Thanks."

Jay turned to Penny. "You ready?"

As she would ever be. "Yes."

Jay greeted the medical examiner, a lean man in his fifties with a shock of dark hair, then introduced Penny. "Dr. Harmon. Doc, this is Penny Crown."

"Hello, Mrs. Crown. I'd hoped to one day meet you, though not like this."

Penny nodded.

"I knew your husband well. He spoke highly of you," the doctor said, pulling himself to his feet with a grunt. "Bad knees."

"I'm sorry."

"Aging is not for wimps." He looked over the frames of his glasses at Jay. "When you're done, we'll move her."

Jay nodded, spoke to Penny. "It is her, right?"

He'd seen her and photos of her. Why was he asking? Penny forced herself to look at Alana. A rush of emotion surged inside her. *Hold it together! Hold it together! Bury it until later!* She swallowed hard and demanded herself to really look at Alana, to engage clinically.

Her nails were broken. Two were missing, her arms and neck bruised purple—she'd been choked by thick fingers, surely male— and she'd taken a hard slug to the jaw, gauging by the dark bruising along her jawline. All of her injuries were awful, but the gunshot wound at her temple was likely what killed her.

"It's her." Penny looked at Jay. "She was tortured." Penny moved around the body, examined the ground. "She wasn't killed here. No blood on the ground or on the trunk of the oak."

"I agree. She was killed elsewhere and then brought here."

Penny spared him a glance. "Why? Why was she tortured?" Penny lifted a hand. "Why abduct her to kill her? Why bring her here?"

"Maybe she knew something the abductors wanted to know. Or not. We aren't clear on motive yet." Jay looked at Alana's gown. "Is that the same dress she was wearing when she was abducted?"

Another question he could already answer from the abduction photos. The delicate peach diaphanous gown. "Yes, though it's worse for the wear." Smudged. Tattered. Torn at the hem. "She fought hard."

"She did." Jay addressed Dr. Harmon. "Was she sexually assaulted?"

"I see no evidence of it," he said. "We'll know more after we get her to the morgue and do a proper examination."

That much Penny could share with Lucas. Grateful for it, Penny backed up a step. "Do you have a suspect, Jay? Anything?"

"Not yet."

As she feared. "If I can help in any way, say the word. I have more latitude." A reminder that latitude had been necessary to solve Mark's murder and Penny would take the inherent risks that came with it couldn't hurt.

"Thanks."

"You'll let me know when Dr. Harmon's report is ready?"

His grim expression soured. "You know I can't release that to you, Penny."

"Release it to Lucas then. Her family is all dead, and he's all she had. Don't treat him as an outsider. He's not."

Jay nodded. Whether or not he would release the report to Lucas remained to be seen, but Penny would get a copy of it, even if she had to call in every favor owed to her or steal it herself. "Thank you, Jay."

"Again, I'm sorry for your loss."

"So am I. Alana was a lovely young woman, full of hope and promise and dreams." Penny's voice cracked and, she lowered her head to block the arrogant glare of the sun from her eyes. Her steps as heavy as her heart, she made her way back to her car. Identifying Alana's tortured body… It should be storming, dark and dreary, not a lovely summer's day.

Seated inside her car, Penny met her own eyes in the rearview mirror. "Don't you dare breakdown, Penny Crown. Don't you dare." Lisa. She hadn't told Lisa!

Fishing for her phone, Penny hit speed dial.

Lisa answered right away. "Mom?"

"It's me, honey. I wanted to tell you Alana—"

"I heard at the meet," Lisa interrupted. "I brought Lucas's car to him."

"Are you still at the Hoff's?"

"Yes. Lucas said you'd be here after you left the park. I'm planning to ride back to my car with you."

"I'm sorry I didn't tell you about Alana myself, but Jay was eager to get to the scene."

"It's okay. You were doing what Lucas asked you to do." She dropped her voice. "I'm glad he didn't have to identify her."

"Me, too." Penny hated the thought of that as much as Lisa. Seeing Alana in that state… it would have haunted him day and night forever. As hard as it had been—Penny's insides were still in knots—it would have been much harder for him. "How is he doing?"

"He's okay. Well, not okay. He's like we were after dad…"

Penny couldn't take that reminder right now. Not right now. "We need to be there for him, like he was with us."

"Yes." Lisa cleared her throat. "You okay, Mom? That had to be—"

"I'm fine," she said automatically, then chose to be honest. "The truth is, I'm wrecked. You never get used to seeing something like that and it's always rough. But I'll be okay." She would be. She just needed a little time. Penny sniffed. "I'm on my way to the Hoff's right now."

"I'll tell Lucas." Lisa paused, then added. "Better call John William before he hears it from somcone clsc."

"I'll do that." A lump rose in Penny's throat. "Lisa, I love you."

Dead silence, then finally, "I love you, too, Mom."

Apparently, they were back to their post-death, mourning truce. Criminal it had taken Alana's death to get them there.

FOURTEEN

June 5th @ 1830

John William hadn't answered so Penny left a message to call as soon as possible. She parked in the driveway of Kyle and Lucas's two-story home and reached for yet another tissue. Strange how everything could look so normal from outside the house, with the wide-columned porch and three dormer windows reflecting the sun and the bushes tranquil and still in their perfected landscaping, while inside the house, the people were shattered, shocked, and stunned, brutalized by the merciless clutches of grief.

She dabbed at her eyes. *Pull yourself together, Penny.* Now, she had to be there for Lucas. Summoning strength, she stuffed the tissue into the trash and took in three deep breaths. When she looked up, Lucas was walking down the driveway toward her. His expression drawn and weary, she didn't have to ask how he was. She could read him clearly. Devastated, holding himself together by a thread, and doing his best to appear in control. *Poor lamb.*

Penny grabbed her keys and left the car, walked to meet him. He looked as unsure of what to say or do as she felt, so she silently lifted her arms and opened them wide.

He walked into them and hugged her hard. "I'm so sorry I asked you to do that. I should have done it myself."

"No, you needed to be with your father," she whispered close to his ear, closing her arms around him. "I'm fine. Just fine."

"You're not. You've been crying."

"Of course." She squeezed him tight.

They talked for a few minutes, Lucas openly expressing his horror and disappointment and doubts about his future without Alana in it. "I'm not sure what to do. I don't know what to do."

"Just breathe," Penny said. "For now, that's enough."

"Was it horrible?" he finally asked.

"Yes." How much information did he want? She tried to gauge, and finally saw the unspoken questions in his eyes. "She fought hard," Penny said, injecting pride into her voice. "She was no match for a gun, but she fought so hard to stay with you, Lucas."

The dam broke and tears rolled down his face.

Penny patted his back and held him while he cried.

Half an hour later, Penny sat with an empty cup at the Hoff's kitchen table. Lisa and Lucas were in the living room speaking softly with an FBI agent.

Kyle Hoff filled Penny's cup with steaming hot tea. "Thank you for going to the park and for comforting Lucas in the driveway earlier, Mrs. Crown. I confess, I watched from the window. He's been bottling up all his emotions, and if not for you, I fear he would still be doing so."

"I'll always be here when Lucas needs me, Mr. Hoff."

"Because you promised his mother?"

"Yes, and because I love him like a son." Penny cast a sideward glance at Lucas's father to see how he received that disclosure.

"Though he has never said so to me, I suspect in respect to his mother, I believe he has always considered himself your son." Mr. Hoff sat down across the table from Penny. "I don't know if you ever realized that."

"Sometimes words are unnecessary." Penny's expression turned tender. "He's become an amazing man. You should be very proud of him."

"I am," Kyle Hoff admitted. "He's known far too much loss and pain for one so young. I would have spared him that, if I could."

"So would I." Penny looked him in the eye. Kyle started to lift his cup. His hand trembled hard, and he set it back onto its saucer. "I don't know your beliefs," Penny said. "But I believe we experience what we do to give us the wisdom, insight, and strength to fulfill our life's purpose. God has important plans for Lucas. I'm convinced of that."

Behind his thick, black-framed glasses, Kyle Hoff blinked hard. "I have always believed that. Which is why I've worked hard to make sure Lucas has the tools he needs to fulfill his destiny."

"As parents, we do our best to give them everything we can, but much must come from them. For all of it, we pray a lot." Penny sipped from her cup.

"Every day of our lives." Kyle offered her a rare smile. "I'm grateful to you, Mrs. Crown. And for you. Many times, over the years you have helped Lucas in ways I could not."

She returned his smile. "Then isn't it time you called me Penny? This mister and Mrs. between us has gone on far too many years."

"You must call me Kyle."

"Kyle." She smiled again, and he sipped his tea.

Lucas and Lisa came in. "Mrs. Crown?" Lucas addressed her. "May we interrupt?"

"No interruption. Join us."

"If you don't mind, I'd like to speak to you privately for a moment. When you finish your tea, of course."

She met Kyle's eyes. "I've just finished." Penny stood up.

"Let's walk down to the water," Lucas suggested.

Together they walked out the back door and down a brick walkway to the water's edge. There was a bench in the shade beneath a towering oak, and Penny sat down on one end of it. "It's lovely here," she said. "Your mother and I shared many a cup of tea on this bench. In the spring, she always had the most beautiful tulips."

"She did." Lucas sat down beside her. "I remember them. All yellow and pink."

"Is something specific on your mind, or did you just need a break?" Penny asked.

He lowered his gaze. "I'm afraid I need your help."

"Okay."

"Planning Alana's funeral." Solemn, he looked Penny in the eye. "Dad can't do it. I had to step in and make the arrangements for my mother. He tried to do it, but… well, we all have our demons and monsters. And that was a small funeral. My parents were very close and allowed few others into their circle."

"And Alana's funeral is more complex."

Lucas nodded. "People say she had no one else but me, yet that's not really true. Alana had legions of friends."

She did. "She touched a lot of lives." And that was before the media explosion. "Okay, so what would Alana want?"

Misery lined his face. "That's just it. I have no idea." He let out an exasperated sigh. "Lisa and I talked about this a solid hour, and neither of us have any idea. She suggested I ask you. I sincerely didn't want to put you through this again so soon, but I'm lost."

So soon after Mark's funeral. "Thoughtful, but I'm fine," Penny said. "Though if I could change this and have Alana well and happy, I would."

He clasped her hand. "Alana and I were busy planning a long and happy life. We never discussed death or final arrangements."

"Neither had Mark and I," Penny confessed. "We were too busy living to think about dying."

"How did you know what to do?"

"I thought about Mark and the kind of man he was, and I did what I thought he would want." Penny patted Lucas's hand. "I didn't know what else to do."

That seemed to relieve Lucas. Some of the stress slid from his face. "Oddly, that makes me feel better."

It did. She could see it. Bare honesty, even if uncomfortable and unflattering, had merit. "Alana loved her friends, but she was private in a way, too."

"True."

Penny thought about that, about honoring both sides of her personality. "What if we plan two services?" She warmed to the idea. "A public memorial service for any who would like to attend, and then a private one for immediate friends and those closest to her."

Lucas paused, staring out onto the water. "I think she would like that."

"Then I'll pick you up in the morning at nine and we'll go make the arrangements."

Lucas stood up. "Thank you."

"Of course."

They walked back up the brick walkway to the back door. "Would you like Lisa and I to stay a while?"

"No," he said. "She's on her best behavior, but I need some alone time to wrap my head around all this."

"I understand." Penny wished for the millionth time she didn't, but she did. "If you need anything, even just to vent, call me. I don't care what time it is or what I'm doing. Understand?"

"I do."

She nodded and walked inside. Lisa sat talking with Kyle at the table. Her teacup was empty. "We need to go."

Lisa's jaw dropped. "Mom, no. I can't leave—"

"They need time alone, honey."

Remembering that feeling, Lisa stood up, carried her cup and saucer to the sink. "I'm sorry. Of course."

She pecked a kiss to Lucas's cheek and to Kyle's. "Call me if you want anything at all."

Penny and Lisa left through the front door.

When they climbed into the car, Lisa squeezed her eyes tightly shut. "I can't believe I forgot that. How everyone hovering drove me crazy." She looked over at Penny. "Thanks, Mom." Lisa frowned. "Did you forget, too?"

"Honestly, no. But that's not why I reminded you."

"Why did you?"

Penny cranked the engine. "I've learned it works best to just ask people what they want and need."

"So, you asked Lucas if we should stay, and he sent us away?"

"Lucas was far more diplomatic," Penny said. "He needed time alone."

"You just asked him?"

"Yes." Penny swallowed hard. "When you're that raw, you don't have the energy for social dictates. You need what you need. Your friends who are aware of that will ask what you need because they trust you'll give it to them without judgment."

"That sounds like John William."

Penny confessed. "I overheard him explaining it to Dr. Mason when your dad died. It was so true. I was ready to pull my hair out."

"I was, too. Everyone was being incredibly nice, and I didn't want to seem ungrateful, but the hurt was so deep… I just wanted to be by myself for a while."

That's what she remembered. Penny nodded. "Same here."

"So how do you know when to come back?"

"Lucas made that easy," Penny said. "Tomorrow morning at nine."

"To make the funeral arrangements." Lisa grimaced. "Sorry, Mom. We tried to figure it out, but…"

"Not a problem," Penny said. "Seriously. It's what he needs."

"You're a good person." Lisa looked so sincere. "You really are."

The praise was totally unexpected, and Penny wasn't sure how to respond. She settled for a lame, "Thank you, Lisa."

Penny held her breath, waiting for the other shoe to drop, but it didn't come. So, she pulled out onto the street a little less sad and more hopeful, and then drove back to Miller University to pick up Lisa's car.

FIFTEEN

June 5th @ 1830

Lucas and Penny worked with the funeral director most of the morning. When Lucas asked if it would be appropriate for Lisa to be buried wearing her wedding gown, Penny nearly lost it. By divine intervention, she didn't, and assured Lucas that would be exactly as Alana would wish.

When the director asked about the service, Lucas told him and Penny he'd received a call from Coach that morning. "Miller University plans a memorial service at 7:00 p.m. on Wednesday. Meet activities conclude at 5:00, which gives everyone an opportunity to change and prepare. Everyone is welcome to attend," Lucas said. "So that takes care of the public service we discussed, don't you think?"

Penny agreed, reminding herself to notify Jay Voigt. The killer was likely to attend. In these type cases, they often did.

"I'd like a private service on Saturday the 10th," Lucas said.

Penny interrupted. "That was to be your wedding day, Lucas." It was also the second anniversary of Mark's funeral. "Are you sure?"

"I'm sure," Lucas said. "If you don't mind her sharing the day with Mr. Crown." He hiked a shoulder. "It makes me feel better to think he'll greet her and help her settle in."

Penny tried to answer but had no voice so settled for a nod. Lucas was putting Alana in Mark's hands for safekeeping. There was something beautiful about that and it spoke volumes of his regard for her late husband.

When they'd exhausted the questions and given the director the information he needed for her obituary, they thanked him and left.

Walking to Penny's car, Lucas cleared his throat. Then, he cleared it again.

"You okay, Lucas?"

"Honestly, I hurt so badly I can hardly breathe." He glanced over at her. "When will that stop?"

Penny clasped his arm and gently squeezed. "I'll have to let you know. So far, it hasn't." Seeing the dread in his eyes, she added, "You do get better at coping with it, but I'm not sure the pain goes away. At least, it hasn't yet for me."

He looked down at the sidewalk. "I was afraid of that."

"You'll be okay. You just need to remind yourself that the circle of life turns for us all. Others get through it, and you will, too."

He grimaced. "Survivors."

Penny unlocked her car. "Yes."

They got inside Penny's SUV and Lucas clicked his seatbelt into place. "I guess then the guilt never goes away either."

"It gets better."

"When?"

Penny stashed her handbag behind the front seat. "When logic and reason remind you that you didn't kill her, and you accept that the only person responsible is the one who did."

"I think I'll have to find them and see justice done to get to that point."

That, Penny understood only too well. She gripped the steering wheel hard. "We will find whoever did this, Lucas. Whatever it takes."

"I don't want you hurt, too." His eyes turned glossy. "Best leave it to Det. Voigt."

To avoid making a promise she would surely break, Penny shifted the subject. "I'll bring you and your father a casserole for dinner."

"No need." Lucas swiped a hand through his hair. "People have been dropping off food since yesterday. The fridge is full. Dad said he'd never seen anything like it."

And she bet the constant stream of people at Kyle's door was making him as crazy as the media reports. Every time she turned on the television, they seemed to be either talking to the police's Public Information Officer or running a promotional for a documentary of all the media events Lucas and Alana had done—something about them or the case. The world had worried with them during Alana's abduction, and it was mourning with them her death. Penny was shocked the media hadn't camped outside the Hoff house. At least, not yet.

"Bringing food is a Southern tradition," Penny said. "When there's a death in the family, everyone brings something or does whatever needs doing so the family isn't bothered with ordinary life tasks for a little while. It's showing respect for the person who passed and for the family who suffered the loss." When Mark passed, Penny had frozen enough food to last for a couple months.

She pulled into the Hoff driveway and stopped. "I'll share the word at the meet today and a reminder tomorrow about the public service. Press releases, too. Is it in the auditorium? Did Coach say?"

Lucas nodded. "I hadn't thought of press releases. That's a good catch. People were pretty invested in our future."

"Definitely invested," Penny said. "What else can I do for you, Lucas?"

"Just be there tomorrow. Can you do that?"

"Of course." She patted his hand. "Try to get a little sleep, okay? You're getting bags under your eyes. Wet a couple teabags and put them on your closed lids for an hour or so."

"Thanks, Mrs. Crown."

"Anything else, you just call."

"I will." He headed up the driveway to the door, then disappeared inside.

Penny started the drive home and tried for the fourth time to phone John William, but still received no answer. This time, she gave him an ultimatum. "Call me in the next two hours or I'm coming over there—and fair warning, I'm in a foul mood."

John William called back before she was halfway home. "I was not ignoring you. I know you have been with Lucas."

He knew about Alana, of course. "I wanted to tell you what was happening before you heard it elsewhere."

"Even if living under a rock, I would have heard," he said. "Nicholas and I have been consulting on the pendant."

Nicholas Ryan. "Did you find out anything?"

"We can discuss that later in person," he said, shutting down the topic. "When is the service."

"The public one is tomorrow night at 7:00, Miller University Auditorium. I'll save you a seat."

"I will be there. You said, *the public one*. Is there another?"

"Saturday at 2:00 in the chapel. Burial follows immediately. You are expected, of course."

"Saturday. The 10th. That Saturday?"

"Yes."

"No." Force filled his voice. "Not on Mark's anniversary."

"It's okay. Lucas finds comfort in turning her over to Mark for safekeeping. She won't be alone."

"Oh, my." John William paused. "There is great sadness in that, but great beauty, too."

"There is," Penny agreed.

He dropped his voice. "Was she violated, Penny?"

"The medical examiner says he doesn't think she was raped—he'll know more after a full exam at the lab—but she was tortured. Lucas isn't yet aware of the torture so…"

John William went silent.

"Are you there?" Penny asked.

"Yes. Complete discretion, to be sure." He spoke slowly, his voice deepened. "I am so sorry."

Someone was trying to call. "Just a second, John William." She checked caller ID, then told him, "Lisa's calling. I'll see you tomorrow."

"Penny, keep a sharp eye on Lisa, and your own head on a swivel. I know you will not stay out of this investigation, so I must say I would feel better if you had some help."

"Who do I dare trust?" She gave herself a shake. "I'll be careful. That's a promise."

SIXTEEN

June 7th @ 1900

Penny saved John William a seat in the auditorium, and a small piece of her felt an enormous relief when he sat down. The service had started and was sad and beautiful and touching in the way that the young can be bold and speak so easily of their pain at losing their friend. Unfortunately, it roused memories in Penny of Mark's service, and the two combined had her attempts to stop her tears failing on a grand scale.

John William sat between her and Lisa and he slipped her a fresh tissue. "Be strong for the kids, Penny. They are watching you for guidance on how to conduct themselves." He clasped her hand and gently squeezed.

She glanced around, and they were watching her. That jerked her out of her memories and back into the service. Lucas was riveted on her also. She chided herself for allowing the distraction. This was not the time nor the place for her to fall apart. "Thank you," she whispered to John William.

For the rest of the service, she focused on Lucas and the swim team members, on all the familiar faces, and on the strangers. Apparently, all the teams and their coaches had come to pay their respects. Was Alana's killer among those gathered?

The service progressed and Alana's friends shared stories of her gentle nature, her kindnesses, and the things they felt were most special about her. Penny thought she had known Alana well, but time after time she heard stories of Alana's reaching out to help others in ways Penny had not known. She truly had been a remarkable young woman.

When the service ended, Lucas and his father stood near the door, thanking people individually for coming.

Gregor stood in front of Penny in line. He wore his sadness in his eyes and on every line in his face. The man who typically guarded him was missing. What was Gregor carrying in that brown leather pouch?

He stepped up to Lucas and shook his hand. "We are profoundly sorry for your loss, Lucas."

"Thank you."

"On behalf of my country and our team, we wish to give you this painting as well as our condolences." He passed Lucas the brown leather pouch. "Please do not open it until you are at home." Gregor's eyes pierced Lucas. "It's important." He glanced at Kyle and then back to Lucas. "The Enchanted Forest was painted before World War II by a prominent artist local to us, Barclay Ernst. There is a legend that the keyhole center depicted in the painting holds the secrets of the kingdom's future."

There was no missing the recognition in Kyle's eyes when Gregor looked at him. They knew each other—or of each other. Before she could ask what nation he was from, Gregor rushed out. Two brawny men followed him.

"Lucas," Penny asked, "where is Gregor's home?"

"I'm not sure." He looked at the pouch. "But the Enchanted Forest he says is in this painting depicts a country from a fairytale my mother used to tell me." She glanced at Kyle. He was collected and yet she sensed he was uncomfortable and agitated.

"Later, Lucas," Kyle told his son. "People are waiting to leave."

Penny's instincts issued a clear warning. Something significant had happened here. Maybe several somethings. Kyle too had told Lucas fairytales about a fictional land. Lucas had shared them with Lisa over the years, though her detail recollection was spotty. One thing not only significant but of concern was that Lucas was too young to have read anything about King Alexander during his lifetime. More significant was that Lucas believed Lovenia was fictional. "We'll meet you outside," Penny told Lucas. It was a lovely service."

He nodded, shook John William's hand, and they exited.

About ten minutes later, Lucas and Kyle stepped out into the warm night air and joined Penny, John William, and Lisa.

"Lucas, this painting interests me," John William said. "Could you share more about it?"

"My mother spoke of it often before she died," Lucas said. "In the stories, Lovenia is a small country between Germany and Switzerland. It's a cluster of villages and farms and forests, including one special forest, the Enchanted Forest."

"Why is it enchanted?" Lisa swiped her hand across her brow. "I kind of remember this one, but not all of it."

"In the fairytale, the king enters the Enchanted Forest. If at the ancient, forked oak he sees a woman, she is to be his bride. Theirs will be a long and content marriage. If she is not at the oak, then his betrothed, if he has one, is the wrong woman. Every king must check the ancient oak before marrying."

One look at Kyle Hoff and Penny was certain. Kyle knew this legend. He had repeated it to Lucas after his mother's death to be sure Lucas wouldn't forget it. Why?

Penny and John William's gazes collided. Kyle knew the legend. Gregor knew the legend. John William knew the legend, or he'd never have asked Lucas about it. Two questions remained in Penny's mind. One she could answer, and one she couldn't.

She couldn't answer whether the legend was fact or fiction.

She could answer the second, and it terrified her. Alana had been left at the ancient, forked oak in Riverside Park.

Alana's killer knew this legend.

"Are you okay, Penny?" Kyle asked.

"Fine. Just a little tired."

"It's been an emotional evening," he said. "Lucas, we need to let Penny and Lisa get home to rest."

"Of course." Lucas leaned in and hugged her. "Thank you again for helping with all this."

Penny nodded. "You get some rest, too."

"I will." Lucas and his father turned and walked toward the car.

John William whispered to Penny. "Alana's killer knew that legend."

"My instincts agree, but I can't prove it. Not yet."

"But you intend to prove it."

"Of course."

"It is too dangerous, Penny. For you and for Lisa."

"We have to try," Penny insisted.

"Lucas did not recognize Gregor, but Gregor—"

"He's been watching Lucas," Penny said. "I've noted it."

"He could be her killer."

"I don't think so," Penny disagreed, recalling his sincere sadness tonight. "He looks at Lucas with admiration and pride, not with anything that suggests harm."

"You cannot be certain of that." John William frowned.

"I know what I see. You must trust me on this." Penny looked from Lisa to John William.

"I trust you, my dear girl. I just think you may be in over your head, and you do not see it."

"I am not going to give up on finding Alana's murderer any more than I gave up on finding Mark's."

"Think of Lisa, Penny."

Penny snapped her gaze to John William. Disapproval burned in his eyes and Penny recalled how closely she had come to getting herself killed in Mark's investigation. "I am. I know what I'm doing. Trust me."

"Jeopardizing yourself and Lisa will not bring Alana back."

NO ONE WAS SUPPOSED TO DIE:

That truth tightened her chest and Penny looked back to Lucas and Kyle. Nearly to Lucas's car. He tucked the pouch containing the painting under his arm, pulled his key fob out of his pocket, then pressed the remote start.

The car exploded.

SEVENTEEN

June 7th @ 2112

"Lucas!" Lisa screamed and started to run toward him and his father.

Penny blocked her, pulled her close. "He's all right. They are both all right." They were on their feet and moving toward Penny, Lisa, and John William. Lucas walked backward, unable to take his gaze off the burning car.

When he was a few steps away, Lisa broke loose from Penny's hold and grabbed Lucas in a hug. "Are you okay?" She looked at Kyle. "Are you okay?"

"We're fine," Kyle said.

The ripples of terror in Penny didn't subside. *Lisa.* She needed to hire a bodyguard to protect Lisa. It would be prudent if Lisa would permit it.

"Lucas," his father said. "We must leave Kerra now."

"I can't leave Kerra," Lucas insisted, swiping his hand across his brow. "Not until Alana's killer is caught. Don't ask me to do this."

"We have no choice." Anguish crossed Kyle's face. "You don't know what is at stake."

"What is at stake?" Lucas met and held his father's gaze. "Tell me."

"We must go now." Kyle glanced at Penny then back at Lucas, clearly fighting an internal war. "We must." His voice calmed and he spoke in low, hushed tones. "I'm going home to pack. After you've spoken to the police about the explosion, come home. We'll be ready to go when you arrive. Hurry as much as is possible, Lucas. It's important." He turned to Penny. "Will you bring Lucas to me after he's finished here?"

"Of course." Kyle Hoff wasn't just rattled by the explosion. He was afraid. And he clearly knew more than he was sharing. Penny feared, much more.

"Thank you, Penny. As soon as possible, son. Please." Kyle turned and ran from the parking lot.

She watched him go. "Lucas, what was your father talking about? Why must you leave Kerra?"

"I have no idea." Lucas frowned, his hand trembling. "He's often cryptic, but this takes it to a new level."

"Whatever it is," Penny said, "it's significant. He wasn't just worried—"

Lucas locked gazes with Penny. "He was terrified."

Penny couldn't agree more. Her confusion was mirrored in Lucas's eyes. "And you have no idea why?"

"Other than Alana's murder and my car exploding—none."

"Thank God for remote access," Lisa said.

Lucas looked beyond her toward the car. Plumes of smoke still rose from it. "The police are here." He started walking toward them.

The police questioned Lucas, Penny, and Lisa quickly, seeing the wisdom in getting Lucas away from the scene where he wouldn't be an easy target. Was he a target? Penny wondered and worried. After Alana, Penny feared he and Lisa might be targets, along with anyone else in his inner circle, including Penny and Kyle. It couldn't have been coincidence that Gregor had gifted Lucas the Enchanted Forest painting on the same night someone had tried to murder him and his father—immediately following Alana's service. It couldn't be.

Inside Penny shivered and led Lucas and Lisa to her SUV. "Stand away until after I've checked out the vehicle," she told them.

"Mom, no."

"The police should do that, Mrs. Crown." Lucas lifted a hand in protest, the painting in its pouch tucked beneath his left arm.

"I know what I'm doing," Penny insisted. "Now stand back." She methodically checked the vehicle for devices and found none. Finally, she felt confident it was safe and signaled Lisa and Lucas to get in.

It was Lucas who objected. "You should never take those kinds of risks. You could have been hurt."

"I'm fine." She moved the gearshift into Drive and left the parking lot. "The officers have their hands full. I've been trained."

"By who?" Lisa challenged her. "You didn't learn that in your Private Investigator courses."

"By my father and yours," Penny said through gritted teeth. "Do you doubt they knew what they were doing?"

"No," Lisa said.

"I don't know." Lucas grunted. "They'd teach you as best they're able, I'm sure. But still…"

"Lucas, life carries risks. You can't protect yourself or anyone else from every eventuality. If someone is determined to kill you, they will find a way…" She paused to let that sink in. "Which is why I think your father is right. You must leave and get somewhere safe."

"What about you and Lisa?" he asked. "What about Alana's murderer?" He exhaled deeply. "I cannot and will not leave until that's resolved."

"I understand your wanting to do that. Probably more than anyone else could understand. But you are at risk in ways we are not, Lucas." Penny looked him right in the eye. "Neither Lisa nor I want to lose you. Losing Alana was hard, but if anything happened to you…"

"You do your best and pray a lot." Lucas fired back at her. "That's the best you can do."

His words resonated, as he no doubt knew they would. Mark had said them over and again during their marriage. To her and to Lisa, and apparently to Lucas.

"I hear you, okay?" Penny glanced from the road to Lucas. "But even Mark would hide you away somewhere safe while he worked out what is going on here. He would, and we all know it."

Lucas went quiet and stayed quiet until Penny pulled into the Hoff driveway. A hand on the door-latch, he paused. "I hear you, too, but I can't do it, Mrs. Crown. I can't run and hide somewhere safe while people I love are targeted. Don't ask me to do that. It's cowardice."

"It's prudent, not cowardly."

He stared at her a long second. "I don't know why any of this is happening, but I know it's significant. My instincts are warning me there is no running from the people behind this. There is no safe place to run and hide. So, it's a moot point." He got out of the car.

"We can't leave him like this, Mom." Lisa opened her door. "We can't."

Penny sighed her agreement and got out of the car then walked toward the front door. She climbed the steps and at the front door, an eerie foreboding coursed through her. With an outstretched arm, she blocked Lisa, tugged her behind Penny. Pausing, she called out, "Lucas! Kyle!"

No answer.

"Stay here, Lisa," Penny whispered. She gripped her gun inside her purse and entered the house.

Furniture upended. Paintings pulled from the walls, slashed and ripped with jagged cuts, tossed haphazardly on the floor. "Lisa, call Jay Voigt. Get him over here right now."

Penny stepped further inside. "Lucas? Where are you?"

Thunderous footfalls sounded on the stairs. Penny's heart hammering against her chest wall, she took cover behind the dining room wall and waited.

"Mrs. Crown. Mrs. Crown!"

Lucas. Frantic. "I'm here." She stepped out so he could see her. "What's happened?"

"The whole house has been ransacked. My father is gone."

"Gone?" As in, dead? As in, not here? "What do you mean exactly?"

"He isn't here," Lucas said. "I checked every room. No one is here."

"He wouldn't leave without you, Lucas."

"No, he wouldn't. Not willingly." Lucas pulled out his phone. "I'm calling the police."

"I already have." Lisa joined them. "Detective Voigt is on his way."

EIGHTEEN

June 7th @ 2230

Penny shadowed Jay Voigt in surveying the damage to the Hoff home. The kitchen was last, and it was wrecked. Flour and cereal, grits and cornmeal dusted the counters and floor. Every cabinet door stood open; its inner contents shuffled. When Jay was done observing and jotting his notes, she asked, "What do you think?"

"Seems consistent with someone looking for something specific. For all the upheaval, there's no signs of a struggle. I take that as good news for Mr. Hoff."

She'd come to the same conclusion. While nothing in the home hadn't been searched, there wasn't the typical you'd expect to see if a struggle had occurred. But there was one thing that bothered her. "Kyle's car is still in the garage. He didn't just leave, and I can't see him ever leaving without Lucas."

"Then it's likely he interrupted the search, or he spotted it and backed off. I lean more toward him spotting and avoiding them than an interruption."

So did she. While a mess, there was a methodical order to it.

Things ruffled through near where they'd logically have been. "That, or someone took him," Jay said. "He could have been intercepted before entering the house."

"Maybe, or maybe he left with them willingly and the house was trashed after he was removed from it."

"Why would you think that?"

An earnest question, free of snide condemnation. At least he didn't minimize her deductive skills. "The sliding door to the patio was forced open and the security bar was not in place."

Jay doublechecked that. "Suggesting they left through it?"

"Yes. But not that they entered through it."

Penny walked through the kitchen to the window above the sink. "No matter how terrified he was, Kyle would never leave here without Lucas. But he might have left to retrieve Lucas, hoping to intercept him. Rationally in that case, he would have taken his car. If he was already here when the intruders showed up, he could have focused on getting out of the house undetected."

"That seems logical."

"If he did, then he'd stay close in case we arrived with Lucas." Penny spotted a bullet hole in the kitchen window. Following the trajectory to the wall, she turned to Jay. "I think he was here before they arrived."

"Why?"

"Did you spot this?" Penny showed him the bullet hole in the kitchen window, the bullet lodged in the far wall.

Lucas and Lisa entered the kitchen, but neither spoke.

Jay walked over, removed, and then examined the bullet taken from the wall. He turned to Penny. "Sniper."

The intent had been to murder. Penny nodded. "Kyle had to be here for someone to take a shot at him."

"A sniper?" Lucas sounded befuddled. "But who would want to kill my dad? He's almost a recluse and never bothers anyone. He rarely even speaks to anyone but me and Lisa."

Lisa frowned. "Mom, is this connected to Alana's abduction and murder?"

"We don't know yet." Penny locked gazes with Jay and saw her fears mirrored in his eyes.

What do the two events have in common? What do the two targets, Alana and Kyle, have in common?

Lucas.

He had drawn the same conclusion and turned to her. "Mrs. Crown, can you help me find my father?"

"Of course, Lucas." Penny looked at Jay. "Forensics on the way?"

"Arriving any minute."

"When they do, we should get out of their way. Come to my house for coffee."

Jay Voigt nodded. He knew exactly what Penny was saying. Get Lucas and Lisa out of here. We brief each other and see what we've got. He already had people searching the area for Kyle, but so far, nothing.

They wouldn't find him. Kyle had every reason in the world to make sure they didn't. He had to be free to do what he had to do to protect Lucas.

About that intention, Penny had no doubt.

"Where are Lucas and Lisa?" Penny asked Jay Voigt.

"They stepped out back. I told them to stay on the patio." Jay frowned. "They vetoed coffee at your place. Lucas is convinced, and Lisa agrees with him, Kyle will come back here for Lucas. I couldn't argue."

The house and grounds were flooded with police. They should be safe enough. "I can make coffee here if you like."

"No, thanks." Jay rubbed at his stomach. "To be honest, I've had all the coffee I can stand for one day."

Penny nodded. "We should talk."

Jay hesitated. "I have to say something first."

"Okay." If he gave her the confidentiality on open investigations speech, she might spit a nail. "Let's go to the porch. We'll be in the way in here."

They walked through to the front porch to assure themselves privacy. The examiner's team streamed in and out, but otherwise, their conversation was protected. Penny sat down in a rattan chair near a small table. "What do you want to say?"

Jay sat down opposite her. "I shouldn't say anything at all. At first, my motivation for talking with you about my findings was out of respect for you and what you did to solve Mark's case."

"A professional courtesy?"

He nodded. "But you're very good, Penny, and I trust you."

"Same here."

"The sad truth is, we've got nothing. Not on Alana. Every turn ends in a dead-end."

"Does that include the coroner's findings?"

His frown deepened. "No suspects, nothing unexpected in the coroner's report."

"Dr. Harmon verified no rape, then?"

"No rape." Jay nodded. "But there was torture." He grimaced. "We're guessing professionals, due to the lack of residuals and evidence at the scene. Usually, we find something, but not this time. We've interviewed everyone even remotely connected to Alana, and we haven't identified anyone with even a grudge against her."

"What about the pendant?" Penny asked, not at all surprised. "That's when all this started."

"Is there a reason someone would want Lucas dead?"

"I don't know yet."

"But it's possible?"

"In a few days, his fiancé has been abducted and murdered, his car has exploded, his father has disappeared, and his home has been invaded by a sniper." Penny couldn't keep the edge out of her voice. "I'd say that makes it pretty clear someone wants him dead." She looked up at the porch ceiling, debating whether to mention the painting, but decided against it. If John William authenticated it, then she would tell Jay. Until then, she couldn't prove it was germane and her feeling it was key just wasn't enough. Jay had confidence in her. If she made one mistake, that confidence would be gone. She couldn't risk losing his trust.

"You need to look into that pendant," she said.

"Honestly, we don't have the manpower. This international swim meet has the entire force pulling overtime. That, Alana's murder, the car explosion and now Kyle's disappearance... We're stretched as thin as paper, Penny, and that's the truth."

"What about getting some help from Atlanta?"

"We're getting help from them. They've had a lot of resignations and retirements in the last few months. They're thin, too."

Penny folded her hands in her lap. "I wouldn't push if it weren't important, Jay."

"I know. But what can I do?" He stood up. "Look, I'm not convinced a pendant that originated in an obscure foreign country is related to my case, but I trust you are, or you wouldn't push it. Bottom line is I can't justify the manpower to the higher ups. If I suggest it without a concrete connection, I'll get shot down so fast my head will swim for a week. If you want to look into it, you have my blessing. Trace any leads you find relating to it. But, Penny, whoever is doing all this is serious. Dangerous. Don't take risks, okay? Mark would never forgive me if I let anything happen to you."

Lip service. A cold chill coursed through her body, feet to fingertips. Jay knew she would take risks. He knew she'd have to take them. So, what was this invoking Mark about?

A gunshot rang out from behind the house.

"Lisa and Lucas are back there!" Horrified, Penny ran toward the sound.

They lay on the ground, huddled, Lucas protecting Lisa with his body. Jay ducked low and made his way to them. "Are you all right?"

Penny joined them, staying hunched and as close to the ground as possible.

"It was close, but we're okay," Lucas said.

"Thank God for lousy sniper shots." Jay's voice shook. "Let's get you out of here." He issued an order to a nearby officer. "Get Mrs.

Crown's car running and pull up as close as you can to the house. I want an escort to remove them and to stay with them. Two cars, outside."

"Yes, sir." The uniformed officer crept back to the house.

Minutes later, the SUV's engine revved. "You're sure you're both okay?"

"Fine, Mom. My ankle's a little sore. I tripped."

"If she hadn't stumbled," Lucas said, "One of us would have been hit."

"It was that close?"

"Inches." His eyes filled with regret and fear. "You've got to get Lisa away from here."

"Don't be ridiculous, Lucas. I'm not leaving." Lisa shot a fierce look at her mother. "I'm not leaving."

NINETEEN

June 8th @ 0600

Penny peeked out her living room window. The patrol car was still in place and the officer was moving inside the vehicle. He was safe. So was the one on the back of the property, parked under her favorite oak.

Breathing a little easier, she went back to the kitchen and poured herself a full cup of steaming hot coffee. The pungent aroma filled the kitchen. She'd need the caffeine kick; it was going to be a long night.

As she put the carafe back onto the warmer, her mobile phone rang.

"Penny Crown," she said on answering it.

"It's John William. What happened with the car…? Is Lucas safe?"

He'd departed after speaking with the police. "Sleeping soundly at the moment."

"Penny, I know telling you to leave this to the authorities is a waste of breath, but you need help. First Alana, then the car exploding at the university… this situation is out of control."

"I agree, it is." She took a hot sip from her cup and walked to her office, then sat down at her desk. "I take it you haven't yet heard Kyle Hoff is missing."

"What do you mean, missing?"

She filled in John William, informed him about Kyle and then about the house being ransacked and Lucas and Lisa's near-miss run-in with a sniper that seemed to vanish into thin air. Before he could start on her needing help again, she added, "I have something else I need you to take a look at and see if it's authentic or a replica."

"Come right away this morning."

She wished she could. "I must deal with the swim meet first. It's Lisa's last event. I'll be there right afterward."

"Is this item related?"

"My gut says it is, but who knows? I'm no expert. I hope you can tell me."

"Be careful, Penny. And get Lisa out of here. As long as she is near you or Lucas, she is in jeopardy, and you know it. Your investigation could get her hurt. It has almost gotten her killed already. I warned you that you needed help. If you will not get it, I will."

"Calm down, John William. Please." He was scared to death for them all. "I know she needs to be moved to safety, and I'm working on it."

"Where are you sending her."

"You know where." Atlanta. To her intrepid school principal mother and retired FBI agent father.

"If anyone can keep her safe, it is them." John Williams spoke as if thinking aloud. "But you still need help."

"I asked for help. Jay says they can't spare the manpower."

Lisa entered the kitchen and the look on her face was furious. "I am not leaving."

"She is," John William said. "Give her the phone."

Penny stretched the phone to Lisa. "John William."

"Will you talk some sense into her, John William?" Lisa said.

"Listen to me. You are going, Lisa. Your mother must give her full attention to keeping Lucas alive. You know I am right. She cannot do that with you in the line of fire. This is not rocket science. She is in dire jeopardy, and you will do nothing to make her work more difficult or more dangerous. Think about it, Lisa. Do you want your best friend dead? Your mother dead?"

"She can't do this alone," Lisa whispered, her voice husky.

"She will not have to."

"What are you going to do? Are you going to help her?"

"I am already helping her. I am not enough. But I know someone who is."

"All right." Lisa acquiesced, though she didn't sound at ease about it. "You've made your point. I'll go. But if anything happens to either of them—"

"I'll notify you immediately."

Lisa passed the phone back to her mother, scowled, and then left the room.

"Thank you, John William." Penny frowned. "But I wish you hadn't mixed my safety into the equation."

"Facts are facts. It is time Lisa realizes it. She is not a child anymore, my dear. That could be why she refused to leave in the first place, but of course, you realize that."

Penny hadn't. Lisa spent so much time wanting Penny out of her life that staying out of fear of her safety seemed a stretch. Was it possible?

"Expect a visitor. If I am able, I will give you more precise details on his arrival."

"A visitor?" Penny groaned. "I've got my hands full, John William. I don't need a visitor now."

"You need this one." He sniffed. "I will update you as warranted. Get over here as soon as you can. And for pity's sake, be careful."

His visitor was her help? Likely. And he'd fight her to the death with any attempt to refuse. Well, at least he'd gotten through to Lisa. Penny guessed she owed him for that. Inwardly, she sighed her resignation. "All right."

Penny muddled through the morning's swim team events. Several of the team members needed to talk, and she patiently listened but learned nothing new that could help her solve Alana's murder, locate the sniper after Lucas and maybe Lisa, or find Kyle Hoff, who still hadn't surfaced.

All of that weighed heavily on her mind, but uppermost was Lisa's luggage in the rear-end of her SUV. She'd compete at 9:00, then they'd leave to meet her grandparents in the designated spot midway between their two homes. And then Lisa would be safe.

Gregor approached Penny, his brow furrowed, his expression stern. "Mrs. Crown?"

She turned and smiled. "Hello, Gregor. How are you this morning?"

"Concerned." He waved the two guards with him further away and lowered his voice. "I heard about Lucas's car last night and that someone invaded his home."

She nodded. "He's fine, Gregor."

Tension eased from his expression. "Thank God."

"Yes." Penny studied him. His relief was sincere. "Why are you so invested in Lucas?"

"Who wouldn't be? He's a symbol of the future. A fine one."

He wasn't telling her the truth. "Gregor, I have noticed your admiration and pride when you look at him. Did you know Lucas before? Why does he matter so much to you?"

He didn't want to lie to her, and his hesitation proved it, so Penny changed tactics. "A sniper tried to shoot Lucas and my daughter last night. Would you know anything about that?"

Worry flooded his face, truth filled his eyes. "I swear to you neither has anything to fear from me. On my life."

"I believe you," Penny said. "Kyle Hoff is missing. Do you know anything about that?"

His upset was visible. His hand shook. "I don't, but I'll see what I can find out."

"Where are you from?"

"I'm a diplomat. Councilor to the king."

Penny's heart thumped hard. "In Lovenia?"

NO ONE WAS SUPPOSED TO DIE:

"Sir." A guard appeared at Gregor's side. "Your presence is required immediately."

"I'm sorry. I must go now." He brushed a hand near the pocket of her jacket. "Be careful, Mrs. Crown, and protect them," he whispered. "It's vital to protect them."

Gregor was invested in Lucas. He was from Lovenia. And he clearly knew a lot more about what was going on here than Penny.

Penny and Lisa were in the SUV driving to the rendezvous point—a shopping mall parking lot halfway between Kerra and Atlanta.

"Coming in second is a solid accomplishment, Lisa. I don't understand why you don't see that. You are the youngest competitor there, too. You should be celebrating."

"It doesn't matter right now." Lisa spared Penny a glance. "I'm glad you're done except for the closing ceremony tomorrow. I hate it that I won't be there, but that doesn't matter either."

Doesn't matter? Was this really Lisa? She was worried about Lucas. Had to be about Lucas. "I regret that you're missing it, too, but the risks…"

"I know." Lisa put on her sunglasses and lifted a hand. "If you're focused on me, you can't focus on Lucas. He's at greater risk. I just feel I should be helping you."

Lisa *was* worried about her. Moved, Penny swallowed hard. "John William is getting me help." Penny was grateful to be able to honestly say that, and prayed his help wouldn't be an albatross.

"Next right," Lisa said. "Look, they're already here waiting for us."

That didn't surprise Penny at all. Her father hadn't taken the sniper news well. Penny pulled into the right lane, preparing for the turn.

"Mom, I know you're bent on protecting Lucas, but protect yourself, too."

"I will." Penny pulled in and stopped next to her parents' Honda Pilot. She waved then looked at her daughter. "I'm not getting out. Dad's orders. He walked around to the back of the SUV and Penny opened it from inside. "They'll keep you safe, but you keep your wits about your own safety, too."

Lisa hugged her mother. "Of course."

Penny shivered. "Take as few chances as you can. Promise me."

Clarity shone in Lisa's eyes. "I know you're struggling to keep it together for me and for Lucas. All this is tearing you up inside. I'm sorry I didn't see that sooner, but I do see it now. You are so strong, Mom." A tear leaked from Lisa's eye. "I haven't much acted like it, but I do love you, and I'm proud of you. Thanks, Mom, for loving me anyway."

Penny wanted to cry so instead she smiled. "Dr. Mason wouldn't agree with you on the strong part. This is kind of new to me. I can't promise I'll be successful, Lisa. I know how important Lucas is to both of us. But you saw yourself last night just how fast unexpected things can happen. All I can promise is to do my best."

"Will you be okay at the Saturday service for Alana? I haven't forgotten it's the anniversary of Dad's death. I feel awful that I won't be there with you."

Penny sniffed. "No matter where we are, Saturday will be hell for both of us. We loved him. How could it be anything else? But we will get through it."

"Yes, we will." Lisa sat back. "For the record, Dr. Mason is wrong. You are strong, and you are a wonderful mother." Lisa clasped her hand and squeezed. "I'll check in if Gramps allows it." She let go, and then left the car.

He wouldn't allow it. But there was nothing he wouldn't do to keep Lisa safe. Lisa would contact her anyway when she could. Penny had to be content with that. Tearful, she watched her mother and father and Lisa drive away.

TWENTY

June 8th @ 1500

Penny checked in with Jay Voigt, who unfortunately had no new developments on Kyle Hoff or on Alana's murder. The case had already grown cold, pointing even more so to professionals, which raised more questions than provided answers. Jay and his team were frantically busy with the foreign teams leaving for their homes today. It wasn't lost on him that once they left U.S. soil, getting them back would be complicated and difficult, if not impossible.

With Lucas's permission, Penny dropped off the Enchanted Forest painting with John William, who said he would get back to her on its authenticity. With his typical flair, John William refused to discuss the visitor he had summoned to help her, but he gave Penny an enigmatic smile and said *he* would arrive unexpectedly and soon.

He seemed to be enjoying this flair of the dramatic. At least she knew to expect a man.

Penny left the museum more than a little flustered and without any new information on the painting.

Realizing she'd forgotten the grocery list, she dropped by the house to retrieve it. Lucas was napping on the sofa. Even in sleep, he looked haggard from intense grieving. *Poor lamb.*

Penny got the list and crept from the house, her heart heavy.

That night at 9:00, John William telephoned. "Is she settled?"

Lisa. "She's fine." Penny's father had left a coded message that they were home safe. Whether that meant they were at her parents' home or wherever he had elected to stash Lisa, Penny had no idea. While she didn't like not knowing, there was a lot to be said for being unable to tell what you don't know.

"And Lucas?" John William asked.

"He ate very little and then went to his room."

"Missing Alana?"

"Yes, and feeling guilty that he couldn't protect her, and that his father is in the wind." Penny sighed and took a sip of wine from her glass. "It would be easier to talk about what Lucas isn't worried about rather than what he is. Poor lamb is so overwhelmed."

"But he is handling it, right?"

"He is. Those who don't know him would say he's coping remarkably well." Penny's throat went tight. "I hate it that he's going through all this, John William. He's suffered through more than enough already."

"We play the cards we are dealt, my dear. None of us get to choose."

"How well I know. But I hate it. I really hate it." She walked into her office.

"As do we all." He paused and then added, "You two are safe there now?"

"Police officers, out front and back. We're okay."

"Good. Good."

At her desk, Penny stretched back in her chair. "Any decision on the pendant or the painting?"

"Nothing final just yet. More analysis is needed, I think. I'm waiting for a consult."

Nicholas. He was taking his time responding on this one. She perused the open file on her computer. Well, well. The remote access camera picked up Bryce Grendel kissing a woman who was not his wife, Karli. Maybe she could identify the woman. Grimacing, Penny jotted a note on her lengthy to-do list to inform her client in the morning. The photo evidence would be welcome news to Karli even if Penny lacked joy in delivering it. Oh, how she hated divorce work. "Did you mention it was urgent?"

"Everything that can be done is being done." John William paused. "Your visitor arrives soon. It will be an unexpected entry."

What did he mean by that? Before Penny could ask, Lucas came out of his room for a drink. His eyes were red. "I have to go. Lucas has surfaced. I think he needs to talk."

"Good night, my dear. Stay safe."

Penny hung up the phone, clasped her wine glass and went to the kitchen table. Lucas poured himself a tall orange juice and took a seat across from her.

"Alana?" Penny asked.

He nodded. "I wish our lives had been more like the fairytales I've been told all my life. Not idyllic, but…"

"Not like this."

"Right." He sipped from his glass. "Maybe more like Alexander and Kerra and the pendant story."

He didn't realize the stories were real and not fairytales at all. That Lovenia was real. Not yet. "Tell me about them."

Lucas glossed over the story of Alexander and Kerra's engagement and their meeting at the ancient oak, but expounded on their marriage and how much they loved each other. It seemed comforting to him to relate it, and when he finished, Penny smiled and asked, "You mentioned there were other fairytales you were told—"

"There are hundreds of them." Lucas nodded.

That surprised Penny. "Are they all about Alexander and Kerra?"

"They're about all kinds of things. Royalty and commoners, festivals and the forests, everyday life and traditions and customs.

Even the law." Lucas smiled. "My parents have or had very rich imaginations."

"Are all of the stories about Lovenia?"

He nodded. "They loved to teach through stories. Too many different places, and I'd be confused." He gave her a wistful smile. "They even created a language. It's a blend of German, French and Italian, though most speak English as well."

Teach through stories. All about Lovenia. "Their legacy to you?" Penny suggested, convinced by his last remark he should conclude on his own that the stories were Kyle's heritage. Lovenia had to be his homeland. Kyle and Gregor had recognized each other. The painting Gregor gave to Lucas was by a Lovenian artist. Penny hadn't yet proven Kyle and his wife had immigrated from Lovenia, though she was working on it. So far, that segment of her investigations had been another dead-end. No Kyle Hoff was found. Yet that had to be part of it with these lifelong fairytales Kyle and Grace had taught Lucas. Why else would they do that?

"I never thought of the stories as a legacy, but I suppose in a way they are." His smile faded. "I just wish I knew Dad was safe. He was so afraid after the explosion."

"Jay will let us know the minute he finds anything."

"I know he will." Lucas blinked hard. "I guess I feel I'm failing everyone. Alana, my dad, Lisa…"

"You haven't failed anyone, Lucas. Some things are bigger than us. We don't fully grasp what is going on, or who is behind what is happening. We just have to do our best to figure things out, and to survive until we do."

"I feel guilty about that, too." He tapped the tabletop. "Lisa was nearly killed. You're in jeopardy, trying to help me. I need to do something to protect you two, but I don't know what to do. I think that's the most frustrating thing of all. I don't know what is happening, so I don't know what to do to keep any of us safe."

"We'll sort it out." Penny patted his hand. "We will, Lucas."

He stood up. "Hopefully before I get you or Lisa killed."

"Lucas, no!"

"I shouldn't even be here." Angry, he left the room.

NO ONE WAS SUPPOSED TO DIE:

Poor lamb. Penny understood his fury and frustration, and her own. His concern and worry and disappointment in everything, including life itself. She would reassure him as best she could, but considering she knew in her bones there was far more at stake here than a pendant and a family fortune, she doubted how much her reassurance would help him. There was a definite tie between Lovenia and Kyle. What it was, she didn't yet know, and why it made Lucas a target, she couldn't imagine beyond the obvious father and son connection. But as soon as the swim meet closing ceremony was over tomorrow and John William got back to her with more information on the pendant and painting, she intended to find out.

TWENTY-ONE

June 9th @ 1400

The swim meet's closing ceremony ended. Penny wished Lisa and Lucas could have attended, but Jay Voigt had adamantly refused, deeming it too risky. Considering Alana and Kyle, she had to agree.

Gregor stood next to a man Penny recognized from the parking lot the night of the car explosion. Dirk, she'd heard him called. He was with Gregor's team and overly watchful. Gauging by Gregor's body language, he didn't like Dirk. Penny wasn't sure what to think of him. He hadn't participated as a coach or even as an assistant, though he was a big bruiser of a man in seemingly tiptop shape. Maybe he was with team security? She could see him in that role, though why he was actually there was anyone's guess.

She and Gregor exchanged a superficial goodbye but his grip on her hand was strong. "Take care, Mrs. Crown."

A warning. It resonated through her. "I will, Gregor. Thank you for participating in our meet."

"It was my privilege and pleasure."

Dirk nodded in her direction. "Councilor, we must go."

Gregor pointedly tapped her jacket pocket, then turned to leave.

Avoiding checking her pocket, Penny left the gathering and got into her SUV. Though tempted, she still avoided her pocket. Why, she had no idea. But she waited until traffic thinned and she stopped for a red-light.

A business card. Gregor's contact information. He hadn't put that in her pocket today. When had he done it? Why had he done it?

He recognized Kyle. He was invested in Lucas.

Who was he to them?

"One thing at a time, Penny." Earlier, John William had texted he had news for her, and she'd promised to join him right after the closing ceremony. She turned right and headed toward the museum.

On Main Street, the flashing lights from police cars reflected on the buildings, and before she parked, she spotted an ambulance right in front of the museum. Her heart thud a staccato beat and fear gripped her bones. Telling herself to get a grip, she turned off the engine. Two EMTs wheeled out someone on a stretcher. "John William!" Penny fled the car and rushed over.

"John William!" Bruised and battered. Had he fallen? She looked to the EMT. "What happened?"

"Are you related?"

"We're family." Penny spoke to John William. "Are you okay?"

His face was swollen, his arm twisted unnaturally. Bruises on his face and neck, on his arms—everywhere she could see. And he tried but didn't answer her.

"Ma'am, I'm sorry. He's been badly beaten. We need to get him to the hospital."

"I'll be right behind you. John William, don't you dare die on me. You hear me?"

He lifted his left arm. "Wait." He licked his lips. "Penny. Come."

She stepped closer.

"Contact Nicholas Ryan."

"How do I find him?"

"Government. Nicholas Ryan. Urgent." He paused for breath. "Type…it…in."

"In what?" she asked. But John William's eyes had closed.

His attendant shouted. "His pressure is dropping. We need to move!"

On the sidewalk, her hands shaking, her stomach full of knots, Penny phoned Lucas.

"Hello."

That wasn't Lucas. She stilled. "Kyle?"

"Is my son all right, Mrs. Crown?"

"He's fine. Under protection." Penny entered the museum and began searching. "Where are you?"

"I've no time for this now."

"Make time!" She lowered her voice. "We've been worried sick. Lucas is beside himself."

"No choice."

"He's with me. Come to us."

"I cannot."

"You left Lucas?" Anger shot through her.

"I could be followed. I cannot risk bringing them to Lucas or to you and Lisa."

That stopped Penny. "John William was attacked. He's on his way to the hospital now."

"Is he how you learned of Alexander and Kerra?"

"Yes," she said for the sake of brevity.

Agitated, he grumbled. "You must keep Lucas safe. You've no idea how vital that is."

"I'm doing my best. Right now, I need to be in two places at once."

"I cannot help you. Call Lucas."

"I thought I had."

"No, you dialed me." He hung up the phone.

What was he doing? Penny stared at the receiver, then dialed Lucas.

"Lucas Hoff."

Startled, Penny said, "Don't identify yourself on the phone. It's too dangerous." She shook herself. "I need a favor."

"All right."

"John William has been attacked at the museum. An ambulance is taking him to the hospital now. He needs something done right away, and I can't be in both places at once."

"You should be with him. What does he need done? I'll do it."

"I must do it." Penny frowned. "Will you go to the hospital and see how he is doing. He looks pretty bad." The two units outside her home would follow Lucas to the hospital. Her voice grew reed thin. "I'll get there as soon as I can."

"Of course."

"Tell them you're family or they won't disclose a thing."

"Got it," Lucas said. "I'll call if there's anything to report."

"Thank you."

Penny closed and locked the museum's doors and activated the perimeter security system. She cleared the building—empty—then began searching for Nicholas Ryan's information. First, John William's phone. Finding it in his office, she checked his contacts. No Nicholas Ryan stored in there. She looked through his desk, feeling as if she was violating John William's privacy even though he had given her instructions to do what she was trying to do. Type it in—*what*? She had no idea.

An hour later, she had looked everywhere that seemed logical and semi-logical and places that defied logic, but she'd failed to find anything on Nicholas Ryan in his computer or anywhere else.

Out of ideas, she used John William's phone and called Lisa.

"Hello."

"It's me. Has John William ever mentioned Nicholas Ryan to you?"

"I met him. He had lunch with us when we celebrated me getting Oxford."

"Seriously?"

"I'll text you a photo we took at the restaurant. He's interesting."

"Interesting?"

"Mysterious but charming," Lisa said. "John William says he's brilliant. Why are you asking about him?"

"I need to get in touch with him and I'm not sure how to do it."

"I can't help you there." Lisa paused, then added. "John William did tell me that I could trust Nicholas—if I ever got into trouble and needed help."

"Why would he tell you that?"

"I don't know. But he did."

"You doing okay?" Penny continued searching drawers, books on the shelf behind John William's desk.

"We're good. I am worried about you and Lucas and Kyle."

"We're fine." She didn't dare tell Lisa about John William. She would be back here in a flash even if she had to walk. "Better go now. I love you, honey."

"Love you, too, Mom." Lisa hung up the phone.

No hesitation in her voice. Their truce was holding. At least, for now.

Half an hour later, Penny still had nothing. She sat back down at John William's computer. He trusted this man and clearly felt she needed Nicholas's help. He worked for the government. That much she knew. She tried the usual databases and locators. Found nothing.

Frustrated, Penny ran a common Internet search.

Nothing of value.

No photograph search that matched the one taken in the restaurant with Lisa.

Her frustration peaked and more in protest than anything else, she ran a search using John William's exact words: *Government. Nicholas Ryan. Urgent.*

A text box popped up on a black screen. "What do you want?"

As it disappeared, she entered, "John William Archer said to find you. He's been attacked at the museum and is en route to the hospital. Need help."

She waited a full five minutes but received no response.

"Enough." She shut down the computer, disarmed the perimeter security system and armed the full system, then locked the door behind her and headed to the hospital.

TWENTY-TWO

June 9th @ 1600

"Have they let you see him, Lucas?" The hospital had that distinct and familiar smell that put knots in her stomach and made her queasy. That *identifying Mark in the morgue* smell. Whether it did or just being in the building triggered her memory, she had no idea. But to her, it was real, nauseatingly pungent, and it was strong.

"No." Lucas leaned forward on the waiting room chair. "The doctor has been in with him. He said he'd come here when he's done."

Penny sat down beside Lucas, put her handbag on the floor at her feet. "Has anyone told you anything at all?"

"Nothing except they're still assessing his injuries."

"Thank you for coming." Penny swiped her thigh with a shaky hand. "That meant a lot to me."

"Did you get your task done?"

Didn't she wish she knew? But without a response, she couldn't be certain. Someone would get the message. But would it be Nicholas? "I did what John William asked me to do." She reached over and patted Lucas's arm. "You look exhausted. Why don't you go home now and rest?"

He gave her a negative nod. "I'll wait with you."

"You don't have to do that."

"I do." He jutted his jaw the way he did at five when he was determined. "I can't rest. I can't go look for Dad or Alana—"

"Why not?"

"Det. Voigt says I'll be in the way. They've got this."

"You don't believe him?"

"I think he's worried the abductors will snatch me, too."

"That is a valid concern, Lucas. If they did, then that wouldn't be good for Alana's case, and it wouldn't be good for finding your dad, right?"

"True." He looked frustrated and beside himself. "I don't want to hinder them in any way, but it's driving me crazy not be out there searching."

"I understand. But this isn't the time for emotional actions. It's the time for logical ones."

He wrestled with that and finally conceded. "Right. I need to be here for you and for John William anyway."

Misplaced guilt. No matter how many times Penny had told him he wasn't responsible for Alana's death. Penny understood it. She'd lived it with Mark. But, oh, how she hated seeing Lucas go through that agony. Still, Lucas and John William had been close for many years. He loved Lucas like he loved Lisa. "All right."

The double doors swung open, and Dr. Handley stepped through them.

His gaze landed on her. "Penny." He walked over.

Fearful of what John William's doctor might say, Penny swallowed hard and stood up.

Lucas rose to his feet beside her. "Dr. Handley, how is John William?"

The skin around his eyes wrinkled, and his expression went even more serious. "He's in a coma." The doctor brushed his silver hair with an impatient hand. "He lost consciousness on the way to the hospital, and he's been in a coma since his arrival."

"A coma?" Confusion riddled Penny. "But he spoke to me at the scene."

"I understand that. The EMT reported it. Nevertheless, he is in a coma." Dr. Handley frowned. "He also has broken ribs, a broken right arm, three fingers that seem to have been hit with a hammer or something like it. And there's significant swelling in his head. We're closely monitoring his cranial pressure. If it gets much worse, I'll have to relieve it surgically. He took a lot of blows to the head, Penny."

"What kind of surgery?" Lucas asked.

"We're hoping to avoid having to drill into his skull to relieve pressure due to swelling. It's a common procedure, though risky of course due to the proximity of the brain. For now, we're continuing with tests and monitoring him closely."

Penny's knees went weak. She stepped back and slid down onto her chair. "Is he... going to..."

Dr. Handley's expression softened. "He's critical but stable. We'll know more after we complete the tests." He cleared his throat. "Try to stay calm, Penny. We're doing everything we can."

It took everything in Penny not to breakdown and sob. She nodded. "Thank you."

Dr. Handley turned and went back beyond the double doors.

After a long moment, Lucas asked, "Are you okay?"

Penny schooled her tone. "Yes. No. I'm as well as I can be right now." She looked at Lucas.

"I talked to the police," Lucas said. "John William had been conscious but not lucid."

He'd been lucid when instructing her to contact Nicholas Ryan. "Did something happen on the way here?"

"No. The officer said it was probably the swelling. He wasn't sure, though."

Swelling, or John William wanting word out he wasn't lucid enough to talk and maybe identify his attacker. Would he fake a coma? She didn't think so, but with everything going on, he might.

"I asked for any news on Alana's murder." Lucas sighed. "Det. Voigt is following leads, looking at everything and everyone in her life. It's like they're still waiting to hear from the kidnapper even though she's dead."

"I hope not. It's doubtful any contact will be made now."

"It's not logical," Lucas said. "Det. Voigt—is he really good?"

"Mark thought so." Jay Voigt couldn't be lingering on that. He had to be looking at other facets of the case. Ones he was keeping close to his chest.

Just after 6:00, Dr. Handley returned. "We've completed our testing. There's no internal bleeding and his organs appear to be intact."

Penny asked, "Has he regained consciousness?"

"Not yet. But the swelling appears to have stabilized. It's gotten no worse. That's good news."

"Can I see him?"

"In a few minutes. We're moving him to a room on the third floor."

"ICU?"

"He's stable, Penny. All the rooms on that floor are on monitors. I need to keep a close eye on him." Dr. Handley clasped Penny's arm. "The nurse will let you in as soon as they have him settled. She'll look for you in the waiting room across from the nurse's station."

"Thank you, Dr. Handley." She focused on Lucas. "Let's move there now."

Minutes after being seated in the Third Floor waiting room, Penny spotted a gurney rolling to halt at the nurse's station. She moved to the entry door of the waiting room. John William rested on the gurney. Two orderlies received the nurse's instructions, then wheeled the gurney into a room two doors down. "It won't be long now," Penny told Lucas.

Ten minutes passed, then fifteen. A third orderly passed by, wearing blue scrubs and hiking boots. Why in the world was he wearing hiking boots? She visually followed him.

He entered John William's room.

Penny started after him, but Lucas caught her arm. "The nurse hasn't yet come for us."

"Did you see that man go into his room?"

"Yes, I did."

"Did you notice his shoes?" Penny took off and shoved through John William's door.

The orderly was about to empty a syringe into John William's IV line. "Stop. Now." Penny shouted. "Get away from him. Do it or I'll shoot you where you stand."

Lucas alerted the staff, elevating his voice enough that everyone on the floor could hear him, including the orderly.

Still holding the syringe, the orderly shoved Penny to the floor, and charged past her, bolting from the room. A cart crashed in the hallway, and he disappeared from sight.

A nurse ran into John William's room.

Penny's hip still hurt like crazy. "Get the police and lockdown this hospital."

Lucas looked at the stunned nurse. "Do it now before he escapes."

The nurse ran back to the nurse's station and put out the alarm.

"I take it you're convinced he's not on their staff." Lucas helped Penny to her feet.

"No, he's not."

"She's right," the nurse said, joining them. "I saw him leave the room. He doesn't work here." Curiosity burned in her eyes. "How did you know that?"

"His shoes."

"What?"

"He wore hiking boots. Muddy hiking boots." Penny swallowed a grunt, rubbed at the sharp pain in her hip. "He was about to inject something into John William's IV line."

The nurse gasped. "An assassination attempt?"

"I'm afraid so." Penny's heart threatened to beat out of her chest. This could be about the pendant and painting or totally unrelated. And her instincts chose now to be on hiatus?

"Why?" The nurse's eyes stretched wide.

Oh, how it galled Penny to admit it. "I have no idea."

She walked over to John William's bed. He looked frail and fragile, swollen and bruised and battered. She swallowed three deep breaths, willing herself not to cry. From his monitors, his vitals were strong and stable.

Lucas stood at her side. "Thank God you were here."

"Thank God I noticed his shoes." Her insides still shook like crazy. If she hadn't noticed the boots, the mud, John William would be dead.

Security came and questioned Penny, assured her they and the police were checking the entire building. There would be a guard posted outside Mr. Archer's door.

Jay Voigt assured her he'd put a guard on John William until the attacker was arrested. "There was supposed to be a guard. He isn't here. Why?" Met with blank expressions, Penny turned to the nurse. "Restrict his visitors to me and Lucas…and Nicholas Ryan," she told Security. "No one else who isn't with the police."

The man from Security and the nurse both nodded. The nurse added, "I'll issue the order immediately, Mrs. Crown."

"Thank you."

Security left with the nurse and Penny turned to Lucas. "I want you to go back to the house now."

"No. You're not leaving him and I'm not leaving either of you."

"Lucas, there could be another attempt. I don't want you caught in the crossfire."

He stilled. "Is this related to Alana's case?"

"I don't know." She answered honestly. Her gut now said it was, but with John William's diverse interests, she still couldn't be sure.

"I'm not leaving you here alone. Don't ask me to do that."

His resolve was unmistakable. Penny gave in and nodded.

Just after ten, Dr. Handley entered John William's room. He checked him over, read the notes in his medical records, then turned to Penny. "Any idea why someone wants my patient of thirty years dead?"

"Not yet." Penny answered. "How is he?"

"About the same." Dr. Handley looked down at Penny. "This isn't going to be a quick fix hospital stay for him," the doctor said. "It's going to take time, which means he's going to need you now and when he's released."

"So, he's no longer critical?"

"He is still critical. At least for now. But the longer he remains stable, the better."

That, at least, sounded encouraging.

"He's now under guard around the clock, Penny." Dr. Handley softened his voice. "I want you and Lucas to go home and rest and do what you do."

Penny grunted. "No."

"You must. Don't make me issue orders." His expression hardened. "Look, I know he's family to you, and I know you're worried. But he's safe here now, and your holding vigil while he's unconscious isn't doing anyone any good. He's going to need you later when you'll be his caretaker and guard. Go home and do what you need to do to make sure no one else comes after him."

"Sorry." Penny looked the doctor right in the eye. "After what happened, I don't trust your people to keep him alive." Jay Voigt had blown a hole in her faith in him, too.

"We didn't know he was at risk then. Now we do. I'm telling you, I'll do everything humanly possible to keep him safe. John William has trusted me for thirty years. You know that. I need for you to trust me, Penny. You know you can. You know I take this attempt seriously and personally." Truth burned in the doctor's eyes. Fierce anger and unvarnished truth.

She needed to investigate to find answers. "You'll call me with any changes?"

"Immediately. Yes, I will."

Praying she wouldn't regret it, Penny stood up. "All right. We're going so I can try to sort this out. But, Dr. Handley, you had better not fail him or me."

"I wouldn't dare." He smiled. "You have my word."

Penny dropped a kiss to John William's forehead, then whispered. "If you're faking, keep faking. If not, snap out of it and let me know." She studied him a long moment, but he didn't move a muscle. She retrieved her purse. "Let's go, Lucas." They swept past the guard, then exited the hospital.

Near the car, Lucas held out a hand. "Keys. I'm driving."

Penny didn't argue. Tears blurred her eyes, and she couldn't see well, anyway. "Let me check the car before you get close."

"You need to teach me how to do that." Lucas stopped a short distance from the SUV.

"When it's daylight." She went over the car twice, signaling she was still shaken by the orderly event and Lucas's car explosion. "Okay, come on."

Lucas got in behind the wheel and Penny slid into the passenger's seat. "I need two white roses."

"Tonight?"

"For tomorrow," Penny said. "One for Alana and one for Mark."

"Two years tomorrow," Lucas said softly. "I haven't forgotten." He pulled out of the parking lot onto the street. "Do you think it's possible he is watching over Alana now?"

"I do." Penny swallowed hard. "I think God puts people in our lives when we need them. Like He did with John William and me. Since the day I first walked into his museum, he's mentored me. Long before Lisa came along, he'd become a second father."

"You love him."

"I do. So did Mark."

"And Lisa." Lucas signaled to turn. "You and Mr. Crown have been like that with me. Mentoring and treating me like a son."

"We love you, Lucas."

"I know." He smiled. "That he's watching over Alana is the only thing that keeps me from falling apart right now. That and you."

"We're family. We take care of each other," Penny said. "I don't know what I'd do if I lost you or John William, Lucas. I couldn't bear it."

"You will always be my other mother. I can't think of you any other way."

About a mile from Penny's house, Lucas's mobile rang. He

answered it, and waited, listening intently. "Fine." He hung up.

Strange call. "Lucas?"

"I need you to drop me off and then go straight home."

"Drop you off? Where?"

"At the corner of Fourth and D."

"What's going on?" Penny couldn't not ask.

"Kyle said for me to come."

That set off screaming alarms inside her. "Lucas, I told you I'd misdialed and gotten him. He was okay and wanted me to keep you safe. He said nothing about you coming to him. Are you sure it was him?"

"It was him."

"You're positive?"

"He used our code word."

"Well, why does he want to meet?"

"He didn't say."

"And with everything going on, you didn't ask?"

"He was afraid, Mrs. Crown."

"Call him back and ask why."

"Seriously?" Lucas frowned. "I can't do that."

"I have a bad feeling about this, Lucas. You ask him why or I'm calling Jay Voigt."

"You don't want me to go. I get it." He spared her a glance. "But I have to do this."

"Why?"

"Because he's my father and he asked." Lucas popped the steering wheel with the heel of his hand. "Look, it'll be a quick talk. That's all. He needs to see me to know I'm all right. That's all it is."

"Why didn't you tell me that?"

"You know my father. He tells no one anything."

He had her there. Penny blew out a deep breath. "Okay. That I understand. But be careful."

"I will." Lucas pulled to the curb at Fourth and D. "You need to go straight home and stay there, okay? At least, until I find out what has my dad so upset he's disappearing. I'll call as soon as I can and let you know what's happening."

"Be careful, Lucas." Dread dragged at Penny's stomach. "When you can, let me know you're safe."

"I will." He got out of the car and walked up onto the sidewalk, then scanned for his father.

A man opened the door on a red truck. "I'm here."

Lucas got into the truck with Kyle Hoff—it was him, Penny saw him clearly—then Kyle drove away.

11:37 p.m.

Penny sat at the kitchen table, staring at the same cup of cold tea she'd been staring at since returning home, begging the phone to ring and for it be Lucas, letting her know that wherever he was, he and his father were safe.

She heard a key in the door and reached over her phone for her gun, gripped it and then held it under the table. Her every nerve stretched to the breaking point, adrenaline surged through her veins, and she waited.

The security alarm being disarmed beeped. Lucas? It had to be Lucas. John William was comatose. Lisa was stashed with her grandfather somewhere. There was no one else with the alarm code.

"You're still up?" Lucas walked into the kitchen. "Why aren't you in bed?"

She stood up and set the weapon on her seat, then hugged Lucas. "You're okay?"

"I am." He hugged her hard, then stepped back. "I'm sorry I worried you. Dad took my phone and left me a burner. I didn't want anyone tracking it to you, so I didn't call."

"What happened?" Penny sat back down. "Where's your father? Is he all right?"

Lucas poured himself a glass of orange juice. For some odd

reason, that seemed to be his substitute for comfort food. "Physically, he seems okay, but he is acting strange."

"What do you mean?"

"He drove me home, told me to get my things together. He started throwing stuff into a suitcase and pulled out a briefcase I've never seen him use before."

"A briefcase?" Penny wondered why. "What was in it?"

"No idea." Lucas sat down across from her. "He wouldn't say. He told me we were leaving, and we wouldn't be back. I refused, of course. Until Alana's case is solved, I am not leaving here."

Penny resisted a groan. "He refused to listen." Easy enough to gather that much. Lucas's confusion was palpable.

"He did. He was gathering weapons, wearing a dark hoodie and skull cap. I didn't know he owned those kind of clothes."

"I've never seen him in them, either."

"Weird. Definitely." Lucas sipped from his glass. "He told me I had to come. To do as he said, and to disguise myself."

"He's concerned about your safety, Lucas."

"Yes, but there's more to it." Lucas's expression darkened. "He admitted that there are things he hasn't told me. That he'd waited too long. *They're here.*"

"Who is here?"

"I have no idea." Lucas shrugged. "But when I refused to go with him, he said he was bringing me back to you, and that I should tell you the fairytales. He wouldn't say why, just to do it."

Penny's heart beat hard and fast. "What else did he say?"

"I asked him again who *they* are. He said they are enemies. I don't know whose enemies or why they are enemies. The whole conversation was bizarre, Mrs. Crown."

"But he explained…"

"Not in a way that made sense." Lucas's frustration came through in his tone. "Enemies of Lovenia. That sent me reeling. How can enemies of a fictional place be after me? Want to harm any of us? It makes no sense." Worry filled Lucas's eyes. "I think he's lost it."

Even now Lucas didn't grasp that Lovenia was real. Understandable, considering he'd had a lifetime of it as a fairytale. "Is that all he said?"

"Just beyond a curve on Forest Road, he pulled over and told me to get out, hide in the bushes for ten minutes, then come straight to you. He took my phone, gave me a burner—his term, not mine—and said to only use it in an emergency."

"Why did he send you to me?" Penny asked, giving time for Lucas to sort through all these oddities.

"I don't know. But he said it twice. Come straight to you—and tell you the fairytales. Not to trust anyone else."

Lucas still hadn't made *any* connections. She considered making them for him, but in his current state of grief and in the current situation that could bring him more harm. That's the last thing he needed, or she wanted. "So, you hid for ten minutes then came here."

Lucas nodded. "I watched him speed away and a black sedan followed him. I tried but didn't get the tag number. I guess I was still shocked by the way he was behaving. I couldn't think fast enough." Lucas was chewing on the puzzle pieces. "Should we call the police?"

Penny thought about it, weighed the pros and cons. "No. He'll call them if it is safe to involve them. We don't know anything to tell them except your father is acting strangely. We have no idea where he's going or why."

"That black sedan was chasing him."

"Okay. I'll let Jay Voigt know about that. He'll have the officers keep an eye out for the sedan." She stood up. "We don't want them in his way, Lucas." Fairly safe to report with no tag number for the sedan. "Your father is doing something he feels compelled to do, and we don't want to complicate his efforts or make things more difficult for him."

"No, we don't." Lucas frowned. "Do you know what things he hasn't told me?"

"No." Seeing Lucas's skepticism, she added, "Your mother never said a word to me, and neither did your father."

"But you suspect something." Lucas leaned in over the table.

"Something specific."

"Maybe. But I'm not clear yet." She started walking to the hallway. "There's a plate in the fridge. You eat while I shower, then you can tell me the fairytales."

"Do you know why he wants me to tell them to you?"

"I'm not sure." Penny hedged. "But maybe after I've heard them, I'll have a better idea."

In the bathroom, Penny phoned Jay Voigt about the black sedan, and he updated her on the rest. The plates on Alana's kidnapper's car were stolen. Unless the police caught a break, they were at another dead-end.

"I'm at the hospital with John William," Jay said. "When the officers guarding him rotate, I will swing by the office and see if there's any developments on the car bomb, though I've already heard the security footage spotted no one going near the car or planting the device."

More than a little frustrated, Penny asked, "What is your gut telling you?"

Jay didn't hesitate. "That Lucas is in a lot of danger."

"Do you have any idea why?"

"I wish I did, but nothing seems connected, except to him. He has no idea why or about what, and I can't find any reason anyone would target him. None of the typical reasons seem to apply here."

She had feared that would be the case. "Thanks, Jay. I'll keep you posted on anything I find."

Penny stripped off her clothes and got into the shower, hoping that by the time she finished the truth about the fairytales would occur to Lucas. Poor lamb had had so much thrown at him so fast... reeling, he'd said.

Who wouldn't be? She stepped into the shower and prayed for the wisdom to handle this right, feeling more than a little fearful she sorely needed that help John William had insisted she needed.

Her insides shook, despite the peppering hot water sluicing over her skin. "Please, let that help be inbound."

Lucas. Lisa. Kyle. John William. Her own life depended on untangling this web...

TWENTY-THREE

June 9th @ 2350

Penny left the shower feeling more confident. Alert and refreshed, she toweled dry, then dressed in turquoise silk pajamas and robe. She slid into fluffy matching slippers and towel-dried her hair, then raked a comb through it and scrunched it into soft curls. For a long moment, she stared into the vanity mirror, hoping, and praying she could absorb all Lucas would relay to her of the fairytales. In her gut, she fully believed these stories were not stories but history. Lucas's heritage through Kyle's side of the family.

She couldn't prove it yet, but all indicators pointed in that direction and the absence of the Richert family fortune, the pendant and the painting reinforced the indications. How else had Kyle survived monetarily all these years? Why else would anyone want Lucas dead?

She glared into her own eyes in the mirror. "You will not fail him."

Turning, she tossed the towel into the laundry bin, then left the bath.

The back of a man with broad shoulders and sandy, golden hair stood in her kitchen, making himself a cup of tea. White shirt, jeans, running shoes.

She looked to the chair. Her weapon wasn't in it. Where had she left it? The bathroom. No, she'd taken it with her to her room, put it in its locked box. That's right. Fear gripped her hard. Was this a good or bad man, and where was Lucas? She should back out and retrieve her weapon. Now, before he spotted her.

"Would you like a cup?" The man asked, his voice, calm and smooth.

When she didn't answer, he looked back over his shoulder at her. "Tea?"

Penny recognized him from the photo Lisa had of him, John William, and her at lunch, celebrating Oxford. "Who are you?"

"You summoned me, Mrs. Crown." He stirred milk into his tea and set the spoon on a saucer under his cup. "Nicholas Ryan. I prefer Nick, but John William is a formal man, as you well know."

Penny got a glass from the cabinet and filled it with cold water. The photo hadn't prepared her for the man. He was gorgeous, of course, with deep-set eyes and a bold nose and mouth, but there was something almost magnetic in him that dared one to look away. "How did you get into my house?"

He leaned back against the counter, his cup in his hand. "Lucas let me in. I'm a friend of John William and Lisa—but you already know that."

"Why did John William tell me to call you for help?"

"I don't know," Nick said, cocking his head. "You need help? I'm with the government and he trusts me? That's the best I can do for you." He nodded at the table. "Mind if I sit?"

She lifted a hand toward the chairs. John William did trust him. He would never consult anyone who didn't have a sterling reputation. "What do you do for the government?" She sat down at the table, across from him.

He smiled. "Mostly, I solve puzzles."

"What kind of puzzles?"

"All kinds."

In short order, Penny concluded Nicholas Ryan was mercurial, mysterious, intriguing, charming and cryptic. But he was trustworthy, or John William would never associate, and they had consulted for each other over many years. He was younger than she expected, guessing Nick was about her age. And he kept details of himself and his life close to his chest. She couldn't fault him for that.

"Have you decided yet?" he asked.

"Decided what?"

"If you're going to tell me what's going on here." He dipped his chin. "It'll make helping you much easier if I know what we are up against."

"We have a cluster of seemingly unrelated events that I believe are related and pose a serious threat to Lucas."

"I know Lucas," Nick said. "More from Lisa speaking of him than from Lucas. What I don't know is why anyone would target him, though the pendant, if authentic and not a replica, could go a long way toward explaining that."

Penny studied his face, his hands. Strong jaw, capable hands. Finally, she said, "I'm going to trust you and not hold back anything. Don't make me regret that decision, Nick. Lucas is like a son to me, and I love him. If you know anything about me from John William or Lisa or Lucas, you know there is nothing I won't do to protect my children."

He leaned closer and whispered, "I do know that, Mrs. Crown. I suspect that's why I'm here, which tells me John William thinks you might be in over your head, and he wants me to help assure you don't lose it."

Blunt and to the point. Nice. "Are you prepared to do that?"

"Provided you tell me everything you know and suspect and you never lie to me, yes, I am." He tapped his cup with his finger. "I have no patience with lies or liars."

Lucas passed through the kitchen, grabbed a glass of juice, and returned to his room without a word.

Nick dipped his chin. "He's nervous and watching over you."

"Lucas is protective."

Nick laced his hands on the tabletop. "I take it you don't want everything you're going to tell me disclosed to him."

"I think it would be best if he came to certain conclusions on his own, and some details would hurt him more than he's already hurt. I'd like to avoid that."

"I understand. My condolences on Alana's death." Nick refilled his teacup from the pot he'd placed on the table. "If I lift two fingers, Lucas is within earshot. Will that work?"

Relieved, Penny nodded, then launched into relaying all she knew beginning with Alana and the pendant, her torture and murder, then to Lucas's car exploding, their home being vandalized, the near-miss sniper incident with Lucas and Lisa, Kyle's disappearance and reappearance, his second disappearance, and Kyle's insistence that Lucas tell her all the fairytales, which she believes could be his father's and his family history.

Three times during the briefing, Nick had held up two fingers and Penny had waited for his all-clear signal. Understandably, Lucas wanted to hear what was going on, but that wasn't in his best interests.

When she finished, she stopped talking and waited for Nick's reaction. Finally, it came. "We need hard evidence to fulfill any objectives," he said.

"What objectives?" Penny placed some lemon cookies on a plate and placed them on the table.

"Find Alana's murderer, find Kyle Hoff, authenticate the painting and the pendant, which I assume Lucas has with him..." Nick paused, lifted a cookie from the plate, then spoke louder. "Lucas, do you have them?"

He walked around the hallway corner. "I do."

How had Nick known Lucas was there? Penny blinked hard.

Lucas stepped closer. "I was told the pendant was a replica growing up, but before I gave it to Alana, I had it appraised. I wanted to be sure it was adequately insured."

"And?" Nick prodded.

"The jeweler couldn't say if it was authentic or a replica. He recommended I take it to John William for analysis. But he did say the two red stones are very rare. They make the pendant priceless. I could ask what I wanted for it—not that I would ever sell it."

"What about the painting?" Nick asked.

"No one has looked at it. John William had it to look at, but then he was attacked and now he's in a coma. I don't know if he found out anything."

"But you have the painting now?" Nick asked.

"I brought it to him from John William's museum after the attack." Penny spared Nick a glance. Saw something... a tenderness in his eyes as he looked at Lucas. It touched her.

"We'll find out if it is authentic," Nick said. "Lucas, can you stay at the hospital to keep Penny updated on John William. Otherwise, I'll get only half her attention on our investigations."

Brilliant move. Penny bit back a smile. Lucas would be under protection at the hospital as well.

"Of course," Lucas said.

"Where is Lisa?" Nick asked Penny.

"Safe and away."

Nick's gaze sharpened. "Your parents?"

"Safe and away," Penny repeated. He hated liars and lies. "I don't know exactly where."

"Got it." Nick stood up and rinsed his cup at the sink. "I'll be back at 7:00 for you."

"Make it 11:00."

His gaze collided with hers.

"Alana's funeral is at 9:00."

"Of course." Nick frowned. "I'm a little worried about the gathering at the funeral."

"There won't be a gathering," Lucas said. "It's a private service. Since my dad and Lisa are gone and John William is in the hospital, it'll just be Mrs. Crown and me. I, uh, wanted it private."

"I understand," Nick said, his body language and the timbre of his voice proving he did. "I'm sorry for your loss, Lucas, and for your troubles. Mrs. Crown and I will do all we can to resolve them."

Nick was sincere and genuine. Penny sensed it. Just as she sensed he would be at the graveside service at 9:00 in the morning.

"Thank you," Lucas said.

"I'd be happy to drive you or to pick you up afterward. We can have a quiet brunch in Alana's honor."

"Thank you." Lucas stiffened. "We'll meet you at Clover Four on Main Street. Mrs. Crown can ride with you to direct you to it."

Penny didn't object. The ride from the cemetery to Clover Four would give Lucas a few minutes alone to settle himself.

"Perfect." Nick smiled at Penny. "Good night, Mrs. Crown." He pivoted. "Lucas, see me out and lock up?"

"Of course."

Penny watched them go, and for the first time in two years, she felt hopeful. Just maybe there could be some kind of life for her after Mark Crown.

June 10 @ 0500

The doorbell persisted, waking Penny from a dead sleep. She groaned, punched her pillow, and put on her robe. Nearly two hours sleep just wasn't enough, and whoever was now banging on her door, threatening to take it off its hinges, better have a good reason.

She peered through the peep hole. Nick. A worried Nick, gauging by his expression. She disarmed the security system and then opened the door. "What's wrong?"

"Sorry to wake you, Mrs. Crown. You need to get dressed. The hospital called about John William."

Lucas stood behind Penny. "Is he...?"

"He's awake and asking for Mrs. Crown," Nick stepped inside then closed the door.

Penny frowned. "Why didn't they call me?"

"I don't know." Nick shrugged. "I do know they called me. Let's go."

Penny and Lucas rushed to dress and met Nick back in the

kitchen. He was downing a large glass of water. "Hope it's okay that I helped myself." He lifted the glass. "I tend to dehydrate on long plane rides."

"Of course." Penny grabbed her phone from its charger and her purse. How long a flight had he been on to get here? Where had he been?

"Ready?"

"Yes." Penny grabbed her handbag and stuffed her phone in it.

On the counter beside the sink, Nick set down the glass. "Lucas, you drive Mrs. Crown's car." He spared her a glance. "Ride with me."

"I'll need to check the car before Lucas gets near it," she said.

"I already have and will check it again as soon as you're ready. Meet me out there."

"I'll check it," she insisted. No way would she abdicate Lucas's safety. That wasn't happening.

Nick must have realized it. "Fine," he said. "Let's go."

He didn't argue. He had realized and understood, knew she needed to check firsthand to know Lucas was safe.

Penny went over the car and Lucas watched, observing her methods. Nick coached him on what she was doing and why. That pleased Penny. He was teaching Lucas how to protect himself.

Minutes later, they were in their respective cars and on the way to the hospital.

Penny adjusted her seatbelt. "Thank you for not fighting me on checking the car. I needed to do it."

"I know." Nick turned on his signal to turn left. "Are you okay today?"

She looked over at him, said nothing.

"Look, I know it's the anniversary of your husband's death, and that's got to be hard. I am a little surprised Alana's funeral is scheduled for today."

"Lucas took comfort in releasing her to Mark."

"That was a loving gesture. I'm sure it meant a lot to Lucas that you would agree to it."

"I can't refuse him anything that helps him get through this." She shrugged. "It hurts too much."

"You loved Mark."

Surprised, she sent him a hard look. "He was my husband. Of course, I loved him."

"Sorry. No offense intended." Nick looked away. "You know very little about me, but I know a great deal about you and your husband, about his murder, and your frustration with his case pushing you to investigate and solve the murder yourself. Very risky."

John William had told him. Or Lisa. Probably both. "I admit, it was risky, and I got lucky."

Nick checked the rearview mirror. "It wasn't luck."

"I was lucky."

"You're a watcher, Mrs. Crown," Nick said. "You noticed details that were instrumental in pinpointing and capturing the murderer." He tapped the steering wheel. "It wasn't luck. It was skill. You have keen observation ability and the courage to use it."

Shock pumped through her. He did know all about her and her family. Too much. Still suspecting John William and Lisa as his sources, Penny wanted verification. Would he give it to her? "How do you know so much about us?"

"John William sees you as his daughter," Nick said easily. "Your family is his family. He's proud of you and Lisa and he enormously respected Mark."

"Nothing John William knows tells you I'm a watcher, Nick, and for the record, I don't abide lies or liars, either."

"Got it." He sighed. "What I said was true, but I also read the case file. You can't tell anyone that."

He read the file? "How did you get access to the case file?"

"That's irrelevant." He stonewalled. "But your skills are relevant and impressive."

Penny frowned. "Well, they don't seem to be helping Lucas, and they sure didn't help Alana." She'd regret that the rest of her life.

"That's not yet determined." He turned into the hospital parking lot. "Why do you think Alana was taken?"

"I don't know yet."

"But you suspect…"

"I suspect her kidnapping is tied to the pendant."

He pulled into a parking slot and turned off the engine. "And the pendant is tied to—?"

"Kyle and Lucas. That's still muddy."

Noting movement through the window, she glanced that way. "Lucas is already here." Penny nodded toward her SUV, three slots over.

He motioned he was going ahead inside, then walked to the entrance.

Penny and Nick followed. They entered the hospital, then took the elevator to the third floor. "I hate that hospital smell," Penny said.

"So do I," Nick said. "Though this one is more pleasant than many."

"It doesn't smell like the morgue to you?" Penny asked.

Tenderness shone in his eyes. "More like antiseptic and lemon."

Penny grimaced. "Then it's me. This is not my favorite place to be."

"Especially not today."

She agreed but held her silence. Sometimes words were just unnecessary lagniappe.

They stepped off the elevator. Lucas greeted them. "He's not conscious."

"So, it wasn't the nurse who called me?" Nick asked.

"No."

"Someone wanted us out of the house," Penny deducted. She pulled out her phone. "I'm calling Jay Voigt."

Nick stayed her with a hand to the phone. "Let's go check out the house first. If anything is amiss, then we'll call Voigt."

Jay had been putting in awful hours. There was no reason to wake him until they knew why they were waking him. "Sounds reasonable." She turned for the corridor to the rooms. "I'm going to check in on John William before we go. Coming?"

Both Lucas and Nick followed her to John William's room.

Penny nodded to the officer outside the door then walked in. The monitors beeped steadily; John William was still comatose. She heard a soft snore coming from the corner and looked over. Dr. Handley was dozing in the visitor's chair.

Oddly comforted, she left the room and rejoined Lucas and Nick. "Dr. Handley is with him."

Lucas shrugged. "Not surprised."

That he was there had surprised her. She waited for Lucas to explain.

"You threatened him if he failed to protect John William."

Nick smiled. "He knew you meant it."

"I wouldn't kill him."

Lucas frowned. "You might. I wouldn't risk messing with John William."

"I wouldn't kill him," Penny insisted, heading back to the elevator.

"I believe her, Lucas." Nick stepped in and pushed the first-floor button.

"I was there, Nick. I saw her face when she warned him."

"She wouldn't kill him," Nick insisted. "But she would make him wish he were dead."

Lucas chewed on his lower lip. "I guess sometimes that's worse."

Penny wisely kept her mouth shut.

Back at Penny's house, Nick asked Penny to watch over Lucas in the SUV until Nick finished sweeping the house for any kind of intrusions. The two patrol cars returned and parked, one in front and one in back. "We don't want to alert them unnecessarily."

Finding no fault with his logic, Penny slid into the SUV's passenger's seat and told Lucas, "Stay put until Nick gives us an all-clear."

The streetlamp cast a stream of light into the car. Penny studied Lucas. He looked tired to the point of dread. "Are you okay?"

"No." He sighed. "You?"

"No." Alana's funeral would be in a few hours. She'd have

Mark's death to deal with again, and Alana's. Penny felt as bone-weary as Lucas looked. "Today will be a hard day, but we'll get through it."

"We will." He let her see the sadness in his eyes. "So much has come so fast. I just want to breathe again. I don't expect things to be normal. I don't even know what normal is anymore, but it's not this."

"Honestly, this chaos and emptiness where everything seems bleak is pretty normal right after the loss of a loved one." She started to stop there but felt compelled to share more. "It's like a broad and deep abyss stretching out in every direction as far as you can see. I remember that desolation. It is almost unbearable, but it does pass. At least, until something triggers it." She glanced over at him. "When I was where you are now, more than anything, I craved a few minutes by myself to just be numb and not feel the pain. Then to just think."

Seeming relieved that she understood, he swiped his brow. "There's too much else going on to take a minute much less a few." Lucas rubbed his eyes. "I still can't believe she's gone."

"I know." Penny sniffed. "That's one of the hardest things to wrap your mind and heart around, and to accept. But with time, things will get better." She saw the lights come on in the house on the first floor. "Then there'll come a day when you go all day without thinking about her and you'll feel guilty. You'll laugh for the first time and feel guilty. And finally, one day you won't feel so guilty anymore. You'll start building a new life and get excited about something in it and feel happy. Each positive emotion you feel will be a trigger the first time or two you feel it. Guilt follows."

"Because I'm still here and she's not?"

"Yes. And because you realize you have a life without her. It might not be the life you imagined or wanted, Lucas, but it can still be good. Dr. Mason says it can be better because you have a deeper understanding of the people and things you most value." Penny swiped her hair back from her face, and saw the lights go on and then off again upstairs. "For what it's worth, I think she's right about that."

"But first I have to get through all this." He turned to her questioning. "What is all this about? It makes no sense to me. Alana was good and kind and never hurt anyone. Why would this happen to her?"

"I wish I had answers to all your questions," Penny said. "But the truth is sometimes we don't get all the answers. We try, and we will continue to try to find them. We look and hope and keep digging for answers, and we find some, but rarely do we find them all. You need to be prepared for that."

"Reasonable expectations."

"Exactly."

He stared out the window. "Maybe sometimes there are no answers."

"For what it is worth, I believe there are always answers," Penny said. "But we find only those that will benefit us."

"Wouldn't they all benefit us?"

"Maybe not. Maybe the questions we can't answer are better for us not to answer in some way."

"Driving us nuts wondering?"

"Kindlier," she said. "Some answers may rob us of peace forever, so not finding them is really—"

"Mercy."

Penny watched the front door. "Yeah."

"You're not saying we should stop looking for answers... or are you?"

"Absolutely not."

He lowered his gaze. "I think I could handle this better if I knew what I'd done. That bothers me most. All this trouble must be my fault but, I don't know what I've done."

"No, Lucas. This is not your fault," Penny assured him. "When things happen, it is natural to look for someone to blame. Anyone to blame, but—"

"It has to be my fault."

"It seems that way to you because of Alana. She was a lovely woman and you two were so happy. You're devastated, of course, and so you feel guilty. When Mark died, I did, too. But here's the thing, dear one. I didn't kill Mark and you didn't kill Alana." Her mouth dry, Penny swallowed. "I wish I had some magic words or something—anything—that could comfort you, but there is no comfort outside of faith. The truth is, sometimes you just have to endure the pain until it subsides."

"And find out who killed her."

"Yes."

Sadness and gratitude mingled in his eyes. "Thank you for helping me do that."

"I'll always do all I can for you," Penny said. "That's a promise."

"You always have." Lucas pointed to a dark shadow coming around the side of the garage. "There's Nick."

It was Nick. And he was on the phone.

When he reached the SUV, Penny and Lucas got out of the car. "Everything okay?" Penny asked, hiking her handbag's strap on her shoulder.

"I found three listening devices, so I called Jay Voigt."

"Did he speak with you?"

Nick looked surprised by the question. "Of course."

Interesting. Jay was typically more reserved on his cases. Penny held her silence.

"I told him I was helping you," Nick explained. "He's sending two new officers to monitor from outside. They'll be here shortly."

"Why the change?"

"He didn't say. Probably because these two are due to rotate off. Just giving us a head's up."

Lucas stepped closer. "Is there any word on my father?"

"He hasn't surfaced again. But try not to worry, Lucas. He's skilled at evasions."

"He is?" Lucas looked baffled.

Nick lightened his tone. "He's done well so far, hasn't he?"

"I guess he has."

Nick knew more than he was saying. Still, Lucas seemed satisfied. "Do you think he'll be at the funeral?"

Lucas shrugged. "I don't know. I hope so, but he could be halfway to Europe right now. He was that scared."

"I won't intrude, but I'll be close in case I'm needed." Nick walked them to the door. "You two get some rest. I'll be out here until the new officers arrive."

"You don't have to do that," Penny said.

"I do." He studied her face briefly. "When John William wakes up, I want to be able to meet his eyes and say I've done what he asked me to do."

"I won't argue," Penny said. "But only because I totally understand that."

"I've already asked Jay why there wasn't a guard on John William immediately after the attack."

Penny stopped and looked back at Nick. "What did he say?"

"He was guarded. The officer he assigned had taken a restroom break." Nick frowned. "You can stand down on the matter, Mrs. Crown. I've already raked the detective over the coals about it. We chew anything more and we'll alienate him. Can't afford that."

"Thank you." Penny genuinely meant it, unsure if she had the energy to spare to rake Jay, especially today. "John William was right about your help. It's good to have a partner."

"I'd have done this with or without you," Nick said. "John William is the closest thing I have to family."

Mulling on that disclosure, she and Lucas walked in, and Penny closed the door.

TWENTY-FOUR

June 10th @ 0900

How dare the sun shine on the lush green lawns of the cemetery? How dare the gentle summer breeze dance through the large oak near Alana's open grave? How dare the minister drone on and on, prolonging the grief and agony of standing beside a coffin holding Lucas's beloved Alana and that blend in Penny's mind with the memory of her standing beside Lisa at Mark's open grave?

Arrogant.

Merciless.

Unrepentant for the pain caused, suffered, and endured.

Lucas whispered softly to not interrupt the minister. "Everything all right?"

Penny sent him a blank look.

"You're shivering." Worry creased his smooth forehead. "Are you cold?"

"No," she whispered back. "I'm fine."

With Lisa removed, Kyle fleeing, and John William in the hospital, only Penny and Lucas stood at Alana's graveside. Them and the minister. He talked and talked until Penny's silent screams drowned out his voice and memories of Mark's funeral filled the void. That angered her. This was about Alana. It was supposed to be about her, and Penny was supposed to be there for Lucas. She shook herself and forced the minister's voice to penetrate her chaotic mind.

Lucas clasped her hand and squeezed.

She looked up at him. Tears leaked from his eyes. Her heart tightened, and she squeezed his hand.

Finally, the words she awaited from the minister were being spoken. "Ashes to ashes and dust to dust…"

A little groan escaped Lucas.

He took one of the three white roses Penny held and placed it atop Alana's coffin. When he stepped back, Penny placed a second.

The minister finished and said a few kind words to them. Over his shoulder, Penny spotted movement in the woods beyond the lush lawn. Nicholas and Voigt, in addition to the two patrol cars parked near Penny on the road behind Lucas.

Lucas thanked the minister, and he departed on foot. Penny watched him go.

"I wish my father were here." He looked at Penny. "I was sure he would show up, but he didn't."

Lucas's disappointment was clear and understandable. He still had no idea what was going on. At least Penny had a little insight. Far from all of it, but something. She locked arms with Lucas. "I'm sure he would have been here if he could have." Kyle Hoff knew exactly what was going on and why. Only his fleeing and absence at Alana's funeral made sense. He was protecting Lucas, leading those who wished him harm away from him. Nick agreed that John William had some information that could assist them about why Lucas was in lethal jeopardy. If only he would wake up and tell it to them.

She patted Lucas's arm. "I'll give you a moment to say goodbye." She looked into his eyes and saw then felt his heartbreak. Too familiar, she walked a short distance away, pressing a thorn from the remaining rose deep into her fingertip to divide the pain running rampant within.

She stopped near the trunk of an oak, pressed a tissue to the blood oozing from her finger, and began a deep breathing exercise Dr. Mason had taught her to use to calm herself.

By the time Lucas joined her, Penny's breathing was nearly normal.

He noticed the rose. "For Mr. Crown?"

Penny nodded.

"Where is he buried from here?"

"Just over there." She motioned a few graves over, on the opposite side of the tree.

"Shall I walk you, or wait here?" His Adam's apple bobbed.

"Wait here." He needed the time to collect himself. His emotions were raw, oozing, and threatening to erupt.

Penny walked over to Mark's grave. "Hi, honey." She swept the sun-warmed stone with her hand, then placed the rose at its base, and whispered a prayer. Then she talked to Mark. "I love and miss you with all my heart. You made life so rich and full." She swallowed hard. "I'm doing my best, though everything is harder without you. If you can, please help me deal with all this. I wanted more interesting cases, but I'm not sure I'm up to this one. I know what I think is happening, but I'm not positive, and I can't prove much. I think this is too big for me, Mark. And I'm scared to death Lucas or Lisa or John William will pay for my ignorance with their lives. Help me."

She went silent and waited, and waited, but heard no response, and felt no reassurance, no comfort, and no peace. Her eyes blurred. She reached up and discovered her face was tear-soaked. Dabbing it dry, she crushed the tissue in her fist and turned from Mark's grave, then walked back to Lucas.

Wordlessly, he held his arms open wide.

Penny stepped into them and hugged him hard.

Nicholas suddenly appeared, joining them. "You both need a little quiet time. I'll drive you to brunch."

"I'll drive us," Penny insisted. "Save you coming back for your car."

"I rode in with Voigt. He left on a call, so I'm stranded." Nick smoothed his tie. "Look." Nick motioned to the street.

From where they were parked all the way to the cemetery gates, mourners, including the swim team members and Coach, lined both sides of the street.

Each person held a single white rose.

1300

After brunch, Lucas took Penny's car to the hospital. He wanted to spend some time with John William and give Dr. Handley a break.

Penny and Nicholas walked the short distance across the stone path to the park and gazebo then on to John William's museum to examine the pendant and the painting. Both, according to Lucas, were secured in the basement vault.

"I'm surprised John William told Lucas there was a vault," Penny told Nick.

"So am I. I thought only John William, you and I knew it existed."

Penny bristled. "He seems to have discussed me with you a lot more than you with me. All I knew was your name, Nicholas."

"Now you know more."

"Not much more."

"You know I prefer Nick."

They entered the museum and Penny found the familiar smells of it soothing. "Tea first?"

"That would be welcome." Nick smiled.

He was an attractive man. Tall, tanned, and frankly drop-dead gorgeous. Trimmed hair, polished and a bit sophisticated. He'd be right at home as a James Bond type character. Cool, calm, and mysterious. "This way." Penny led him to the kitchen and put the kettle on for tea, then readied a tray.

Nick sat down at the table. "Go ahead, Mrs. Crown. Ask your questions."

Penny could step back, but before she opened John William's vault, she wanted a better feel for her partner. "I know you and John William consult with each other and have for a long time. I thought you'd be older."

"I began consulting not long after hitting double digits," Nick said. "Twelve, to be precise." He cocked his head. "Not many experts trust the findings of a twelve-year-old boy."

"But John William did."

"Yes, he did."

"So, you do consults full-time?" Penny placed the teacups on the table.

"It's an important part of my work."

"Who employs you?" She added cream, lemon, sugar, and cookies to the table.

"The government."

That surprised her. "Ours?"

He smiled.

"I noted your accent. British." She sat to wait for the kettle. "So, what else do you do for the government?"

"I told you, mostly I solve puzzles. To be more precise, I address a long list of things which are of little interest in what we're doing now." He folded his hands atop the table. "A gentle reminder, Mrs. Crown. I am here at your request."

"John William's request."

"Yes. My point is, John William trusted you enough to tell you how to contact me. I trust him enough to respond and show up to help you. He's family to both of us, as I explained." Nick paused a long moment, then added, "To state the obvious, if we want everyone involved to survive this, we have to trust each other."

She added cutlery and sat down across from Nick. "We've already lost Alana and maybe Kyle."

"Do you have information on Kyle you haven't shared?"

"No, but I suspect he's avoiding contact to lead Alana's murderers away from Lucas. I also suspect he knows exactly what is happening and why. That's speculation and I can't prove it, but that's where I am at the moment."

The kettle whistled. Penny poured hot water into the teapot then returned to the table with it. They sat in silence until Penny poured the tea.

"I have a few questions—if that's all right." Nick added cream and sipped from his cup.

"Of course." His asking was fine. Her answering remained optional.

Nick placed two cookies on his plate. Apparently, the zesty tang of lemon appealed to him. "Did Voigt note anyone of interest at the memorial service held at the university?"

"Not that he's mentioned to me," Penny said. "Neither did I, for what it is worth. There were so many people there."

"Has Lucas heard from his father since the black sedan incident?"

"Not yet." She thumbed the rim of her cup. "I've been looking into Kyle Hoff, but I can't find anything from before the time he arrived here. It's as if he appeared in Georgia out of thin air."

"Did you check—"

"I checked every database, everywhere I could check. Nothing."

Nick pulled out a satellite phone and made a call. "Adam, good," he said when someone answered. "I need deep background on Kyle Hoff."

He listened, then asked, "Who sealed the file?"

Another listening pause, then Nick added, "I want it as soon as possible."

Nick locked gazes with Penny then disconnected the call.

"State Department or Homeland Security?" she asked.

"State."

"Who sealed Kyle's records?"

"Secretary Dawson."

"Will Adam be able to get the file for you?"

"If anyone can, Adam will. He'll be in touch."

"Interesting." Penny's mind reeled.

Nick paused and then asked, "What does Kyle do here?"

"He works from home is all I can tell you. I've never seen evidence of him doing anything except caring for Lucas."

"So, he has no visible means of support?"

"Not that I've seen, but he is very private, so he could be doing anything and it's likely no one except maybe Lucas would know it. Lisa is welcome, but their home is nearly off-limits to everyone else."

Nick mulled that over. "They live well. Beautiful home, nice vehicles."

"Lucas's was nice, until someone bombed it." It wasn't as if Penny hadn't thought about this. "Maybe there was a hefty insurance settlement after Lucas's mother died?"

"What happened to her?"

"Grace had cancer. We got to know each other through the children when Lisa was an infant. Lucas and Lisa are very close."

"I know," Nick said. "John William talks about them both a great deal. Was this a long time ago, that Kyle's wife died?"

Penny nodded. "It's been over a decade. Maybe twelve or so years. Lucas was young, but old enough that he remembers a lot about her."

"And there's no one else in Kyle's life?"

"I've never seen or heard of anyone else being in his life. Just him and Lucas. Kyle doesn't associate with others, doesn't like others in his home—besides Lisa—and he never socializes. I've stood in as parent on all Lucas's school events since his mother died, and all the media events for the swim meet. Honestly, I was half-surprised Kyle showed up at their engagement party."

"And you never asked why?"

"No, I didn't." Penny fidgeted. "Kyle is a very private person. Alienate him, and where does that leave Lucas? Alone. I couldn't risk that."

"Why is it a risk?"

"I promised his mother I'd watch over him. As I said, Lucas and Lisa have been close friends since she was tiny."

"And because you love him."

"I do," Penny admitted. "So did Mark."

"I understand. Lucas was like your son."

"He still is, Nick, and he always will be." She noted his empty cup. "More tea?"

"Please." He nodded. "What's the most significant thing about either of Lucas's parents that you know?"

"They totally and completely love Lucas."

"Okay." Nick sighed. "Let's take a look at the pendant and painting now."

At ease, Penny agreed, and stood up.

Nick dipped his chin. "Why don't you tell me what you really wanted to say was most significant?"

Not surprised he'd picked up on that, Penny disclosed the truth. "Kyle instructed Lucas to tell me the fairytales he and his wife told Lucas. He's going to do that tonight. I hope that will give us more insight about Kyle."

Nick cocked his head. "So, what troubles you about that?"

"Lucas will do as his father asked, but I'm certain he has no idea why the stories are significant."

"But you do know why?"

She feared she did. But without proof… "I'll have a better grasp after I hear what Lucas has to say. Until then, I'm reserving judgment."

For the next hour and a half, Nick examined the painting and the pendant, using only John William's equipment in the room with the vault. Did he not know about the lab? The plethora of equipment in it?

"What's this?" Nick glanced from the pendant to Penny. "Did you pick up on this splotch under the arch?"

"I saw it, but even under magnification, I didn't see anything significant. Of course, I'm no John William."

"It could be significant. Interesting, at least." Nick took another look. "We need expert analysis."

"You and John William are the experts."

Nick smiled. "There are others with testing equipment John

doesn't have." Nick straightened up. "Don't worry. We have a trusted associate. We will visit that lab tomorrow."

"Where is this expert?"

"New York." Nick returned the pendant to the inner vault safe. "I'll handle our transportation." He pulled the painting from its pouch and placed it on the exam table across from Penny. Then, he studied it.

Finally, he looked at her. "This is a forgery, but a very good one." He moved it to Penny's side of the table. "Look at the center of it, through the keyhole."

She examined it closely. A jagged line appeared. Her heart beat hard and fast, her pulse raced. "There's something underneath it—an under-layer."

"Yes," Nick said. "Our associate can help us with that, too."

"What do you think will be found?"

"I'm not sure." His gaze locked onto hers. "But my guess is that whatever is there is the reason Alana was killed and Kyle has vanished."

Nick's declaration resonated deep inside Penny. "I wish I could disagree, but I can't." Puzzled, she added, "I don't know what it could be. Do you?"

"Not yet. But I'm certain it's something…significant."

She felt so, too. "Wait a second. Tomorrow is Sunday. The lab in New York will be closed."

Nick nodded. "Monday. I meant Monday. I'm still out of sync from the travel. I'll pick you up at 9:00 Monday morning. Will that work?"

"Yes." Penny returned the painting to its pouch, closed, and then locked the safe. Stepping back, she checked her watch. "I need to get home. Lucas will be coming for our story hour shortly."

"I'll drive you." Nick double-checked the safe inside the vault and the vault, then the door. "Security system is enabled?"

Oddly comforted by his attention to detail, Penny smiled. "Check."

TWENTY-FIVE

June 10th @ 2000

The kitchen smelled great. A chicken casserole the swim team had delivered was heating in the oven. Penny pulled the makings for salad from the fridge, grabbed a cutting board and knife. Working at the bar, she heard the door and paused. Lucas came in looking weary and beaten. "Good timing," Penny said. "I'm working on dinner."

"I don't think I can eat."

"Of course, you can. Grief requires fuel, as does clear thinking. We need clear thinking. Grab a drink and sit down." She diced a tomato. "How is everything at the hospital?"

He reached for a glass from the cabinet and filled it with ice. "Dr. Handley appreciated the break. He got a shower and a good nap, he said."

"Good." Penny added tomato to the salad bowl and reached for an onion. "And John William?"

"No change." Lucas filled the glass with water. "He's stable but still not conscious. Dr. Handley says not to worry."

"Was his door guard alert?"

"Definitely." Lucas sat down at the table. "Have you talked to Lisa?"

"Yes. She checked in shortly after I got home."

"Anything new?"

"Nothing you haven't already been told." Penny added diced onion to the salad. "What about your father?"

"No word at all." Lucas took a sip of water from his glass. "He's not even answering our dedicated phone. Something is wrong, or he'd answer it."

Penny didn't necessarily agree but held her tongue. "What does Jay Voigt say about that?"

Lucas twisted his mouth. "I phoned the detective this afternoon, not that he had anything to say."

"Nothing?"

"Nothing. They haven't found any leads on Dad or Alana's murderer." Deep sadness riddled his eyes. "Nothing at all."

More disappointed than surprised, Penny finished the salad and washed her hands at the sink. She snagged a dishtowel to dry her hands. "Maybe your father is with a friend? Or one of your mother's relatives?"

Lucas spared her a glance. "She had no relatives and my dad's a loner." He turned his gaze back to the clear water in his glass. "Before Mom died, there were often people around. But not since then. Dad stays to himself."

Penny put the bowl on the table, then tossed the salad. "What does he do with all his time?" She passed the tongs to Lucas.

Lucas filled his salad bowl. "He gardens mostly. And cooks. He loves both but has little interest in anything else."

"Must be lonely."

Lucas nodded. "I often thought so, but he denies it. Says he's dedicated to his purpose."

Penny sat down at the table. "What is his purpose?"

Lucas shrugged. "I don't know."

That response she didn't expect. Filling her salad bowl, Penny mulled on it and decided. Kyle Hoff was a man with a lot of secrets he wanted to keep secret… or a man with a lot he wanted to forget.

By the time they finished dinner, Lucas seemed nearly overwhelmed with grief. Funeral day for Penny had been hard. But funeral night had been an endless nightmare. She pulled a business card from her pocket and placed it on the table near Lucas.

"What's this?"

Penny cleared the dishes. "It's one of Dr. Elizabeth Mason's cards."

"Your therapist?"

"Grief counselor." Penny stacked the plates on the countertop near the sink. "Lucas, when you lose someone so special to you, grief hits in ways you expect, but in ways you can't expect, too. At least, it did me." She sat back down at the table, across from him. "When Mark died, it was bad. There were people around and coming in and out with food and to check on Lisa and me. That was hard, too. But in short order, they got busy with their own lives, and then it got worse. That's when I ran into trouble dealing with it."

"John William and I were here."

"You were, and that helped so much. But the nights stretched on forever. The house was quiet. I was essentially alone with my thoughts, and they were brutal." Penny shuddered at the memories and pain of those nights. "I fought going to grief counseling and waited too long. Dr. Mason could have spared me a lot of agony by warning me of what was coming and how to cope with it." She reached across and covered Lucas's hand with her own. "I don't want that for you."

"I don't see how she can help. She didn't even know Alana."

"She didn't know Mark, and I didn't see how she could help, either. But she did. It's not fun, and I won't say it was easy. But she did help." Penny stared into his eyes, her own pleading. "Promise me you'll consider talking to her about all this, okay?"

He lifted the card and tucked it into his pocket. "I'll talk to her about Alana."

"Thank you." Penny smiled at him and returned to the dishes.

"Mrs. Crown?"

"Yes, Lucas?"

His eyes shone overly bright. "Does it ever get easier?"

God, didn't she wish? "I'm so sorry to say that it doesn't. But you will get better at coping with it." She let out a deep breath. "I know that isn't want you want to hear, and it certainly isn't what I want to say, but I won't lie to you, Lucas. What I told you is the truth as I know it." She filled the dishwasher. "Faith helps. I honestly don't know how anyone survives grief without it."

"I don't know how anyone survives life without faith. So many ups and downs," Lucas said. "Seems logical that wouldn't exclude death." He looked up at her. "It helped when I lost my mom. And I know it helped Dad, too."

Penny closed the dishwasher. "Sometimes, faith helps me feel strong enough to keep moving, and for a few minutes, I forget. Then I remember and I feel guilty for forgetting. That part is getting better, Lucas, and it will for you, too. When it does and you feel guilty, remember that everything happens as it does for a reason."

"What do you mean?"

"Mark and Alana died. We didn't. We don't know why but I believe that one day we will know. That belief is enough reason to keep going. Oh, dying with them would have been easier. Grief is miserable. Has no mercy. It chews us up at every turn, trying to drag us even deeper into the abyss."

"The abyss?"

Penny nodded. She'd told him, but he had been too overwhelmed at the time to take it in. "That dark place grief takes us that makes us question life. Is this all there is? If this is all there is, why bother?" She shivered. "But then faith whispers in our ear, promises to reveal the purpose we didn't die. The reason we're still here."

"I haven't heard that yet."

"When you most need it, you will, and then you'll have to choose. To keep going to fulfill your purpose, or to lose it, too. Faith in our purpose keeps us out of the abyss."

"I'm still not clear on the abyss."

"You've felt it," Penny said. "I've seen it in your eyes." She sat back down. "It's when you feel empty and lost and like nothing could possibly ever matter to you again. It's the place of nothing.

Not good or bad things, not anything. Just dark empty space and nothingness. It's awful. More terrifying than hell because there is seemingly no escape and no hope. The abyss is the absence of everything. Nothing to see. Silence. Nothing to touch. Just dark space and nothing."

"What can reach you there?"

"Only one thing. And it can be hard to find when you most need it."

"What?"

"Faith." Penny smiled. "I remember the first time for me. I was deep in the abyss, and I called out. Well, I railed against the nothingness and then I called out. A little speck of light burned through the darkness. I was never so glad to see light in my life. I moved toward it in my mind. And the more I did, the bigger it got, and I finally recognized it."

"What was it?"

"Hope." Penny sniffed. "It was hope, Lucas."

His forehead wrinkled in a frown. "Did Dr. Mason tell you about the abyss and hope?"

"Unfortunately, I had to find that out on my own. I guess it is one of those things where you have to live it to really understand how important it is." She tapped the table. "Dr. Mason is more of the it's different for everyone and she tries to tell you things to help you resolve what grief is doing to you."

Lucas sat silent, clearly processing all this. Finally, he asked, "How do you handle it?"

"At first, I just did what needed doing. I'd get up, get dressed, go to work, eat and sleep—not well even now, but much better than I did at first."

"Just do what you need to do?"

Penny nodded. "Take things a day at the time, and when a day is too much, take them an hour at a time, or even a minute at a time."

"Sometimes a minute seems hard."

"Take a second, then." Penny sipped from her water glass. "The first day I didn't think about Mark until in the afternoon, I felt so guilty, Lucas. I cried half the night, angry at myself for forgetting him."

"But it was just for a morning."

"I know." Penny lifted a hand. "After the trip to the abyss where I discovered faith fosters hope, I finally got it that life moves on, and moving on doesn't mean you forget. It means you focus more on life than on death. For me, that was the first sign I recall of any kind of healing."

"So, are you healed now?"

"Honestly, I'm not sure. I don't cry every day anymore. I can think of Mark without feeling lost and empty. Actually, I remember good times, too. Not all the time, but often. Is that healed? I don't know. But I don't feel as dead inside as I did at first. I've asked myself a million times if there was life after Mark Crown. Not so much anymore. I know people need me, and I've learned that I need them, too. So you tell me if I'm healed."

"You're getting there," Lucas said. "You laugh more again, and you don't have that sad look in your eyes all the time. I'll be glad when I can look in the mirror and not see anything but sadness and me being broken."

"So will I." Penny stiffened. "This has been a hard talk, Lucas, but I hope it has helped you. And I hope you will contact Dr. Mason."

"If you insist," he said. "But to tell you the truth, talking to you does me more good than talking to someone I don't know and who doesn't know me."

"She'll help you even more." Penny stretched. "Now, do you feel up to talking about the fairytales?"

"Not really," Lucas admitted.

"It's been a hard day." The funeral. His father not being there. John William still comatose and Lisa being away. "Would you rather wait until the morning?"

"No." His eyes darted. "One is coming to mind that fits. I need to take a shower and get it clear in my mind." He stood up. "I won't be long."

"Take your time. I'll be right here."

Soon the shower was running, and the phone rang. Penny answered it. "Hello."

"It's Nick. Have you learned anything yet?"

"No, sorry. We needed to talk about grief."

"Did it help?"

"I think so. He doesn't look as haunted or weary as when he came in."

"I don't think he does either. Eating a little helped. Well done, Mrs. Crown."

Nick could see them, talking in the kitchen? "Where are you?"

"Outside. I'm giving the patrol officers a break."

"I can handle this, Nick."

"Of course, you can. But remember, John William. I won't risk disappointing him."

That, she understood. She'd rather die a thousand deaths than have John William wake up and have to tell him she'd blown it. "I understand."

"If you'd crack open the window, I could hear, too."

"No way. I can't violate Lucas's trust."

"But you will let me know what he tells you afterward."

"With his permission, yes, of course."

"I guess that's as good as it is going to get."

"It is."

He hung up, and Penny winced. It wasn't what she would have wanted, either. But it was the best she could do.

Lucas returned. "Was that the phone?"

"It was Nick. He wanted to be sure you'd gotten back from the hospital okay."

"Is he here?"

A test. He'd heard. "He's outside. Giving the officers a coffee break."

"That's good of him." Lucas sat down on the sofa. "Come over here. It's more comfortable."

Penny took a seat in her favorite chair, opposite the sofa. "You look like you're feeling better."

"Revived."

"Are you ready then to tell me about the fairytale that fit?"

Lucas nodded. "King Arthur of Lovenia died. His son, Alexander, was coronated and crowned—and grieving. The new king knew he had to be strong for his people and his country. The people had loved the old king very much, and Alexander believed it was his duty to set an example for them. To grieve his father privately, he would walk through the woods surrounding the castle—the Enchanted Forest in the painting. He'd always walk the same path, to an ancient, forked oak."

A forked oak? Penny swallowed hard. Alana's body had been found at the forked oak in the park. "Was that oak significant?"

Lucas nodded. "Alexander prayed there, and cried there, alone so no one else witnessed it. Every day at twilight, he walked to the forked oak, and one day, he discovered he was not alone."

"His guards?"

"No. He'd ordered them to stay away. He felt this touch on his shoulder. A comforting touch. When he turned around, he saw a beautiful woman named Kerra. Silent tears soaked her face. Alexander asked Kerra how long she had been coming to the tree. She told him since his father had died. She couldn't bear the thought of Alexander grieving alone. He was a king, but also a man. So, she came to grieve with him, but she didn't want to intrude."

"That's lovely."

"It is," Lucas agreed. "They talked and held hands."

"Did she meet him there daily then?"

"She did. They prayed together, cried together, and talked until one day, they didn't cry. Alexander fell in love with Kerra under that oak, and he eventually married her, and she became his queen. They had two children, Prince Stefan, and Princess Brigit. They were happy and beloved by the people of Lovenia."

"I love that story," Penny said, processing it. "How did your dad hear of it?"

"He and my mother created all the Lovenia stories to entertain me. They loved telling stories." Lucas's expression turned to puzzlement. "Though, I can't for the life of me understand why Dad insisted I repeat them to you."

Penny wasn't sure. It seemed obvious Kyle Hoff had some connection to King Alexander. But how, she didn't know. Kyle was too young to be a relative of King Arthur and too old to be Prince Stefan. Besides, both children died long ago, according to her research. So why had Kyle insisted Lucas share the stories?

She focused on Lucas, seeking more information. "You said there are many stories, right?"

"Yes, but it's late and I need to check in with Det. Voigt and then settle in for a while. I'm emotionally zapped, Mrs. Crown. I'm sure you are, too. We'll share more stories in the morning." Lucas rose then headed off to bed.

Penny watched him go, knowing the poor lamb was in for a long night. She fisted her hand in her lap. He was right about today. It had been hard. And if things kept moving in the same direction, the coming days were unlikely to be easier... or less dangerous.

TWENTY-SIX

June 11th @ 0930

Penny awakened early, dressed in jeans and a blue pin-stripe blouse, then put on coffee and had her first cup at her desk. She checked her email and cases, viewed some video footage, and spotted nothing new or significant to report but touched base with her active clients to brief them and to let them know she'd be out of town until Tuesday.

When she finished that and had checked her calendar and moved two Monday appointments to Wednesday, she phoned the hospital for an update on John William.

The charge nurse transferred her directly to Dr. Handley, and not knowing if that was good or bad news, Penny waited breathlessly for him to get on the line.

"Good morning, Penny," he finally said.

"Good morning." She braced for anything. "How is John William this morning?"

"Strictly speaking, there's been no change, but he had a good night."

"Still stable but comatose?"

"Yes. And his vitals are better. I can't say for sure, but it wouldn't surprise me if he regained consciousness soon. We were able to avoid relieving pressure on his brain. That's a good sign."

"Very." Penny exhaled, finally daring to breathe. "I'll be up to see him later today. Is the guard staying on his toes?"

"He is… or they are. They work in shifts," Dr. Handley said. "Thus far, I'm relieved to report, there have been no further incidents."

Praying that truth held, Penny said, "That's good to hear. I wanted to let you know that I must go out of town tomorrow. I'll try to be back tomorrow night, but it's possible I won't return until Tuesday."

"On the case, I expect."

"Yes."

"What about Lucas?" he asked.

"I thought I'd ask the Coach to come stay with him. His wife is visiting her parents in Virginia."

"Why not have Lucas come here? He could be with John William and under close guard. We'll bring in a bed so he's comfortable, and I'll be available if he needs to talk."

"That sounds wise." She should have thought of it herself. Too many irons in too many fires. "I'll run the idea past him and let you know." Lucas not being alone and being closely watched would ease her mind. She'd half considered sending him to her parents, too. Dr. Handley's suggestion would be safer for all of them.

"Happy hunting, Penny. Take care."

"Thank you, Dr. Handley. If there's any change, you can reach me on my mobile."

"Will do."

Penny hung up then dialed Lisa on her burner phone. She answered on the first ring. "Good morning."

"Morning," Lisa said. "Is everything okay?"

"We're fine. And you?"

"We've been examining the college thing. She's pro UG. He's pro Oxford."

Penny imagined her parents vigorously discussing the pros and cons, trying desperately to influence Lisa's decision. "Who is winning the debate?" Lisa would listen, of course, but then she would do what she wanted to do.

"No one just yet, but they're both strong contenders." Lisa changed the subject. "After yesterday, are you really okay?"

"I am. We all got through it."

"Yes, we did." Her voice grew stronger. "That's a win."

It was. Penny studied the leaves blowing outside her window. "I wanted to let you know I'll be out of town."

"For how long?"

"A day or two. If you need me, use this number, okay?"

"Okay." Lisa hesitated. "Is this trip work-related?"

"It is."

"How is John William?" The tremor in her voice proved she'd been afraid to ask.

"As of this morning, no change, but his vitals seem more stable." Before Lisa could ask, Penny added, "Lucas is worn to a frazzle, but hanging in there."

"What does Jay say?"

Penny worked to keep her tone bland, burying her frustration. "They've found nothing on Alana's murderers. It's as if they abducted and killed her then vanished into thin air." That led Penny to believe they'd left with the swim teams and were now safely out of the country. She hoped she was wrong about that. "No word on Lucas's dad, though they think he chose to disappear again intentionally."

"Without Lucas? I don't believe it. Why would he do that? It makes no sense."

"I don't know why. Not yet."

"Well, find out, Mom."

There was no missing the challenge issued. Penny frowned. "I'm trying."

"I know you are." Regret laced Lisa's voice. "I'm sorry. I'm just worried."

The apology was unexpected, and welcome. "We both are. And I'm sure you're tired of being banished from home."

"That, too."

Penny's doorbell rang.

"I have to go. Someone's at the door. I love you, honey."

"I know you do." Lisa sighed. "Be careful."

Disappointment rippled through Penny. No *I love you, too* from Lisa. The mourning truce was apparently over. She teared up and forced strength into her voice. "I will. Bye."

Penny heard the disconnect then went to answer the door. Shock rippled through her. *Lucas?*

She opened the door wide. "What are you doing out there? I thought you were still asleep."

"I went for a run." Sweat beaded on his forehead and his breathing was still labored. "Sorry. Didn't mean to upset you." He entered the house.

Penny closed the door behind him. "Tell me the officers went with you."

"They did." He got a glass of water at the fridge and drank a long swallow. "I had to burn off some energy before story time this morning."

Energy or emotion? Probably both. "Did you sleep at all?"

"Some." He cast her a you-know-what-it's-like look. "My mind just wouldn't shut down."

"That gets better, too." She reached for a skillet. "How about an omelet?"

"Sounds good." He hooked a thumb toward the hallway. "Can I grab a quick shower first? I smell rank."

"Sure."

Penny poured her third cup of coffee and diced the makings for the omelets. When Lucas returned in jeans and a t-shirt, she began cooking, and filling him in on her phone calls with Lisa and Dr. Handley.

"Stronger vitals must be a good sign."

"Dr. Handley thinks so, and I agree." Had John William heard her advise him to continue to appear comatose? Penny pointed with the egg flipper. "Put some toast in, will you?"

"Dr. Handley's suggestion seems logical." Lucas grabbed the

bread and moved to the toaster. "Is that what you think is best? For me to stay at the hospital?"

"From our options, it would be safest for you." Penny looked over at him. "What do you think?"

He gazed back over his shoulder. "I think if you'll worry less while you're away knowing I'm there, then that's where I need to be. You need your whole focus on finding out what you need to know so you're safest and I won't have to worry as much."

Thoughtful as always. "That works for me. It's decided then." She sprinkled in cheese, then paused. "But what if your dad comes here looking for you?"

"I'll message him on our dedicated phone. He'd figure it out anyway."

John William. Lucas was close to him, like Lisa and Penny. "I bet he would."

After breakfast, they settled in on the patio and Lucas began relaying his parents' stories of Lovenia. Penny took copious notes and became even more convinced that there was a strong connection between Lovenia and Kyle Hoff.

That afternoon, Penny visited John William. The wires and tubes were still disconcerting, but the steady rhythmic beeps emitted reassured her. Sitting at his bedside, she leaned close and whispered. "Lucas will be with you and Dr. Handley. Nicholas and I are going to have those special items tested. I'll be back on Tuesday, and I sure hope you're awake by then. I love you, John William. You keep fighting and come back to us." A tear leaked from her eye. "We need you."

Lucas stood near the door. When Penny joined him, he said, "I don't feel good about you being home alone tonight. I'm coming with you, and I'll come back here in the morning."

Nick joined them. "We're all checking on John William this afternoon."

"We are," Penny said. "I'm just about to leave. Lucas will be staying, giving Dr. Handley a much-needed break."

Lucas frowned at her, then looked at Nick. "She'll be home

alone tonight. The guards will be with me. I don't feel good about that, but she's being—"

"Stubborn?" Nick suggested.

"I'll be fine." Penny insisted.

Nick turned his back to her and mouthed "I'm on it" to Lucas. "While you two duke this out, I'm going in to see John William. Do play nice."

Penny resisted the urge to roll her eyes back in her head. "I'm fully capable, Lucas."

"I know you are. I'm just concerned. Too much happened, too fast."

She hugged him. "I'll be back before you know it."

"Don't get hurt, okay?" Lucas's Adam's apple bobbed in his throat. "I can't lose you, too."

"You won't," she said in a whisper. "It's not that kind of a trip. I'll be fine."

That sparked curiosity in his eyes. "What kind of trip is it?"

"Specific research and confirmation. That's all."

Gauging by his expression, her disclosure relieved some of his worry. For that, Penny was grateful. "I'm going to go home and pack." The hospital smells on top of the funeral and cemetery yesterday colluded and threatened to overwhelm her. She had to get out of here. She hugged Lucas. "Be careful and let me know if you hear anything from your dad or Jay." When he nodded, she turned and called back to Nick. "See you."

From John William's bedside, Nick lifted a hand and waved.

TWENTY-SEVEN

June 12th @ 0900

Penny stood ready and waiting for Nick on Monday morning. Though she was a little bleary-eyed, she was more eager to determine what he knew about her 2:00 a.m. visitor. There was little doubt in her mind he was behind it. And plenty of doubt in her mind why he felt inclined to prompt that visit.

Nick arrived promptly at 9:00 and drove them to the airport, skirting the main terminal and drawing to a stop near a parked jet. Surprised, Penny said, "I didn't realize we would be on a private flight."

"It's necessary for my work," Nick said. "I travel a lot." He shifted the subject. "How did it go last night for Lucas?"

"Fine."

"He stayed at the hospital then?"

"Yes."

"Did he tell you about Lovenia?"

"Not all the stories. The night of the funeral, he told me one about King Alexander and Kerra and how they met after Alexander's father died. They married, and had two children, Stefan and

Brigit. They were happy." She sighed. "Lucas was too wiped out to do more, but yesterday morning, he relayed a lot. I took notes. You can read them on the plane."

"Sounds tame enough," Nick said. "So why are you puzzled about it?"

"I'm not really. But I am wondering how Kyle connects to King Alexander, and why his heritage was relayed as fairytales and Lucas hasn't picked up on it yet."

"Are you sure he hasn't?"

"Relatively. He's said nothing that indicates he has a clue that the stories are real."

"He's too bright to not have made the connection."

"Maybe under normal circumstances, but right now all he can focus on is grief and catching Alana's killer. Combine that and a lifetime of being told they are fairytales… Under these circumstances, that's a lot to overcome and see clearly, Nick."

Nick seemed perplexed. "So even knowing Lovenia is real, Lucas doesn't realize Alexander was a real king?"

Penny looked over at him. "Have you ever lost someone you loved?"

"No, I haven't. Well, my parents, but I have no memory of them—they died in a plane crash when I was an infant."

"I'm so sorry." She wanted to ask who had raised him, but this wasn't the time to intrude on his privacy. He valued it too much to be open. "My point was when you lose someone you know and love, you understand that grief consumes you. It smothers out everyone and everything else."

"Like it did when Mark…"

"Yes."

"I understand yesterday was the second anniversary of his funeral. Det. Voigt mentioned it at the cemetery."

"It was."

"Is it better? The grief?"

She stiffened. "Not yet." She hiked a shoulder. "I gave Lucas my grief counselor's card. Whether or not he'll use it, I have no idea. I hope he does, and he's spared as much pain as possible."

"Whether or not he sees Dr. Mason," Nick said, "take comfort. She can't do anything for him you aren't already doing."

"I doubt that. I'm not a trained counselor."

"Lucas acknowledges that. But you are experienced, and you love him. She doesn't."

Clearly Lucas and Nick had discussed this, and her. "I'm not sure that's enough."

"Love always trumps training, Mrs. Crown." Nick smiled. "Alana wouldn't want Lucas to give up on life anymore than Mark would want you to give up. You didn't, and neither will Lucas."

"There's some truth in that." Penny gazed through the window. "I came close several times, but I always sensed Mark pushing me to go on and not give up or quit."

A man appeared near Nick's window and Nick waved. "Time to board."

A second man pulled the luggage from the trunk and put it on the plane.

Penny and Nick boarded and then took their seats. Decorated in tan leather and pale cream, the plane was lush and soft on the eyes, and the oversized seats were comfortable.

After takeoff, when the plane leveled out, Nick asked, "Did you find out why Alana had worn the pendant at the engagement party but not after it?"

"Actually, I did. When her body was recovered and the pendant wasn't, I told Lucas I was sorry it had been lost. He said it wasn't. Alana had returned it to him just before they left the party. That's why she'd removed her wrap and forgotten it. She wanted to keep the tradition intact, so Lucas was to hold the pendant until their wedding."

"The groom gives it to the bride then. That's the tradition?"

"Yes." Penny confirmed it. "She only wore it early because Kyle suggested Lucas expand the tradition, since they had to delay the wedding until after the swim meet." Kyle's suggestion confirmed for Penny that Kyle wanted Lucas in the media's eyes—and to keep himself away from them. Being seen in public, Kyle believed, protected Lucas.

"I expect Lucas is glad now he agreed."

Penny nodded. "He said he was glad he got to see her wearing it."

"How did you get him to agree to let us bring the pendant and painting to New York?"

"I told him we needed experts to run tests for trace evidence on them." Penny lowered her eyes. "He assumed we might find something to help us identify who abducted and murdered her."

"It might." Nick studied her. "Probably not, but it's possible." He reached over and patted her hand. "Be at peace, Mrs. Crown. You didn't lie to Lucas, you spared him more pain."

Penny swallowed. "That was my intent. We'll see whether that is the result."

He propped his elbow on the armrest. "May I see the story notes now?"

Penny passed them to him. "I hope you can read them. My penmanship is rusty."

"No problem. So is mine. It's typical now for everyone who does most of their work on electronic devices."

Penny pulled her laptop from her briefcase and glanced at Nick. He was deep into reading already. She ran a more extensive check on Gregor. His giving Lucas the painting and his obvious admiration and pride in Lucas still niggled at her...

An hour later, a loud clink interrupted Penny from her research. Startled, she jumped.

Nick stood beside her, his hand on a glass of fizzing soda. "Sorry. I thought you might be thirsty."

Gorgeous and thoughtful. She smiled. "Thanks, Nick. I'm parched." She reached for the glass and took a long swallow.

He sat back down in his seat.

"Have you gotten through all the stories?" she asked. He'd set her notes on the seat beside him.

"I have. He's quite the storyteller."

"I thought so, too. It's obvious he's heard these stories repeatedly."

"His whole life, I would say. The details he recounted make that evident."

"Did you note any that struck you as embellished?" Penny rephrased that question, fearing she'd worded it poorly. "Ones that seemed added in by him, is what I mean."

"I didn't. That's what led me to believe he had heard them many times." Nick's brow furrowed and his expression went serious. "It's as if they were schooling him on all things Lovenian." Nick lifted his chin. "What have you been working on?"

"A man named Gregor." She looked over at Nick. "We met at the swim meet, and I watched him. He showed more than interest in Lucas."

"What do you mean?"

"It was odd, really. More than interest in a competitor. Gregor had this expression—"

"What kind of expression?"

"For some reason, he took enormous pride in Lucas. His admiration was clear." She let Nick see that puzzled her. "Then he gave Lucas the painting. I want to know why."

"Did you ask him? What did he say about it?"

"I tried to find out, in an indirect way, but he said nothing."

"So, you're investigating him on an intuitive feeling?"

Whether or not he considered that a flaw was unclear. People in their line of work functioned on intuition a lot. "Based on observation, and intuition. Which has led to a lot of relevant material." Penny turned in her seat to face Nick. "Gregor is actually Christopher Gregor."

"Sounds familiar, but I can't place the name."

"He was King Alexander's Chief Councilor in Lovenia. Now he remains on the new king's council, but a new Chief has been appointed."

"That's common. Rulers want their own people in key positions."

"True." Penny went on. "Gregor has never married and there's nothing—and I mean nothing—on him. He's so clean he squeaks when he walks."

"That invites trust." Nick leaned forward, his arms on his knees. "What relevant material have you found?"

"A little history. Alexander and the new king, Berthold Richter Franke, were half-brothers. The Queen Mother, Adelphia Richter, was widowed. She remarried Fredrich Franke to secure her throne. Alexander was a young boy at the time. Adelphia and Fredrich parented Berthold."

"Okay." Nick made small circles with his hand, urging her to move along.

"Don't get impatient. Why you need to know that is coming." Penny referred to her notes. "Adelphia's second husband, Fredrich, was rumored to be a war criminal who funneled stolen art from Germany through Lovenia to art dealers in Switzerland. From there, the art was sold to private collectors."

"Was he charged or investigated?"

"Not charged, no. But his activities were being investigated when Alexander and his family were murdered sixteen years ago."

"And now Fredrich's son Berthold is king, and the investigation has been halted and buried." Nick frowned. "Sixteen years ago. . . What happened?"

Penny suffered a chill. "There was a coup d'état that killed King Alexander, Queen Kerra, and their two children, Stefan, and Brigit. The Queen Mother, Adelphia, was also murdered that night."

Nick's eyes burned interest. "Is the story of the coup one of Lucas's fairytales?"

"Not that he's said, but I'll ask." Penny frowned. "His mind is on Alana, of course, and the life stolen from them."

"Mine would be." Nick paused, his gaze darting wall to wall in the plane. "Interesting."

"What?"

"I'm curious as to why King Berthold would send a council member to a swim meet in America. The council is mainly involved in internal legal matters or diplomatic ones. There was no obvious need for Gregor to be here."

Penny countered. "Unless they anticipated trouble and sent

Christopher Gregor as a preventative measure. Surely, he has diplomatic immunity."

"Yes," Nick agreed. "Anticipating trouble could be possible."

No customs. Diplomatic immunity. Penny's thoughts went into overdrive. "Especially since Gregor gave Lucas the painting."

"Berthold wouldn't want Lucas to have the painting."

"No, he wouldn't. Yet Gregor gave it to him." Penny took a sip from her glass and processed their discussion. "I'm curious, too."

"About what specifically?"

"Why would Gregor, who still resides in Alderburg, Lovenia, single out Lucas and give him the painting—original or forgery—by a Lovenian artist?"

Nick locked gazes with Penny. "Good question."

"It was deliberate and has to be significant." Penny felt that down to the marrow of her bones. "There has to be a connection between Kyle and Lucas to Lovenia. The nature of that connection well might lead us to Alana's murderer. And maybe to John William's attack."

Nick rubbed at his jaw. "And to the attacks on Lucas and Kyle. The house and car."

Penny stared at Nick. "It could all be connected."

"Maybe," Nick said. "But how? That's the question—and the reason we need these experts to examine the pendant and painting."

"Exactly." Penny's mind whirled. "There is something to be found in both the pendant and the painting."

The pilot's voice came over the speaker. "Prepare to land. We'll be wheels-down in about ten minutes."

"And the hotel?" Nick asked.

"Is expecting you and Mrs. Crown later, sir. We'll get the luggage to your rooms."

"Thanks," Nick said, checking his watch. "We have time for a little lunch before our 2:00 meeting at Crowlee."

"Great." It was amazing how smooth travel could be when you weren't shuffling through airports, waiting on trams, shuttles, and taxis. Penny glanced at Nick. He must be independently wealthy. Few working for the government could afford these types of luxuries. She needed to find out more about him, though John William's calling him in to help was really endorsement enough. Learning more wasn't a necessity, she admitted to herself, but a curiosity.

An appealing curiosity.

@1400

The Crowlee Institute was on the south side of Central Park near the pond. Penny and Nick walked the four short blocks to an imposing modern building that stretched into the sky and had no windows on the first two floors marring its white stone exterior. All floors above the first two reflected images of the water in long banks of darkened-glass windows. A uniformed security guard stood posted at the main entrance door. "Good afternoon, Mr. Ryan."

Nick nodded and they went inside.

Penny stood on the cool marble flooring beside Nick and welcomed the blast of air-conditioning. It was hot and sticky and still outside, but inside the air felt light, breezy, and blissfully cool on Penny's heated skin.

A second uniformed guard joined them and addressed Nick, who didn't seem at all wilted from the heat. "May I help you?"

"Yes, please," Nick said. "We have an appointment with Dr. Amanda Brentwood. Nicholas Ryan and Mrs. Penny Crown."

"Of course," the guard said. "One moment please." He walked over to a tasteful desk and picked up the phone.

"It won't be long," Nick told Penny.

"I should have freshened up first."

"You look fine." His eyes twinkled. "Cooler."

Penny slid him a killer glare.

A woman soon exited an elevator and approached them. In her mid-thirties with sable-brown cropped hair and a studious expression on her pretty face, she was dressed in navy slacks and a white lab coat.

"Amanda." Nick smiled. "It's good to see you."

"Of course, Nicholas." She smiled, then turned to Penny and offered her hand. "Amanda Brentwood. And you are?"

"Penny Crown." She shook Amanda Brentwood's hand.

"Well, let's get started." Amanda guided them to the elevator. They rode up to the third floor, then stepped out into a bright, sunlit lobby with scattered blue leather sofas and lime green and peacock blue artwork on the walls. "If you'll have a seat here, I'll summon my team and then take you to the conference room." She took two steps, stomped her foot, then turned back to them. "Will you require something to drink?"

"No, thank you." Penny and Nick answered simultaneously.

Penny took a seat on the nearest blue sofa, and Nick dropped down beside her. "Don't be fooled by her feigned social awkwardness. Amanda is respected internationally for authenticating and examining art in many forms. Her team is a group of twelve experts—all with reputations as stellar as hers."

"Why do they work under her, then?" Penny asked.

"Amanda's expertise crosses mediums. The twelve excel in their chosen medium. Frankly, as good as they are, they ride on her reputation and clout."

"Can they be trusted?"

Nick sent her a digging look. "Would I come here if they couldn't?"

"So, she does her own work, and they largely assist her?"

"In a manner of speaking." Nick checked the empty lobby, then added, "They are all heavyweights, Mrs. Crown. The best collection of experts in the nation."

"Better than John William?"

"He's on par with Amanda, but he can't be blasted out of Georgia, I suspect, because of you and Lisa and Lucas. That renders him a little less accessible, especially to international clients."

Penny never considered she was holding John William back. "Surely, he wouldn't sacrifice something he wanted—"

"He's very content there with your family," Nick said. "I just meant he'd be more in demand if he were in New York."

"I see." Penny shrugged, imagining John William living in New York. "He wouldn't be happy here, you know."

"Not unless the three of you were here," Nick said. "No, he wouldn't."

Amanda returned and led them to the conference room. The twelve on her team were already seated around a long table. With a nod to Nick, Amanda accepted the painting and then the pendant. She reverently placed each in the center of the table, roughly four feet apart.

A little nervous, Penny watched closely. The twelve rose and moved around the table, viewing both objects from all angles. No hands touched the table, or attempted to touch the objects, and when they completed the full circle around the table, they sat back down in the seats they had previously occupied. Oddly, each of them nodded to Amanda.

Obviously, the team had done this routine many times. What did those nods mean?

Amanda faced Nick and Penny and smiled. "I can't permit you into the lab, but my team and I will run the tests to authenticate on both objects. We'll start now and do all we can before the lab reopens at 8:00 a.m. tomorrow. Others will require access to it then, and I wish to respect your privacy on this. We'll start with precursory testing and see where that leads, then do more extensive testing, if required. Whatever time allows."

Uncomfortable with the objects being out of her possession despite Nick's assurances they would be fine, Penny asked, "Are the tests you have in mind going to damage either object?"

"No." Amanda said softly.

"All will be well, Mrs. Crown." Nick nodded, adding weight to his claim. "Amanda and I have worked together many times. Flawlessly."

"All the same, we should wait out in the lobby," she told Nick then looked at Amanda. "I gave my word the objects wouldn't leave my possession. I can't violate that trust."

Amanda's surprise was evident. Her gaze darted to Nicholas, who signaled her to agree. "Of course." She nodded to the team, and they exited the conference room. "When I have anything to report, I'll come and tell you."

"Thank you, Amanda." Penny stood and then followed Amanda back to the lobby.

"If you need me," she told Penny and Nick, "I'll be in the lab. Reach me through any house phone."

Phones were posted on each wall. "Thank you, Amanda."

When Amanda returned to the elevator, Nick made a call from his mobile. "It's Nicholas. Stop any exit or entrance to the building except through the main lobby door." That's where he and Penny were seated. "No exceptions."

He stowed his phone in his inner suit pocket.

Penny stared at him.

"What?"

"Who did you call?" she asked.

"Associates."

Government associates. "Why?"

"Security. If these items are authentic, they're invaluable."

"I thought you trusted these people."

"I do. That doesn't mean I'm going to rely solely on them to protect property we promised to protect."

That disclosure made Penny feel better. She settled in on a blue sofa and opened her laptop to check on her clients at home...

Hours passed, and at 8:00 p.m. there still had been no word from Amanda or anyone else in the lab.

"That light lunch wore off hours ago," Nick said. "I'm ready for dinner."

"So am I." Penny closed her laptop and stowed it in her briefcase.

"Do we order in or go out?" Nick asked.

She wasn't leaving Lucas's treasures. "Order in."

He reached for a house phone. "Amanda, we're ordering dinner. Would you and the team care to join us?" He paused for her answer, then added, "How about you join us for dessert then?" Another pause, followed by, "Great. We'll call when it's ready."

Penny gave him a cheeky grin. "You're sly."

Nick feigned innocence, but Penny wasn't fooled. He wanted to pump the team for interim information.

"Per Se is close by. Columbus Circle," Nick said. "Lobster, okay?"

"Great." One of Penny's favorites, typically reserved for special occasions.

Nick was still on the phone ordering when the tables arrived and were being set up, transforming the lobby into a dining room. On the far wall, a long table was placed. All tables were draped in pristine white.

Soon, Per Se arrived with their dinner and when they'd finished eating, the long table was filled with desserts. Penny recognized the Crème Brûlée and Chocolate Torte, and of course the Cannoli Shells, but not several of the others. They all looked appealing, garnished to ignite a tastebud frenzy. If the sugar high wouldn't have her buzzing for a week, she'd risk a sampler. Two silver coffee urns were placed at the end of the table, she presumed, one decaf and one caffeinated, and a third urn and elegant setup for tea was arranged beside it.

Nick phoned Amanda and invited her and her team down. When they arrived, they looked pleased with the assortment.

Amanda enjoyed a Cannoli Shell and watched Nick work the room. He was exuding charm, definitely on the hunt for preliminary findings.

As Penny ate her dessert, Amanda dropped onto a seat beside her, and though subtle, she peppered Penny with questions on her relationship with Nick. Penny offered little and never raised a question on the team's progress.

Clearly, Amanda expected she would, and finally volunteered. "We've completed the preliminary tests and are moving on to more advanced ones."

Penny swallowed her last bite and set down her fork. "Does that mean you've not revealed either to be forgeries?"

Amanda smoothed her hair, but an excited light danced in her eyes. "Not yet."

Penny's heart beat hard and fast. She pondered the implications.

Until this moment, she hadn't dared to believe that either object was authentic. Now, she did, and the possibilities of what that could mean sent her mind reeling.

The lobby settled down and the team returned to work in the lab. Penny and Nick settled on the blue sofa and Nick dropped his charm and let Penny see his frustration.

"Never have I encountered such a closed mouth group. None of them would utter a word about their preliminary findings."

"None of them?" Penny was surprised by that.

"Not one." He grunted his irritation. "Amanda has trained them well. I couldn't even back into getting them to reveal anything at all. And believe me, I tried."

He had. Penny had observed his efforts.

"If it helps," Penny said, "they've finished the preliminary tests and are moving on to the advanced ones now."

Surprise flitted across Nick's face, sobered his expression. "Who told you that?" He lifted a hand. "I watched you. You sat at the table the entire time."

"I did, though many of the team members stopped by to say thank you for the desserts."

"Which one of them told you about the testing?"

"None of the team members. Amanda mentioned it voluntarily." Penny smiled. "I then asked if that meant they had failed to prove either object was a forgery or replica."

"And?"

"She said, 'Not yet'."

He smiled. "Well done, Mrs. Crown."

"I'm wondering what it means on a broader scale."

"As am I." He stared off at the wall of windows, gazing far beyond them and into the recesses of his mind. "What have you concluded?"

"Nothing yet," she said. "But I'm feeling more and more certain that all of this is connected to Lovenia—the real one, not the historical fairytales—and that Kyle, and perhaps Lucas, are at the heart of it."

"Lucas?" Nick hooded his eyes, shielding his emotional reaction to that disclosure.

Penny nodded. She was about to explain further when her mobile rang. *Lisa's ringtone.*

"Excuse me." Penny answered the call. "Hello."

"Mom, I had to let you know," Lisa said. "Oh my gosh, I can't believe it."

"Believe what? Let me know what?" Penny went on alert.

"It's John William," Lisa said. "I was on the phone with Lucas, and he was in the cafeteria at the hospital getting a snack."

Every nerve in Penny's body stretched taut, setting off a firestorm of tingles. "Lisa, what's happened to John William?"

"He's awake. John William is awake."

Penny shot a look at Nick, who sat silently studying her. "John William is out of the coma. He's awake." She addressed Lisa. "You're sure? The hospital hasn't called, and neither has Lucas."

"I'm sure. I told you, I was on the phone with Lucas when the nurse called him in the cafeteria. John William's awake and seems fine. Lucas said to tell you that tomorrow, after he talks with Dr. Handley, he will call you with a report. He doesn't want you to worry."

"So, John William has his faculties. They're intact."

"That's what *he's fine* means, Mom."

"It's such wonderful news. I just wanted to hear it again." Relief washed through Penny. She nodded to Nick. Their gazes locked and the tension in him dissolved.

"I'm going home tomorrow," Lisa said. "Lucas could use the help at the hospital. Dr. Handley is worn to a frazzle."

Penny had to tread lightly, or Lisa would totally ignore her and do the opposite. "That's thoughtful of you, honey, but it's not a good idea just yet."

"You sound like Lucas."

"We both have our reasons."

"Which neither of you wish to share over the phone."

Grasping that straw, Penny added, "Please, just stay put a little longer." *Let her listen. Please, let her listen.*

"If you think it's best."

No anger or sarcasm. That stunned Penny. Pleasantly stunned. "I do."

"Okay, I'll wait for now."

Gratitude seeped through Penny, then suspicion. Normally, Lisa would argue. She always argued. "You're agreeing?"

"I am." Lisa paused and her tone deepened. "I think you have enough worries right now and I don't want to add to them."

Penny's heart melted. "I appreciate that, honey."

"I see, Mom."

Confused, Penny frowned. "See what?"

Lisa struggled to find her words, stumbled a little and settled for the truth. "I see how hard everything you're doing is for you, and yet you're doing all you can to keep everyone safe and get the answers others need. It's really kind of extraordinary, Mom."

Lisa thought Penny was extraordinary? Shock rippled through Penny. A good kind of shock. Was it genuine? Penny pinched herself. Felt the sting and was oddly reassured by it.

"When will you be back?" Lisa asked.

"I'm not sure yet. The tests could take a while."

"Keep me posted."

"I will." Penny softened her voice. "Stay safe."

"Night." Lisa hung up.

Penny stowed her phone and noted Nick's broad smile. It wasn't his intentionally charming smile but the authentic one that crinkled the skin beneath his eyes. She liked it best. "What?"

"That's wonderful news about John William."

"It is," Penny agreed. "I can breathe again." He gave her a strange look she couldn't decipher. "Why the odd look? What is it?"

"That's my question for you." Nick's intense scrutiny penetrated. "Lisa stunned you. That much is clear. But with what?"

"She wanted to come home. I objected and she didn't argue. That was stunning."

"Young women her age often argue, asserting their own authority."

"True. Not that it makes it less exhausting."

"But your strongest reaction came after that. It's the one I am talking about."

Penny flushed. "She thinks what I'm doing is extraordinary."

"You're her mother. Of course, she recognizes your work on all this is extraordinary."

"No, Nick. These days, Lisa rarely has a civil word for me. It's all about me needing to get my own life. Being overbearing and intruding into her life. Her saying anything positive about me or my actions is stunning. And suspicious."

"You think she is planning something anyway, like going back to Kerra against your advice?"

"It wouldn't surprise me."

Nick pulled out his phone and dialed. "Det. Voigt. Sorry to intrude on your evening, but Mrs. Crown and I are away on business, and we have reason to be concerned that Lisa may return home prematurely against our advice. I wonder if you'd be so—" Nick paused and listened. "Thank you, Jay. I appreciate your keeping an eye on her if she should return, as does her mother." Another pause, then Nick added, "Good night."

"Thank you," Penny said.

"You wanted to do it but hesitated because of Lisa's *smothering* accusations."

"True." *Smothering.* Had Lisa told him and John William about her favorite accusation? Surely one of them had, and Penny wanted to know which one but didn't ask.

Nick clasped her hand. "You do realize her attitude is just a part of her growing up, right?"

"I suspected it until my grief counselor sided with her. To be fair, I suppose I earned it," Penny said, comforted by the warmth of Nick's hand. "I've always wrapped my world around her and Mark. I guess, after he died and his murder was solved, I heaped all I had to give onto Lisa. It was too much."

"It was natural," Nick said softly. "You feared losing her, too."

"I still fear losing her," Penny confessed. "I tried to ease up on her. Took art classes, the private investigator training, and more. Not that in her view any of it helped much. She's chomping at the bit to leave for college."

"When is that?"

"Less than a month." Penny sighed. "She doesn't realize she's all I've got now."

"And perhaps you don't realize she isn't." Nick paused until Penny looked into his eyes. "You have yourself, Mrs. Crown. You're very good at what you do. Methodical, thorough and precise, and you work with integrity. That's rare these days, and it's a potent combination." He leaned back on the sofa, resting his head against its back. "Beyond that, you have John William and Lucas, and now, me."

Much calmer, she leaned back, too, and relaxed. That he didn't judge her helped more than it probably should. "And all of you have me."

TWENTY-EIGHT

June 13th @ 0700

Penny and Nick sat chatting over morning coffee when the elevator bell finally sounded. The door opened and Amanda emerged then walked over to them, carrying the painting in its leather pouch and the pendant.

"Good morning." She sat down in a chair across from them and removed the painting. "I need both of you to sign for the objects."

Penny examined them, then reached for the transfer of possession form and pen Amanda extended. She affixed her signature, then waited. When Nick had finished examining the objects, she passed the form and pen to him.

He signed then returned a copy to Amanda and retained two copies, one for himself and one for Penny. "So, what did you learn?" he asked Amanda.

"Let's discuss the pendant first." Amanda referred to her notes. "We're confident it is the original."

Penny swallowed a gasp.

"We can't enlighten you on how it got to America or how your client gained possession, I'm afraid, but we've concluded the pendant is the one King Alexander designed with his royal crest and gifted to his bride, Queen Kerra, on their wedding day."

"The stones?" Nick asked.

Amanda nodded. "They're impossible to duplicate. We are prepared to certify them as one and the same."

A light frown creased Nick's brow. "But not the pendant itself."

"Correct. You'll need additional testing that we can't perform here." Amanda sighed. "But for what it is worth, I found nothing that proves the pendant is not authentic or the original."

Questions fired in Penny's mind. "King Alexander was called Red Richter."

"Yes," Amanda confirmed it.

"I understand the Richter. It was his surname. I don't understand the Red."

"That came about at the time of the pendant," Amanda said. "It could well be because of the two stones under the double arches on the pendant. The stones are nearly identical, extremely rare red diamonds. Actually, they are the second and third largest red diamonds known to exist in the world."

"I see." Penny felt gobsmacked. Where and how had Kyle gotten the pendant?

"And the painting?" Nick asked.

"It's very interesting," Amanda said. "Typically, we can get within forty years on dating an object, but this one is dated the last year in King Alexander's reign, just over seventeen years ago. It isn't visible to the naked eye, but with infrared, the date is quite clear."

Amanda looked at the painting in Penny's lap. "The artist didn't sign it. However, we know King Alexander commissioned a painting from photographs of the original. It went missing during the war. The identity of the artist has never been disclosed."

Amanda again looked at the painting. "The original was painted by Barclay Ernst and named The Enchanted Forest. He gifted it to his home country, Lovenia, before World War II. To Alexander's father, Arthur. It was stolen during the war and has never surfaced."

"So, this is not the original painting?" Nick asked.

"It is an original, just not the one painted by Barclay Ernst,"

Amanda said. "King Alexander had a fondness for the painting. He played in those woods as a child and prayed in them as an adult. In his last year as king, he commissioned an unnamed artist to paint The Enchanted Forest again. The artist accepted the commission, but he did not sign the work. He was reportedly also Lovenian and felt complying with the king's request was his civic duty."

Penny didn't have to look. There was no signature on the painting. "He painted it for love, not recognition."

"So it is said." Amanda smoothed her hair back from her face. "I believe this is the commissioned painting."

"Which means it's a forgery?" Penny asked.

"No. If it is the original painting for King Alexander, and I believe it is, it is authentic and very valuable."

Nick rubbed at his neck. "Then we'll need further experts to verify and issue certifications on both objects."

"I'm afraid so." Amanda stiffened. "I can do a history but not a chain of custody."

"That said, you're confident." Nick pushed her.

"As much as I can be with the variant," Amanda said.

"What variant?" Penny asked.

"There's an underpainting, which isn't uncommon. Artists often paint over used canvases. But in the underpainting, we noted squiggly lines in the center of the keyhole arch that were painted at the time of the new rendition. Why, we have no idea."

"Interesting." Nick mumbled.

Penny recalled what Gregor had said to Lucas when giving him the painting. "It is said that the keyhole center holds the secrets of the kingdom's future."

"Very interesting." Amanda's eyes gleamed. "There is a method that might reveal more on this, but I can't test it here." She frowned. "It's new and not readily accepted yet by those who fund us, so we lack the equipment and, of course, we can't certify the results. It's the modified LAM method originally created by Cotte and his team."

"Modified, how? Who can do it?" Nicholas asked.

"Technological advances are responsible for the modifications.

The way they are implemented is truly innovative and remarkable. As for who, someone reliable," Amanda said. "The best, of course, would be the creator of the modified LAM."

"Who is?" Nick asked.

Penny, not Amanda, answered. "John William Archer." She looked at Nick. "He's spoken of it often."

Nick suppressed his surprise, but Penny saw it flash through his eyes.

"That is correct," Amanda said. "Sorry I couldn't do more here."

"We're grateful, Amanda." Nick stood and shook her hand. "Thank you."

Penny stowed the objects in the leather pouch, stood, then shook Amanda's hand. "Thank you."

"You're most welcome, Mrs. Crown," Amanda said. "Do say hello to John William for me. He speaks of you often when we talk."

Oddly pleased, Penny smiled, relieved that he was conscious, and she could pass on that message. "It'll be my pleasure."

On exiting the building, Nick turned to her. "I can't believe he never mentioned the modified LAM to me."

"Perhaps he had Amanda put it through its paces or something." That was as far as Penny could go without breaching John William's confidence.

"That would make sense." Nick phoned the pilot and asked for the retrieval of their things from the hotel and to ready the plane.

They were going home.

@ 1100

Penny glanced through the window of the plane, eager to see John William, then go home and stretch out in bed for at least a few hours.

Nick napped through most of the flight back to Georgia. His

soft snore was oddly comforting. She glanced over at him. Gorgeous man. His hair was sleep-ruffled, and his expression was totally relaxed. How did he manage that?

Her mobile rang. Lucas's ringtone.

Hoping not to awaken Nick, she answered quickly. "Hello."

"It's me, Mrs. Crown."

Lucas. "How are you?"

"Honestly, I'd be better if Det. Voigt could catch a break."

"Nothing on Alana?"

"No, and nothing on my father."

Penny's heart tugged. "Sometimes it takes a while. How is John William?"

"He's the reason I'm calling now," Lucas said.

"Is he…all right?" Penny's breath caught.

"He's insisting he be released from the hospital. Dr. Handley is at wit's end, trying to talk him out of it."

"Why?"

"Because John William says he's leaving even if he must tie sheets together and exit through the window."

"Does he feel at risk there?" Penny couldn't imagine him doing this. He had to have a compelling reason.

"Do you hear that chattering in the background?" Lucas asked. "That's John William. Hold a moment, please." Lucas's voice carried to Penny. "I am telling her, and you can explain to her why you're behaving this way. You've been awake less than a day. She likely will be very annoyed with you." Lucas paused, began speaking to Penny. "Now he's attempting to justify himself. I'm going to put him on the phone. Maybe you can talk some sense into him."

"Lucas, wait. Is Dr. Handley opposed to releasing him?"

"He's opposed to him leaving without security. For what it is worth, I wholeheartedly agree."

"Wise decision." Penny steeled herself. "Put him on the phone."

"Penny?" John William's voice soothed her.

"I'm so relieved you're okay. You are okay, right?"

"I am fine."

"Great. So, keep your fine self parked right where you are until we get home. Then you can get released, but not one second before then. Don't press me on this, John William. I've been an emotional wreck, I'm tired to the bone, and I'm in way over my head on all this, though the pieces are coming together. I do not need you further complicating things right now."

"But Penny—"

She used her best mama bear voice. "I mean it, John William Archer."

"Understood." He paused, then added, "Where are you? Is Nicholas with you?"

"He is, and we're in flight, on the way home."

"Did Amanda certify?"

"No, but she's confident. We need the modified LAM." Penny stopped suddenly. "How did you know about Amanda?"

"Stop playing games, my dear. She is the best. Naturally, Nicholas went to her. Why did she not authenticate?"

"She couldn't. She found an anomaly."

"What kind of anomaly? Oil?"

On the oil painting. "Squiggly lines under it. It's a different original." He knew too much. Entirely too much for a man who'd been in a coma. And Lucas couldn't have told him what he didn't know. "How are you tied up in this?"

"Later, my dear. Just get to the museum as soon as you are able."

"I need an hour and a half or so." Penny doublechecked her watch. That should be plenty of time.

"We will meet you there."

"No, John William. Stay put. You're going to give Dr. Handley a heart attack."

"He is fine, and so am I," John William insisted. "Now, if you do not want anyone else to die, get to the museum."

The chill in his voice set every nerve in her body on edge. "Have the security guards and Lucas go with you," she said. Clearly, the man had no intention of staying put. "Time your arrival for after we get there. Lucas will drive. I mean it. Don't you leave there without them."

"Of course not, my dear."

Penny frowned. He'd gotten exactly what he wanted. Again. "Did Amanda phone you?"

"To schedule the modified LAM test." He sighed. "The truth is, we're running out of time, Penny."

The chill in her turned to ice. "On Kyle?"

"On the offspring." John William hung up.

"I'm confused," Nick said.

He'd awakened during the call and apparently had gotten both ends of the conversation between Penny and John William. "About what?"

"When you suggested Kyle, he said 'on the offspring'."

"He had to mean Lucas." Penny shared her interpretation. "Which means John William knows a great deal more than he's disclosed."

"Why would he say, 'the offspring' rather than 'his offspring' in a direct question about Kyle?"

"I don't know, Nick. Maybe it was a slip of tongue and means nothing."

"John William uses precise language. You know he does, Mrs. Crown."

"Typically, yes. But the man's been in a coma."

"Coma or not. He is still himself. And he is precise. I think he was sending you a message. Lucas is there with him. It had to be intentional."

"I'm not totally convinced, but your logic holds merit. Regardless, we'll know soon enough," Penny said. "He and Lucas are meeting us at the museum in just over an hour."

"*The* offspring," Nick said again.

"If you're right, and that is significant—"

"John William is telling us that Lucas is not Kyle's son."

TWENTY-NINE

June 13th @ 1405

Though precious art filled the museum, with John William not being there, it felt empty. Penny stowed her purse in the bottom of the curio where she'd kept it all the years she had worked for John William, then told Nick, "I'm going to do a walk through to make sure everything is in order before he arrives. I don't want him upset after his hospital stay."

"He isn't going to forget what happened here that put him in the hospital," Nick warned her.

"No, of course not." She looked back at Nick over her shoulder. "But if everything is in order, I'm hoping he will be more inclined to tell us what happened to him."

"He hasn't told Det. Voigt."

"You see my point then." Penny walked on.

When she returned to the main room near the entry, Nick was admiring the art. "Is everything in order?"

"It is now," Penny said. "My guess is they were after the painting and pendant and failed to locate the vault."

"I agree or the objects wouldn't have been in it before we left for New York."

"I'll put the kettle on for tea. No doubt John William will be eager for a good cup. Then I want to search a bit on King Alexander's council members."

"We know Christopher Gregor was Chief Counselor then."

"We do," Penny said. "What we don't know is why he would give Lucas the original painting at the swim meet."

"You're thinking there's a strong connection."

Penny nodded. "I am. If I'm right, a very strong connection."

"Kyle is too old to—"

"I know." Penny stopped, turned to Nick. "But Gregor didn't give the painting to Kyle. He gave it to Lucas."

"Which means what to you?"

"I have my suspicions but I'm seeking hard evidence. Until then, I think I'll follow my normal protocol and keep those suspicions to myself."

Nick's eyes gleamed. He admired her unwillingness to speculate. "May I recommend something?"

"Of course." In the kitchen, she filled the kettle at the sink and put it on to heat then readied a tea tray."

Nick watched her closely. "Forget preconceived notions and deductions from your research and follow only what you determine to be fact."

Placing cookies on a plate, Penny paused. "Is there any other way to properly investigate?" She selected her favorite teapot from his collection, an 18th Century Thuringia Strawflower Porcelain, and filled it with hot water from the kettle.

"Interesting choice," Nick said. "Germany. Hand-painted. Not the most rare or expensive one, but not the least either."

"I like it." She gave him a cheeky grin. "Always have."

"That's the best reason to select, isn't it?" Nick smiled.

"I think so."

"I see my investigative advice was unneeded. I hope it didn't offend you?"

"Of course not," she said.

He leaned against the cabinet. "You were tutored by John William long before your formal training."

"I was, and he isn't someone I have ever been inclined to deliberately disappoint."

"May I ask why you are so devoted to him?" Nick slid onto a chair at the table.

"Because she loves me." John William said from behind Nick.

"John William, you're home!" Penny ran to him and hugged him hard.

"Easy, my dear." He lifted his casted arm. "I am still sore all over."

She gentled her touch. "Do your ribs hurt much?"

"Only when I breathe."

"I'm sorry. But you're here and all right, aren't you?"

"I will be fine. Everything is healing nicely." John Williams took his usual seat. "Lucas is parking the car. Before he comes in, Penny, I must tell you and Nicholas about the attack." He leaned closer. "Two men came into the museum. I can identify one of them. The second scoundrel sheltered his face with one of those knit masks."

"Please, tell me he wasn't Gregor." She hoped she hadn't misjudged his admiration for Lucas.

"No. But we have seen the man. He was in the parking lot when Lucas's car was bombed. In the photo, remember?"

"I do. But we haven't identified him." Penny thought there was something familiar about him, but the photo was just too grainy to say with any degree of authority.

Nick spoke up. "May I see the photo?"

John William frowned. "It is on my phone, which is currently secured."

"I'll get it." Penny retrieved his phone and then passed it to him.

He located the photo he wanted and then studied it. "Yes. Yes, that is the man." John William passed the phone to Nick.

Nick examined the photo, and then turned to John William. "His name is Dirk," Nick said. "I've encountered him before."

"Who exactly is Dirk?" Penny asked, vaguely familiar with the name from somewhere. Wait. She slotted where she had seen him.

"He accompanied the Lovenia swim team here for the meet. I saw him with Gregor. He didn't seem to like the man much and never introduced him." She asked John William, "Did you share this with Jay?"

"No. I've been in the hospital in a coma. The phone has been locked away here."

Nick and John William exchanged a look warning Penny they both knew more than they had disclosed. "Well, what aren't you two telling me?" she pushed.

Nick answered. "Dirk works directly for King Berthold. His position is somewhat muddy."

"Muddy?" Penny voiced her confusion. "What exactly does that mean? What is his position?"

"It doesn't formally exist," Nick admitted. "His own refer to him as the enforcer."

"Of what?" Penny filled her own cup and sat down.

Nick answered. "We suspect he enforces any order given to him by King Berthold."

"Including bombing Lucas's car?" Penny asked. The implications of that disclosure had her mind spinning. "Abducting and murdering Alana?"

John William placed a hand atop Penny's on the table and nodded toward the door. Lucas was making his way to the kitchen, and clearly John William didn't want this discussed in his presence.

Penny greeted Lucas then excused herself for a moment. Let them assume she was going wherever they chose. She closed herself in John William's office, ran a search on Dirk, which led to a flood of images. Kyle Hoff and Christopher Gregor knew each other. Penny had seen the recognition in their eyes. Dirk, of course, would follow the orders of the king. So that part of the puzzle was resolved. What wasn't resolved was how Kyle Hoff connected to King Alexander. She found nothing pertinent in the photos of Dirk, then searched for photographs of King Alexander's council.

She scanned them, and on the third page of images, she came to a photograph of The Royal Council. Christopher Gregor was easy to recognize. She studied the others and came to a dead stop.

Kasper Hoffman, Chief Financial Officer.

A younger man but the facial structure, his eyes, and his ears… The ears were always very telling…

She located and read supporting documents, biographies on the council members, paying particular attention to Kasper Hoffman. The most significant finding was that he reportedly had died during the coup sixteen years ago.

And yet, unless she was sorely mistaken, he wasn't dead.

He was Kyle Hoff.

Penny returned to the kitchen embroiled in uncertainty. She needed time to think—seriously think—how best to inform Lucas of everything going on. He'd deal with the now all right, she thought. But the past sixteen years… he'd be confused and devastated and likely angry. How would he react? Should she tell him? Should Kyle? What would be best for him? And what about the complex complications? What could this all mean to him and his life?

She gripped the back of a chair at John William's table. "Where is Lucas?"

"He went to your house to shower and change clothes," John William said. "He's grown into a remarkable man, Penny. I told him to rest for a while. He's been at the hospital with me during your entire absence." John William gently rubbed his temple. "He is vigilant."

"Vigilant?" Penny frowned. "Did something happen?"

"On his watch? No." John William smiled. "Our Lucas had a healthy distrust of everyone except Det. Voigt and Dr. Handley. He required credentials even from the hospital staff, including the janitor."

"He was guarding you. Of course, he was cautious. Need I remind you we stopped an attempted assassination attempt while you were comatose?"

"Dr. Handley informed me." John William nodded. "I was

touched by Lucas's devotion. Yours, I have long since come to appreciate."

"Lucas loves you," Penny said. "You shouldn't be surprised by that after all these years."

His eyes glistened. "It has never been quite so evident."

"You weren't threatened before," Penny reminded him.

"Not that others knew of, anyway," Nick said.

Penny lowered her teacup to its saucer. "John William, you were threatened before?"

"Nothing that relates to the matters at hand, my dear." He quickly turned the subject. "So, what did you find?"

"When?"

"In my office. You were researching, were you not?"

She stared at him and Nick and let them see her disapproval. "I found my suspicions were correct."

"What suspicions?"

"Two, really." Penny didn't lift her stare. "One, Kasper Hoffman reportedly died during the coup against King Alexander. Hoffman was the king's Chief Financial Officer."

"And the second confirmed suspicion?" Nick asked, his face a mask giving nothing away.

Not a word about her disclosure confirmed her second suspicion. She pivoted her gaze between the two men at the table. "Both of you are withholding information from me about all of this."

"What do you mean, Mrs. Crown?" Nick said.

"Don't even try to pretend, Nick. You know exactly what I mean. And," she swung her gaze to John William, "so do you."

"What are you talking about, Penny?" John Williams asked.

"Kasper Hoffman is Kyle Hoff, and both of you knew it. Yet you let me continue to puzzle through his connection to King Alexander. I want to know why."

The men locked gazes but neither spoke.

"Don't bother denying it," Penny warned them. "I have proof."

"Proof?" Nick asked.

"Photographs and Kasper's bio. Three authenticated sources."

John William smiled. "I told you she would find them," he told Nick.

"You did. But not that she would do so this quickly."

They'd meant for her to find the information on Kasper. John William even looked proud of her. What was she to make of that? "You two have some explaining to do."

"We do," John William said. "Unfortunately, my dear, we are not in a position to explain. It would require… a breach of trust that neither of us dare to break."

Penny absorbed that. Nick worked for the government. Did this mean that John William did also? Unsure, Penny went silent, then she changed the subject. "I received a text from Dr. Handley. You checked out of the hospital against medical advice?"

John William sighed. "It was necessary, Penny."

"More necessary than your health?"

Nick muttered. "I knew she wouldn't like this."

"You warned me," John William said, "though it was predictable."

Penny folded her arms. "John William, I'm waiting for you to explain yourself."

"My dear, there are more lives than mine at risk." That lacked the desired impact, so he tried again. "Have you ever known me to take foolish risks?"

She stared at him.

"All right. The truth is, I am fine, and we need those modified LAM tests on the objects and the results as soon as possible."

"Mrs. Crown," Nick interjected. "We need John William. Otherwise, it would take three experts to do what he can do, and one of them is out of the country for the next two weeks. That could be too late."

There was a threat, and the urgency in acting was preventative. Or preemptive. Either way, it had to be done. That interference could have been behind the attack on John William. Leaving little wiggle room for him to avoid a straight answer, she asked, "Why did Dirk attack you?"

Again, that gleam in John William's eye shone brightly. "I

requested information on King Alexander and Queen Kerra from the Royal Archives in Alderburg, Lovenia. The people there were not, er, receptive. However, the day of the attack, I was told the materials would be coming, provided I agreed that my source would remain confidential."

Penny didn't bother asking him for the source. Wild Horses and sodium thiopental couldn't drag it out of him. "You agreed?"

"Of course." John William sniffed. "And as promised the materials were delivered by messenger shortly thereafter. I had just stowed them in the vault and gone back to the museum to lock up when Dirk and his companion arrived."

"So you haven't yet examined them?" Penny asked.

"I have."

"When?" Nick asked.

"When I had Lucas retrieve the package and bring it to me at the hospital."

That stunned Penny. "Risky, John William."

He sent her the most sober look she had ever seen on his face. "I want Lucas to live."

Nick frowned. "What is in the package that threatens Lucas?"

"Nothing." John William blew out a sharp breath. "But with the attempts on his life, there is something somewhere."

Penny tossed out one of many theories. "In the Lovenia coup, the royal treasury was emptied. CFO Kasper was reportedly killed but clearly survived. Perhaps he took the money, and the new king wants it back."

"Logical deduction," Nick said. "Mrs. Crown, you examine the package. John William and I will run the tests and hopefully authenticate the objects." Nick frowned. "We have less diagnostics to do on the pendant," he told John William. "Amanda authenticated it."

Penny folded her arms. "Actually, Amanda authenticated the diamonds, not the pendant, so work on it must be done as well." Penny spoke to John William. "If it were me, I'd run all my own tests."

John William's eyes stretched wide. "Amanda is very good, Penny."

"Yes, but you're better," Penny agreed. "And I fear she missed something."

"Like what?" Nick asked.

"I don't know," Penny answered honestly. "But think about it. These two objects are linked. There is a reason for that. Something on the pendant that wasn't noted—or at least, wasn't shared with us by Amanda—secures that link. Whatever we're meant to find takes both objects and both links."

"How do you know that?" Nick challenged her.

Penny shrugged. "It's simple logic."

Nick disagreed. "Amanda wouldn't withhold information from either of us, much less both of us."

"I didn't say she withheld anything. I said she missed it. I don't know why she didn't connect the two and discover the link or reveal it to us, but she didn't. Yet there must be one, and it must be extremely significant for Gregor to come all the way from Lovenia to Georgia to hand deliver the painting to Lucas now."

John William looked her right in the eye. "My dear, what are you really thinking?"

If Penny were totally honest, he would think she'd lost her mind, but her instincts were insistent. Queen Kerra and Kerra, Georgia? Of course, that connection was deliberate. But it was so obvious that it likely did nothing more than confirm that connections were there and should be sought and found and weighed into any deductions made.

"I'm thinking as soon as the pendant was revealed in the media, Gregor appeared in Georgia with the painting. Perhaps the two objects contain clues to lead us to the missing money?" That's as far as she was willing to go. "Perhaps Lucas is being attacked because King Berthold fears Lucas has access to the money." She took a deep breath and went one step further. "Remember that Kyle Hoff has no visible means of support and yet he and Lucas live well and have for the sixteen years they've been here."

"This would explain Kyle's fear and disappearance." John William tapped the table.

"But not his abandoning Lucas." Nick countered.

Penny swallowed a scoff. *Abandoning Lucas? No way. Caring for Lucas is Kyle's career.* "What you see as abandonment, I see as disassociation to shield and protect. Kyle is attempting to take Lucas off the gameboard to prove he is not involved."

"Likely," John William conceded. "Kyle loves Lucas. That is undeniable and always has been."

"Which is why Lucas will never be off the gameboard," Penny said. "No enemy would willingly forfeit that leverage."

"Valid points." Nick rubbed at his neck.

The rest of her thoughts Penny kept to herself. Suggesting that perhaps Kyle was protecting an even greater treasure than the royal treasury would be a bridge too far to span based on her current evidence. She needed incontrovertible proof.

John Williams drained his teacup then stood up. "Come, Nicholas. We had best get started."

John William and Nick left the kitchen and headed down to the lab. Penny retrieved the package from the vault, then returned to John William's office to examine the contents.

Something niggled at her. Something significant. *Why Lucas?*

If Kasper had been the CFO and the money had disappeared when he "died" during the coup, why seek out Kyle or Lucas now? Perhaps they'd just located them. The media attention. But if Kyle was the thief, why would he summon them? Why would they come after Lucas? She thought a long second. Maybe because Lucas was Kyle's Achilles' heel? His most vulnerable point?

That was true—Kyle devoted himself solely to his son—but was their reason for targeting Lucas an accurate deduction? Or was there another reason? One less apparent?

The echoes of betrayal between the coup in Lovenia sixteen years ago and now troubled Penny. Almost as much as trying to understand why the protective Kyle would allow the pendant to be paraded publicly if he knew it would put Lucas in jeopardy. That seemed the last thing Kyle would want to do. So why hadn't he stopped it?

Unsure, Penny set her questions aside and settled in at John William's desk then opened the package from Lovenia.

Before she surpassed the history she had already reviewed, her mobile rang. She recognized the ringtone and answered it. "Hi, Lucas."

"Mrs. Crown, Det. Voigt just called and asked me to come to headquarters right away."

"Why?" Penny began stowing the neatly stacked papers back into the large envelope.

"He thinks they've found the place Alana was held, and he wants to know if I know anything about it or of a connection to her."

His voice was unsteady. This development shook him deeply. Penny imagined, down to the depths of his soul. "I'll come and go with you."

"No," Lucas said, forcing strength into his tone.

"Why not?" He really shouldn't see the place alone. If Jay Voigt was right, Lucas would discover there Alana had been tortured. Penny couldn't let him face that alone. "I think I need to be with you."

"I can do this," he insisted. "Whether or not you're there, Alana will still be dead. My father might still be alive. What you are doing is trying to help him, right?"

And so much more! Penny squeezed her eyes shut. "Yes."

"Then you stick with it, and I'll handle this with the detective."

"All right, Lucas." Penny hesitated, choosing her words carefully. "But prepare yourself. There will be blood stains and likely signs of restraint and all that goes with being held hostage. Remember, I told you that she fought to stay with you."

"You did, and I will be prepared."

He thought he would, but nothing could prepare him for what she expected he would find. "I'm here if you need me. When you're done, come here. If I need to come and get you, just call me."

"I'll be okay, Mrs. Crown. It's just after hearing nothing for so long, his call surprised me. I'm fine now."

Lucas wasn't fine, and he sure wouldn't be fine afterward, but she admired him for this attempt. He wasn't a child anymore, and this proved it. "Lucas, remember how much you are loved, and that so long as those who love you breathe, you will never be alone."

"I won't forget. I'll be there when I can."

He hung up and Penny clutched the phone, bowed her head, and prayed he was as ready to do this as he believed he was, and that the experience wouldn't fling him deep into the dreaded abyss.

THIRTY

June 13th @ 1900

Penny returned the documents to the vault, still semi-dazed. Never in a million years had she expected to find what she had in the package. Now, John William's *the offspring* made perfect sense.

She returned to the kitchen starving, called down to the lab and asked John William what he wanted for dinner. He responded with one word: *Chinese*.

Knowing him well, she placed the order for delivery, certain to get enough food for the three of them and Lucas as well. He should be leaving Jay Voigt and arriving here before long. He'd need something normal to diminish the horrors of what he had witnessed. Nothing could be more normal than dinner. And food would absorb the acid churning in his stomach because of what he'd seen.

Penny just hoped the poor lamb could swallow. Odds were, he would be too upset to eat, which meant they all would have to work that much harder to make dinner normal.

Twenty minutes later, the food arrived, and John William and Nicholas joined Penny in the kitchen. When they were seated with their food, Penny said, "I need to share what I found in the documents from Lovenia before Lucas arrives. He can't be much longer."

"Go ahead then," John William said, pausing his fork over a heap of Shrimp Lo Mein.

Penny stopped eating. "The first point of interest happened during the coup against King Alexander and his family."

Nicholas swallowed a sip of wine. "So much began that night."

Penny nodded. "I think Alexander's son, Stefan, could be in exile—likely with the royal fortune."

"He died the night of the coup," Nicholas said. "There were witnesses."

"Supposedly, he died." Penny reached for a spring roll. "But it was rumored that Stefan was smuggled out of the country."

John Williams frowned. "No less than six authorities saw his corpse and attested to it, Penny."

"Those same six people saw Kasper Hoffman's corpse, too. Yet here we are."

"What's your point?" Nick asked.

"Kasper Hoffman is alive. So my point is, if Kasper wasn't dead, maybe Stefan isn't dead either."

"If that proves true, who loses most?" John William dabbed at the corner of his mouth with a white linen napkin.

"The current king," Penny said. "Berthold Franke."

"These documents prove this?" John Williams asked.

"They don't offer hard evidence, which is why we can't tell Lucas any of this without first learning more. But we can ask questions that could lead us to that hard evidence."

A tap at the door signaled Lucas's arrival. Penny went down to disarm the security system and let him in. "Lucas, are you all right?" He looked tense but not frazzled.

"I will be fine in a few minutes. But, Mrs. Crown, I hope I never have to go through a crime scene like that again for as long as I live."

"It's horrible, I know." Penny clasped his arm. "Go wash up for dinner. It's on the table."

He nodded and minutes later joined them in the kitchen.

John William and Nick studied Lucas, and thankfully neither of them mentioned what he'd seen at the scene with Jay Voigt.

"Penny ordered enough food for an army." John William looked at Lucas. "I hope you brought a healthy appetite."

"It smells good." Lucas loaded his plate with a sampling of everything.

John William guided the conversation. "We were discussing the fairytales your parents shared with you about Lovenia. Penny disclosed many of them, but that has me wondering."

"What?" Lucas asked.

"Were there any fairytales about the coup? I find I'm especially interested in Prince Stefan and Kasper Hoffman."

Lucas spooned fried rice onto his plate. "There are several stories about the coup, and the prince and Minister Hoffman."

"I'm eager to hear them." John William said.

Penny bit her tongue to prohibit a gutsy "me too" from escaping her mouth.

"I'd like to hear them, too," Nicholas said, unrestrained. "Tell us."

Lucas took a bite, slowly chewed, then swallowed. "There's one about King Alexander coming here."

"To Kerra?"

"Yes, before the coup. He was in the country for a State visit, and discovered there was a Kerra in Georgia. He insisted on visiting it because it shared a name with his queen, who was traveling with him. Queen Kerra thought our Kerra was charming, and said if she ever lived outside of Lovenia, it would be in Kerra, Georgia. There was talk of the king establishing a scholarship at the university. It would have pleased the queen. But then the coup... Well, everything changed."

Penny felt a tingle at the base of her spine.

"Then there's one about the night of the coup," Lucas said. "King Alexander had caught wind of what was coming. He arranged to get the queen out of the country. She and her lady's maid switched roles to get the queen to the plane. Queen Kerra was to smuggle out their daughter, Brigit, and the pendant. But at the last minute, Queen Kerra refused to leave. She stayed behind with King Alexander."

"Why?" Penny asked.

"So that no one would suspect King Alexander had also planned to smuggle Prince Stefan out. The queen knew she would die, staying in Lovenia, but it was most important that the people believed Stefan had died that night, too. Otherwise, the new king would come after him and kill Stefan."

"What about Prince Stefan and Kasper Hoffman?" John William asked.

"There's a story about them that night, too." Lucas paused to take a few bites and to sip from his glass. "The story goes that their deaths that night were staged."

"But there were witnesses," John William reminded Lucas.

"There were—King Alexander's trusted allies," he whispered. "A small group of men stowed Stefan and Kasper in drums and smuggled them onto the plane. They were hidden in the belly of it the whole time, until just before the flight took off and flew them to a distant land to wait… for the boy king to grow up and claim his crown." A thoughtful look settled on Lucas's face.

Lucas. Before John William or Nicholas spilled it all out, Penny interceded. "But to reclaim the crown, he would need irrefutable proof he is indeed Stefan." She slid John William and Nick a warning look to silence them into saying nothing to Lucas until they held that proof in their hands.

Lucas paled, seeming oddly out of sorts. "May, um, I be excused," Lucas said. "I need a few minutes."

He hadn't eaten much, but he had gotten down more than expected. Penny nodded. "Of course."

"Rest in the guest room, Lucas." John Williams lifted his gaze. "You know the way."

"Thank you." He left the kitchen.

"Do you think he knows?" Nicholas asked.

Penny answered. "If he doesn't, he's beginning to wonder."

John William frowned. "It's a process. I'm convinced it's

occurred to him that Lovenia is real and there is something of truth in the fairytales."

"He'll let us know when he's ready," Penny said. "Until then, we gather proof."

Nicholas passed John William his phone. "Verify for me this photo is of the man who attacked you in the museum."

"I showed you the man's photo, Nicholas."

"I haven't forgotten, John William. I just received this photo from Adam. It is more clear."

"I see." John William clearly knew who Adam was and studied the new photo. "That is him." He looked up at Nicholas. "Who is he?"

"I told you, Dirk."

"Yes, I know his name." John William's expression was blank. "But who is Dirk?"

Penny waited but Nick didn't answer so she did. "He's a fixer for King Berthold. They call him the Enforcer. He enforces whatever orders Berthold gives him." Penny cocked her head, more than a little concerned. "Are you all right, John William? We discussed this earlier."

"I'm fine, my dear. Just residuals from the injury, I expect."

He had taken multiple hard blows to the head. Should she call Dr. Handley? More information was needed to determine that. "Is this memory lapse your first since waking from the coma?"

"I am just not recovered yet, my dear, and we're sharing a lot of information. I really am all right. Just not yet back at the top of my game."

That eased her worry, but it didn't alleviate it. If John William admitted to being less than normal, he had to be bone-weary. "You need to rest for a while then."

"Not yet." John William looked at Nick. "Obviously, Dirk's skills include assassination."

Nick shrugged. "I would assume so."

"Penny?" John William looked to her for an opinion.

"Possibly, but I can't say what I can't prove. The Enforcer was here. Alana did die. Attempts were made on Lucas's life, and on

Kyle's. Dirk being an assassin seems reasonable, but we can't prove it. He did stick like glue to Gregor at the meet. Frankly, that had me doubting and concerned about Gregor. But his distaste for Dirk was clear from the start."

"I need to report Dirk to my people," Nick said. "You're sure about Gregor's reaction to Dirk, Mrs. Crown?"

"Positive."

Nick stepped away and made a phone call, and then returned to the table. "If he's still in the U.S., they'll locate him and pick him up."

"If not?" Penny asked.

"If he's back in Lovenia, he's out of our reach." More than a little resentment etched Nick's tone.

"He is long gone," John William said. "He was safe on Alana's murder until I survived his attack. I can identify him."

They could make dangerous connections for Dirk. "You're probably right. He would be a fool to not have returned to Lovenia with the team." Penny looked down at her food. Dirk was out of reach, but he wasn't out of Stefan's reach…

Or he wouldn't be once Stefan returned to Lovenia.

Compared to the imposing Crowlee Institute in New York, John William's compact lab was likely not as sprawled out or flush as Amanda's, but it was impressively well-equipped. Over the years, Penny had spent a lot of time on this floor, but from Nick's reaction, he was seeing it for the first time.

"I had no idea this facility existed," he whispered to Penny. "All this equipment is his?"

"Would John William have it any other way?" Penny stepped away, hung the painting on the wall a foot away from where the pendant hung, then stepped behind a ten-foot lab table distant from John William's modified LAM. "The modified Layer Amplification Method testing equipment is his latest edition and addition."

Nick examined it, seeming as fascinated as Penny had been

when John William first had shown it to her. He followed the drum section connected through blue tubing to receptors on a tripod type piece of equipment with multiple camera lenses that he aimed at the painting.

"How does this work?" Nick asked from beside her. "It's significantly different from the original."

Nick knew exactly how it worked but was testing her knowledge. Again. Since meeting her, he had tested her repeatedly on people, background information, historical events, deductions—nearly everything. She lowered her voice so as not to interrupt John William at work and indulged him. After all, she had been testing him, too. It was prudent to know how a partner's mind worked.

"It shoots intense light and measures the light that bounces back to the lens and sensors, as Cottes' original LAM did, though more intensely and in deeper detail. That peels the layers of the painting and pendant like an onion. Each layer then appears as a separate image on one of the four monitors so all layers can be viewed and studied simultaneously." She pointed to the monitors, atop a second lab table behind which John William stood. "All four screens connect to a single terminal, hence to one keyboard. From the monitors, he can closely examine and manipulate each of the layers individually."

Penny and Nick stepped behind John William to view the screens.

"Interesting," Nick said, rubbing his jaw. "On the second screen, the long series of squiggly lines Amanda spoke of are visible. Definitely intentional."

They were uniform and exact, yet blurred and indecipherable. "Agreed." Penny frowned. "Is there a way to make them readable, provided they are text?"

"They could be text," John William said. "But something required to enable reading is missing. Whatever it is, I suspect only it can make the message clear."

"Red Richter," Penny said. "Perhaps the pendant? We know there is a link between the two objects." Requiring both to decipher the message made sense, though the experts in the room could deem her crazy for suggesting it. She was the least experienced and no expert. *In the painting, the keyhole held the nation's future.* At most, they would ignore her suggestion and she'd look silly. So what? It was worth a shot. "John William, is it possible to view that portion of the painting through the diamonds in the pendant?"

He thought a moment, then shrugged. "The facets in the stones will affect the light."

"Reflections will be distorted," Nick said.

"Maybe distortion is what's needed," Penny said. "It can't be read without them."

"True," Nick agreed. "But we risk damaging the painting."

"We don't," John William said. "I adjusted for distortions in my modifications. We can't damage either object by trying it."

He moved the pendant into position, then returned to the computer, released a strong burst of intense light, and four new images appeared on the monitor screens.

"Oh, my." Penny gasped. The squiggly lines became a visible row of sets of numbers.

"Brilliant, Penny!" John William treated her to a rare smile.

A rush of excitement raced through her, and she smiled.

"The numerical sequences are consistent with Swiss bank accounts," Nick said. "Unfortunately, they are useless to us."

"Why?" Penny asked, her elation fading to disappointment.

John William answered. "No password."

Penny studied the screens. "It must be on the pendant. Can you test it without the painting?"

John William positioned the pendant, ran the test, then examined it. Finally, he looked back at Penny and Nick. "There are two separate areas with embedded writing."

"What do they say?" Nick asked.

"The first reads, 'Berthold's coup.' The second reads… Oh, my." He darted a look back at them.

"What is it?" Penny pushed. "What does it say?"

John William's eyes stretched wide. "Stefan lives!"

Lucas! "Stefan lives has to be the password."

"Nicholas," John William lifted a hand. "You must try it."

"Are these computers secure?" Nick asked.

John William nodded. "Use that one." He pointed to a computer on a desk in the corner.

Nicholas tried the password. "It worked…but it isn't giving me access to the accounts."

"What is it giving you?" Penny asked.

He held up a staying finger. "A moment, please."

Nick looked at Penny and John William. "It triggered a message."

"What message?" John William asked.

"A parcel will arrive within forty-eight hours. Guard it well."

Penny sucked in a strong breath, her body tingling head to foot. "Alexander arranged his son's escape and more. And his plan was successful. He will receive the parcel."

"We don't know what the parcel is," John William reminded her.

"He's right." Nick shut down the computer and rejoined them. "It could be a ruse to bring in a team of assassins."

Penny disagreed. "Why would the instructions say to guard a team of assassins well? They wouldn't." Sometimes brilliant men got mired in minutiae and missed the obvious. "Alexander created these accounts. He wouldn't trigger assassins against his son. Whatever this parcel is, it's coming."

"Coming where?" Nick asked.

"To Lucas." Penny tilted her head. "He has to be Stefan. Kyle is Kasper. Alexander charged him with keeping Stefan safe until he was grown and able to claim his crown. The royal fortune is in these Swiss accounts."

"I agree," John William said. "Lucas being Stefan is the only thing that makes all of the events that have occurred logical and reasonable, including Alana's death."

"It doesn't explain why Kyle didn't keep the pendant out of the media. That did put Lucas in jeopardy, which is why we must now go to Lucas and tell him the truth." Penny began shutting down the lab.

John William hesitated, shut down the Modified LAM. "I am not sure telling him everything at once is a good idea, Penny. This is a lot for a young man to absorb. He is so grieving Alana." John William returned the painting and pendant to the vault. "What do you think, Nicholas?"

"I agree with you. Alana's abduction and death, the car bombing and home intrusion and sniper attack, Kyle's disappearances, and then the attack on you." Nick rubbed at the back of his neck. "He is in so much pain. Learning Kyle isn't his father could be the last straw."

Penny resisted the urge to roll her eyes back in her head. "Don't be absurd. Lucas is a survivor. He'll deal with this. True, it won't be easy, and he will be shocked, but better he be shocked than dead."

"Dead?" Nick looked stunned.

Penny frowned. "The more he knows, the greater the danger to him. That's true. But what he doesn't know is deadly to him. Do you think Berthold is just going to forfeit his crown without a whimper? Or that those who killed Alana and attempted to kill Lucas and Kyle are just going to suddenly stop? What about the sniper, the people who tossed Lucas's home? None of them are going to just quit fighting and hand over Lovenia to Lucas. Of course, we must tell him everything, and the sooner the better. It doesn't matter whether he's Lucas or Prince Stefan, he can't defend himself against the unknown."

While the men debated, Penny phoned Lucas. The call went straight to voice mail. She then called Jay Voigt. "Detective, have you any idea where Lucas might be at the moment?"

"No, I don't. He left me hours ago. Has something happened?"

"I'm sure everything is fine," she said. "If you should hear from him, please have him call me."

"He was pretty upset at the scene. Sad and angry. We talked about it. Hard to see a young man in that kind of pain." Jay sighed. His breath crackled static through the phone. "I expect he just needed to be off by himself for a while."

She should have talked to Lucas about that sooner. "Thank you, Jay." Penny hung up. Then she dialed Lisa.

"Hi, what's up?"

"Have you talked to Lucas recently?"

"About an hour ago. He had some word on his father and was going to check it out."

A shiver raced up Penny's spine. "A word from whom?"

"He didn't say." Lisa's breath hitched. "Mom, is he in danger again? He told me he was safe."

"Let me see what I can find out." Penny avoided a direct answer. "I'll call you as soon as I can."

When she stowed her phone, John William caught her attention. He was so tired he was wobbly on his feet. "John William," Penny said. "You're exhausted and need to rest. Now." She turned to Nick. "You check Lucas's house to see if he's there." Penny grabbed her handbag. "I'll call as soon as I've located him."

"When she gets bossy, it is wise to just agree with her," John William whispered to Nick.

He smiled. "She's worried about you."

"It's annoying."

John William didn't look annoyed. "It's charming," Nick said.

"Fine," John William said. "I will rest, my dear. But I think we should tell Lucas about things together. He will no doubt endure a wide range of emotions and have a lot of questions."

"Agreed. Turn on the alarm then go straight to bed," Penny said as she headed out the door and to her car. "Call me, Nick."

"Will do." He got into his rental and departed.

Penny shut the car door and paused. "Where would Lucas go?" Her mind reeled and she forced herself to focus. Suddenly, the answer seemed clear. She cranked the engine and took off.

Before she arrived at her destination, her phone rang. "Hi, Nick," she said.

"He isn't here, and there's no sign he or anyone else has been here."

"That's not too surprising, but we needed to know for certain."

"Penny, what if we're too late? What if someone in the Lovenia contingent in Kerra for the meet stayed behind and has gotten to Lucas?"

The possibility had occurred to her more than once. *Chilling.* "Did your people pick up Dirk?"

"He's back in Lovenia," Nick said. "That's confirmed."

"I can think of only one other place Lucas might be. I'm on my way there now."

"Where?"

"Alana's grave."

Penny parked at the cemetery, grabbed a flashlight, and headed toward Alana's gravesite. In the darkness, she spotted a silhouette seated near it. *Lucas.* Relieved, Penny walked over. "Lucas, may I intrude?"

"You're never an intrusion, Mrs. Crown."

She sat down beside him. "Why are you out here?"

"I just walked to talk to her."

"I understand." Penny swiped her hair back from her face. "I come out here a lot to talk to Mark." She had since his burial, though she had been coming far less these last few months.

"I started to call you, but I didn't want you to think I was losing it. Some people think it's crazy to talk to a dead person."

"They're wrong, and you're not losing it. It's normal."

"It is?"

"Of course. You miss her, and you two talked about everything. Lucas, you lost your fiancé and your best friend."

"I'm still getting used to it," he said. "It's hard."

"It is. But give it time. It will get better."

"Yes, you're proof of that."

She wasn't so sure she was a good example, but now wasn't the time to increase his doubts about anything. "I need to talk with you about some things, but I wanted to do that with John William and Nick."

"I have something to tell you, too." Lucas checked his watch. "I heard from my father. We're to meet in a few minutes at Bayside Park, near the oak."

Kyle was still alive. *Thank you, God.* "You spoke to him directly?"

When Lucas nodded, she added, "Did he say why he wanted to meet?"

"He has something to tell me," Lucas said. "I'm not sure what it is about, or why he's hiding. With everything going on, it could be anything." Lucas stood and extended a hand to her. "Ride with me?"

"I have my car, but I'll meet you there."

"Thanks. He hasn't been himself lately, so I'm a little uneasy. You being there could help. You bring out the best in him."

That surprised her. "I'll meet you there, then."

Penny returned to her car and phoned Nick. "He's meeting Kyle in a few minutes. Bayside Park at the forked oak."

"Where Alana's body was found?"

"Yes. I'm on the way there now." She paused to think. "Nick, maybe you should observe covertly. Lucas is uneasy about the meeting. Frankly, I'm not totally comfortable with any meeting arranged in that specific spot. It's the last place Lucas needs to be."

"I'm glad to hear Kyle's alive," Nick said, his relief evident. "But him setting a meeting with Lucas there is odd."

"And painful for Lucas." Penny looked at the choice through a mother's eyes. "Maybe Kyle thinks no one would ever consider them meeting there."

"I suppose that's possible. Regardless, be extra cautious, Penny Crown. I'm on my way."

Penny Crown. Using her given and surname rather than his habitual *Mrs. Crown.*

Nick too was uneasy.

The park was still and quiet, bathed in deep shadows and soft light cast from the lamps lighting the stone walkway. Lucas stood waiting in the parking lot. Kyle waited at the base of the tree.

Parked and out of her SUV, Penny joined Lucas. "If you wouldn't mind, I'd like to speak to your father for a minute before you two talk. Is that okay?"

"Of course." Lucas stared at the tree.

Penny could only imagine the images running through his mind. Instinctively, she brushed a hand across his shoulder. "You can do this, Lucas."

"I can. But I wish I didn't have to do it."

"I wish you didn't have to either, but here we are."

"Here we are... and there's my father."

Penny clasped Lucas's arm. If Kyle was being forced to bring them here, Lucas would at least have the length of the lush lawn between them to escape in his favor. "Wait here."

He stopped without question.

Penny walked on, her hand inside her purse, gripping her gun, and met Kyle near the oak. "Lucas will be here in a moment. Coming to this spot is hard for him."

"It always will be, but it's also the last place anyone would ever expect to find him."

So that had been his rationale. Feeling easier knowing it, Penny relaxed. "I'd like a word with you, Kyle, if you wouldn't mind."

"What is it?" His eyes burned with genuine concern.

He'd once appreciated her straightforward speaking. She hoped he still did. "I know the truth."

"What truth is that?"

The door was open, and Penny marched through it. "Echoes of betrayal."

"I don't understand."

"Everything happening here aligns with the events in the Lovenia coup. What I don't understand is why you didn't keep the pendant out of the media. You knew it would put Lucas and yourself in danger."

Kyle hiked his chin. "I don't understand."

"I know Lucas is Prince Stefan and you are Kasper Hoffman."

Silence.

"I suspect you've been following King Alexander's instructions on caring for his son."

Still, no response.

"This will go more quickly if you'll acknowledge what I've said,

Kyle. Time is of the essence with Lucas waiting, and the message I have for you."

"Message? Has someone been in touch with you?"

"In a way. The painting and the pendant provided the message."

"You discovered it?"

"We did. John William, Nicholas Ryan, and me."

"What is it?" Kyle stilled, board stiff. "Please, tell me."

"First, you tell me why you permitted the pendant in the media. Why you deliberately put Lucas in jeopardy."

"I had no choice. It was time. That predetermined sign signaled the long, silent wait was over."

That confused Penny. "What long, silent wait?"

"Our wait for Lucas to grow to a man and be ready to return to Lovenia." Kyle paused, then added, "It was determined in King Alexander's plan for Lucas's protection."

On solid ground now, Penny shifted her perspective. "You knew the media attention would also alert hostile forces, and public exposure was Lucas's best defense? His protection?"

Kyle's relief swept across his face. "Exactly. We couldn't wait any longer. Lovenia is in dire financial straits."

Dire straits. So that is why Berthold sent Gregor to Kerra. To find and retrieve Lovenia's money. Gregor, with diplomatic immunity, could avoid customs and safely return the fortune to Lovenia. But Gregor didn't do it. Couldn't do it at the time he departed for home, though the silent interaction between him and Kyle proved Gregor wouldn't have done it anyway. He stood firmly in Lucas's corner. Satisfied with that explanation, Penny nodded.

"The message?" Kyle prodded. "Please, Mrs. Crown."

"Lucas will receive a parcel shortly, which means Berthold—I'm guessing he is responsible for the coup that resulted in the deaths of his family—is very likely who is after you and Lucas."

"His people are already here. As tragic as Alana's murder was, it warned us of that. As a result, we've survived several close encounters." Kyle shot a glance toward Lucas. "Does he know all this?"

"Not yet. But it's too dangerous for him not to know now. If you don't tell him, I will."

"I agree he must know." Kyle stared into the treetop for a moment, clearly thinking. "But I must be the one to tell him... so he can prepare himself for what is to come."

"The truth should come from you," she said. "He will be deeply disturbed about Alana being caught up in this unaware."

"His resentment will be just." Kyle regretted that. It shown in his eyes.

"But he is in grave danger from Berthold." Logical deduction, but Penny wanted confirmation her deductions were accurate.

"So long as Berthold breathes." Kyle nodded. "He murdered the royal family, including his own mother."

Something odd in his tone alerted Penny. "But not just for the crown?"

"The crown was only part of it," Kyle said. "The family fortune was only another part of it. Fortunately, Christopher Gregor and King Alexander and I were successful at putting the royal holdings out of Berthold's reach."

There was more. Penny urged Kyle to elaborate. "What is the other part?"

Kyle paced a short path before Penny. "It started with Berthold's father, Gerhard Franke. During World War II, he facilitated a gateway through Lovenia to traffic stolen art between Germany and Switzerland. Art dealers there would sell to private collectors. The funds were deposited into Swiss accounts." Kyle swiped at his neck. "Berthold's father amassed quite a collection of art, jewelry, artifacts, rare documents, and books—anything of value that could be stolen and trafficked. When he died, Berthold inherited his business. He had worked for his father most of his life." Kyle paused and then added, "Rumors began swirling about war crimes charges coming against Berthold. He grew panicked and asked King Alexander to intercede and protect him. King Alexander refused. He insisted Berthold face the accusations for his own good and the good of the country."

"King Alexander didn't believe his brother could be involved in something like that."

"No, he didn't." Kyle stared off into the distance. "Until he had no choice but to believe. That's when King Alexander deduced any man capable of those actions would react with even more deadly ones to bury the truth. He expected that Berthold would seize control and install himself as king. The crown would insulate him from his accusers." Kyle stopped pacing. "Alexander prepared for a coup. Tactically, it was Berthold's second-best move. The first was for him to disappear, but his ego and greed would not permit that. His lust for power was insatiable."

In her mind, Penny imagined the turmoil and upheaval. "Alexander arranged to get Queen Kerra, Brigit, and Stefan out of Lovenia, but Stefan was separated when the queen decided to stay. She and Alexander placed Stefan in your care. You were already part of the fortune being hidden in Switzerland. You were to raise him as your son until he was old enough to claim his crown?"

Kyle nodded. "Queen Kerra refused to leave the king. Her maid was to get Brigit out of the country. We don't know if she was successful. Christopher Gregor has been searching for her ever since the coup, but he must be cautious."

Penny speculated. "If Berthold discovered Gregor's search, he'd kill him and everyone around him to secure his position."

"Exactly." Kyle cleared his throat. "The night of the coup, bodies were produced that could have been the children and the maid. We attested that they were. But whether or not that was true about Brigit and the maid, I can't honestly say."

"But you died that night, too."

"Yes, supposedly, after testifying as a witness before the council." Kyle paused, swallowed hard. "The escapes were the first phase of the mission—Phantom I. To save as many of the royal family as possible."

"And the second phase?"

"Phantom II is active now. In Phantom I, deaths were unavoidable. But Phantom II was different." Kyle looked her right in the eye, his own laden with sorrow that had to be ripped from his soul. "No one was supposed to die."

Alana. "I am so sorry."

"As am I." Kyle dipped his chin. "We never considered he would choose a bride before returning home." Kyle looked up at Penny. "We failed him. I failed my son."

"You've kept him alive and prepared him to rule, Kyle." Penny's heart broke with his, parent to parent. "No one can predict every eventuality in life. Things happen. Lucas knows that, and he will, given time, understand."

"I pray you're right, Mrs. Crown."

"Thank you for sharing all this and confirming what I suspected." Penny glanced at Lucas on the distant lawn. "He must be told now. It's far too dangerous for him to be in the dark a moment longer." Penny looked back at Kyle. "Is this why you wanted to meet him here?"

"I need to speak to him about it all, and about the parcel."

"It's probably best if we tell him his history together," Penny said. "I'll get John William and Nicholas to meet us in the private room at Café Vere in an hour. Will that give you enough time?"

Kyle nodded. "Father to son." His voice cracked. "This will be our last conversation father-to-son."

"It won't," Penny assured him, her chest tight with compassion. "You know his every bruise and wound and heartbreak, Kyle. That will never change. Trust him."

She turned then walked back to where Lucas stood waiting. "Sorry it took longer than I expected. We're all going to meet in an hour at Café Vere. He's fine, Lucas."

That seemed to ease his mind and Lucas walked quickly to his father. They embraced.

After the discussion, she prayed Lucas would remember how much Kyle had sacrificed to be a father to him. At least, once the shock wore off. He did truly love the man, so she dared to hope that wouldn't take long, though Alana's death would be a huge obstacle. Lucas was going to need all the support he could get.

Berthold, being ruthless and evil enough to kill his own mother and attempt to murder his brother's entire family, would see to that.

Walking near a thicket of bushes beyond the lush lawn, she phoned John William and filled him in, ending with instructions on the meeting.

"I'll secure the private room," he said.

She returned her phone to her handbag and heard a rustling in the bushes.

"Don't shoot. It's me." Nick revealed his position and he and Penny returned to his car. "There's no one out here except for them. We can leave."

"No, Nick." Penny fisted her hands. "We need to keep watch."

Seated inside, he didn't start the engine. "You and Kyle talked a long time."

"We did."

"And?"

Penny spared Nick a glance. "He confirmed our suspicions."

"Lucas is definitely Stefan."

"Yes." Penny bit her lip and resolve to protect Lucas filled her body and soul. "And Berthold is a ruthless murderer who will try anything to kill him."

Nick looked away. "Unless we stop him."

"And his assassins."

"We will stop them all, and we'll have help, Mrs. Crown." Nick reached for the door. "I need to report in."

She nodded, watched him leave the car and retrieve his phone.

He returned abruptly and lifted his chin toward Kyle and Lucas. "They're leaving."

Penny checked her watch. They'd spoken forty-five minutes and had just enough time to get to Café Vere on time. "Drop me at my car. We meet them and John William in fifteen minutes."

Nick started the engine. "John William is already there. He's secured the private room."

So, he had reported in to John William. She had assumed Nick had been reporting to his government associates, but he had made only one call. Perhaps John William was one of his government associates? "Good." Penny grabbed the door handle. "I'll meet you there."

"Check your car before getting in. It wasn't always in my line of sight."

"I will." Outside the car, Penny stopped. "Is there a reason you suggested it?"

"Just a precaution. I advise you always check it. At least for the foreseeable future."

"Okay." Penny closed the door, certain Nick was keeping secrets. In his line of work, that was to be expected but she still didn't like it. When they had a moment, she would discuss the matter with him. But now was not the time.

She had to steel herself to bring Lucas's world crumbling down around his ears, and pray he still trusted her enough to permit her to help him pick up the pieces…

THIRTY-ONE

June 14th @ 0700

Penny sat with John William and Nick in the private room at Café Vere. The warm autumn tones and muted lighting seemed the perfect choice for the conversation they were about to have. Lucas and Kyle had not yet arrived.

On the way in, Penny had phoned Lisa with an update, but held back on disclosing Lucas's true identity. No matter how many times Penny swore Lisa to silence until he was told the truth, it would be just like her daughter to phone to console him. She had picked up on the fact Penny was withholding information, but Penny did not cave in and tell Lisa. She did plead being short on time and promise to phone later with a full accounting of events.

Penny hoped she didn't live to regret that.

Lucas came in. Alone. He didn't look shell-shocked, so that was good. "Where is Kyle?" Penny asked.

"He had a stop to make," Lucas said, taking a seat beside Nick and across from Penny. "He'll be here."

John William and Nick talked about the modifications on the LAM method used to test the pendant and the painting. Lucas feigned interest, which would have been odd—typically, he was fascinated by John William's work—but considering his discussion with Kyle, seemed normal.

Penny poured Lucas a cup of coffee. "Are you okay?"

His eyes burned overly bright. "I'm not."

John William and Nick fell silent. Penny again spoke to Lucas. "What's wrong?"

Pain settled in his eyes. "My fiancée is dead, and my father isn't my father." He took in a shaky breath. "I've lived a lie my whole life."

John William started to speak. "Luc—"

Penny lifted a staying hand. "What lie, honey?"

"Apparently, I am a dead heir. King of a country I believed was a fairytale."

"Lovenia?" Penny asked.

Lucas nodded. "Learning that, who could be all right?"

"No one," Penny said softly.

Realization burned in his eyes. "You knew?"

"I—We just discovered the truth. Today, Lucas." Penny stiffened.

"Then you tell me. Am I the reason Alana is dead?" He swallowed hard. "Was she killed because of me?"

"Alana is dead because others murdered her. You loved her enough to propose marriage and spend the rest of your lives together. You didn't harm her in any way."

"If I hadn't given her the pendant and the media hadn't seen it…"

"Reality is what it is," Penny said. "Did Kyle tell you about Berthold's duplicity and all your parents sacrificed to ensure that you lived?"

"As much as time would allow," Lucas admitted. "Kyle and Grace sacrificed a lot, too. Everything. They took enormous risks for me."

"They did," Penny agreed. "And they loved you every day of your life. Kyle still does, Lucas." She reached across the table and covered his hand. "Most children are very lucky to have one set of parents who love them enough to sacrifice everything for them. You were blessed with two sets willing to forfeit all, including their lives."

"I'd rather they lived."

"Of course, you would. But you didn't get to choose, honey. You got to live with the fallout of other people's choices. And I mean Berthold and his traitors, more so than either set of your parents. They protected you."

Penny went on to relate what they'd learned about King Alexander working with Kasper and Christopher Gregor.

Lucas's eyes stretched wide. "The same Christopher Gregor who gave me the painting at the meet?"

"The same," Penny said. "I spoke with him several times and watched him closely during the meet, Lucas. He looked at you with such pride and admiration."

"He knew who I was before I knew."

Penny nodded, shared the truth about his mother, sending her maid to try to get Brigit out of the country safely. "She knew none of you would be allowed to live. Against your father's wishes, she stayed with him to remove any suspicion that anyone else was smuggled away. She protected you and tried to protect Brigit. The cost was forfeiting her life. The maid wore the pendant—or so Berthold thought. But the original pendant left with you and Kyle. Did he tell you his real name?"

"Kasper Hoffman." Lucas nodded, absorbing. "So how did the maid get a pendant, too? Was there more than one?"

"The one she took was an early iteration, I suppose. Back then, when a piece was commissioned, the designer made a prototype, so to speak."

"So, Brigit is dead?" Pain flooded his eyes.

Penny shrugged. "There is no word on her or the maid. We've done an exhaustive search from here, but found no mention of either of them, beyond Brigit being identified as among the dead the night of the coup."

"She was killed then." Lucas looked down at the table.

"Not necessarily," Penny said. She waited until he looked up at her, then added, "You were reported dead that night and so was Kasper Hoffman."

"Forces loyal to King Alexander protected us."

"It appears so." Penny sipped from her cup. "My guess is Christopher Gregor, who was the Chief Councilor at the time, was among them."

Lucas's jaw snapped shut. "Which means Berthold hadn't known the maid's pendant in his possession wasn't the original until the media exposed Alana wearing it and I revealed the tradition."

"Perhaps." Penny couldn't confirm that, but it fit. "If in that position, I'd have left a forgery in place, so Berthold thought he had it, and sent the prototype with Brigit, hoping it would provide her safe passage. But I can't know that's what happened, of course."

Lucas stared at her a long moment. "Why didn't you tell me about all this? I should have known Lovenia was real at the meet, but with what happened to Alana—"

"You were distracted, then grieving. And I couldn't share what I didn't know to be true, Lucas. None of us could." She motioned to John William and Nick. "But we have worked diligently to find the truth for you." She patted his hand. "With everything that's happened, we couldn't risk passing on anything unconfirmed. You were already heartbroken and wounded. Surely you understand that."

He sighed. "I do, Mrs. Crown." He cleared his throat. "You were doing what you always do, proving you love me unconditionally. Like a second, or now, I guess, a third mother."

He understood. Or he'd forgiven her. Regardless, she was grateful for the reprieve.

Kyle came in. "Mrs. Crown has always loved you unconditionally, Lucas." He looked at Penny. "No forgiveness for anything you've done or haven't done is necessary. No birth mother or surrogate could have done more."

"Thank you, Kyle—or do you prefer Kasper?"

"Kyle, please. And Lucas should remain Lucas until he returns to Lovenia to reclaim the crown." He let his gaze travel between the two of them. "It's safer."

Kyle sat down beside Penny and addressed the group. "Gregor has just made contact. Berthold has ordered Stefan's assassination."

Penny frowned. "I think he did that long ago."

"I agree." Kyle nodded. "But now he has done so officially."

Nick frowned. "Is Gregor to execute the order?"

"No, but he believes the assassin is already in Kerra."

"Then it isn't Dirk," Nick said. "I have confirmation he is in Lovenia."

"That information might be unreliable." John Williams interjected.

"Why?" Penny asked.

"It's illogical." John Williams poured himself another cup of tea. "Dirk is Berthold's enforcer. He was here. Why bring him back to Lovenia before this is resolved only to turn around and send him here again? Especially when one has no idea what developments would arise in the interim."

Penny looked at Nick. "Good points," she said. "Are you certain your confirmation is authentic?"

"I'll have that doublechecked right away." Nick pulled out his phone and stood. "Either way, it's time to bring in the authorities—on a limited basis."

"The fewer the better. Need to know only." John William stared at Nick. "You'd best inform the secretary."

"I'll contact Jay Voigt," Penny said. "You contact the necessary federal sources."

Nick nodded and left the table.

Penny also left the table and paused just inside the private room to phone Jay. When he answered, she greeted him then immediately followed with a warning. "This entire conversation is confidential. Strictly need to know, and the fewer who know anything about it, the better."

He agreed and she briefed him on the essentials. "The rest, I'll tell you in person."

"What do you need right now?" Jay asked.

"To sequester Lucas and Kyle." Until the parcel arrived, that was essential.

"I'll arrange a safe house and get back with you," Jay said. "Give me five minutes."

He understood the urgency and the risks.

She walked back to the table but before she could sit down, Jay phoned back. "I have a house."

When he told her the location, she refused. "No way."

"Why not?"

"It was compromised on the Merc case."

"How do you know that?"

"I was standing beside Mark when the call came in telling him his star witness had been murdered in that house."

Jay paused, then sighed.

"Perhaps the feds have more secure resources," Penny said.

"They probably do," Jay said. "They're going to take over the case anyway."

"But you will still do all you can…"

"Absolutely, Penny. Anything you need."

Penny stowed her phone in her pocket and returned to the group. Nick was already there. "We need a secure safe house. I refused the one the locals suggested."

Surprise flitted over John William's face. "And they allowed it?"

"It was compromised in an earlier investigation. How could they refuse?"

"Well done, Mrs. Crown." Nick's eyes gleamed admiration. "I'll handle it."

June 15th @ 1940 p.m.

"Nicholas, could you please stop pacing?" John William frowned. "A man can hardly digest food with you stomping a path the length of the table."

"Sorry." Nick sat down. "We should have heard on the parcel by now."

At the request of Secretary Dawson, Penny and John William were in a safe house just outside of Atlanta with Lucas, Kyle, and Nick. Four federal officials were stationed outside. It was the third location the group had been moved to in the last twenty-four hours. "Delivery is scheduled, Nick," Penny said. "Tomorrow morning at 5:00." Kyle had told them the parcel would arrive then via armored truck, and extra security measures had been put into place. Nick was to retrieve the parcel from a secondary location not yet provided. Gregor insisted only Nick's biometric signature would be accepted. Without it, the parcel would not be released.

Gregor obviously trusted Nick.

And Penny had been right. Nick had known more about this case long before Penny knew there was a case. He'd led her and confirmed her findings as they occurred, but he had not offered new information to her during the search. She caught that earlier but because of his association with John William, she put it down to him testing her. He likely was, but he was keeping his secrets, too. Now, she believed John William was also more aware. Was he a confidential informant to the government? A human resource? An employee like Nick? He had some affiliation. That much was clear in his insistence that Nick contact the Secretary.

After dinner, Lucas joined Penny in an informal den. She sat on the sofa, and Lucas asked, "May I join you?"

"Sure." She motioned to the other end of the sofa.

"If it's okay, I need to talk." Lucas bent his arms and rested them on his knees. "I should have told you this before, but honestly, I'm still absorbing everything."

"It'll take some time, I expect." Penny set aside a book she'd been reading on Lovenia.

"I haven't been totally honest, Mrs. Crown." He worried his lower lip with his teeth. "It's humiliating to admit that to you after all you've done for me."

"About what?" She rested her hands in her lap.

"I suspected there was more to the fairytales than fairytales." Lucas couldn't meet her eyes. "I probably wouldn't have thought too much of it, but it was both my mother and father—I mean Grace and Kyle, those parents. My whole life, they taught me everything about Lovenia. The politics, the law, the traditions, the people."

"When did you come to suspect there was more to the stories?"

"I don't recall exactly," he said. "I was young. But I convinced myself they were relaying stories of their lives, not mine. And their heritage. I guess that sounds foolish now."

"Not to me. Your instincts were alerting you, but these were your parents. Of course, you trusted them."

"Looking back, knowing what I know now, I can see they were preparing me for my future."

"Reclaiming your crown."

"And my heritage."

"It was clever of them to prepare you in the way they did, Lucas. And heaven knows you'll need all you learned when you challenge Berthold's claim to the throne."

"I will, if I challenge him." Lucas dropped his voice. "I'm torn, Mrs. Crown."

"I expect you are. Kerra is your home. It's all you've known, as is Kyle as your father."

"Everything's changed." Lucas squeezed his eyes shut. Finally, he reopened them. "I'm not sure where I belong anymore."

Penny's heart twisted. "You just need time to come to grips with your changed circumstances."

"Duty or desire, right?" Lucas shook his head. "I know I have obligations there, but I have a life here. I don't know if I want to be a king."

Penny lowered her feet to the floor and sat beside him. "You are who you are. You can't change that."

"They changed it for me."

"To save your life," Penny said, suspecting this wasn't so much a matter of duty or desire. It was fear of the unknown. She clasped his hand. "You're prepared to fulfill your duty, Lucas. Grace and Kyle saw to that."

"They taught me what they thought I needed to know. But—"

"King Alexander, your father, knew exactly what you needed. With all his plans, do you believe he didn't instruct them?" Penny didn't. "Those stories they used to teach you. Do you think they were Kyle and Grace's stories, or King Alexander's?"

Surprise crossed his face. "I don't know."

"I believe Alexander wrote them, and Kyle and Grace learned just as you did. He was the king and knew exactly what you need to know."

"They never said they created them. I assumed that."

"You had no reason not to assume it. They relayed them all to you. I can't imagine that Alexander didn't leave you with all the wisdom he could." Lucas's surprise faded and she added, "For what my opinion is worth, I think you'll make a wonderful king that will make your birth mother and father proud."

"Really?"

She nodded. "But I don't see that becoming king means you must forfeit your own life."

"My own life will be thousands of miles away."

"No, honey." Penny pressed a hand to his arm. "Your own life will be with you always. You are the author of it, Lucas. Your life will be what you create no matter where you are. And I think you'll best serve your parents and your country by simply being yourself."

"You think I should challenge Berthold."

"Do you really have a choice?" She paused to give him a moment to consider her question. "As I said, you are who you are, and that is King Alexander's son. You're the rightful heir. Whether or not you challenge Berthold or wear a crown, you will always be your father's rightful heir because you will always be your father's son and heir. This really is not about a crown or power or holdings, Lucas. It's who you are. Does that make sense?"

"It does." Lucas leaned back. "Which means my life here is over."

That much was true and couldn't be softened. "Boys who grow to men all leave home and chart their own course. It's their destiny."

"The people there could reject me."

Penny rolled her eyes. "Don't be ridiculous. You will charm them as you do everyone, and they will love you as much as they loved your father."

"You believe I can do this." He flattened his lips. "I would never want to harm them. I've been prepared, but was that enough?"

"I know you can do this. You'll have loyal advisors, like Gregor, to help you. And Kyle, though they'll no doubt refer to him as Kasper at some point, and you as Prince Stefan. Well, at least after you are coronated."

"If that day comes, you and Lisa must be there."

"Of course." Penny smiled. "We wouldn't be anywhere else."

A strange look crossed Lucas's face.

"What is it?" Penny asked.

He sobered even more, and worry settled in his eyes. "I failed to protect Alana. What if I fail to protect the people, too?"

Penny should have expected this. "Firstly, no one knew Alana was at risk. You will always think some subject is at risk. Just be diligent in protecting them. That's a worry of every good monarch. If you are diligent and give your people your best, that's all you or anyone else can do. You'll have to be at peace with that."

"You're not angry I didn't tell you about my suspicions on the stories sooner?"

"Lucas, you're far too bright to not have known something was not as it seemed. I wondered what held you back." She could say the same about John William and his governmental connection.

"It was Mr. Crown," Lucas confessed.

"Mark?" That surprised Penny. "What did he do?"

"When Lisa and I were little, we played police."

"I remember. When he could, Mark played with you. You were his recruits."

"He always said, "Never accuse what you cannot prove.""

Penny smiled. He did say that. Often. To the children and to her. "Yes, he did."

"Well, I couldn't prove, so…"

Penny laughed. "Mark meant a great deal to you, too, Lucas."

"He still does." Lucas looked from the wall to Penny. "I learned a lot from him, and from you. I don't know if I've ever told you that."

"You have told me everything in many ways, honey. Sometimes

words are just lagniappe. The important stuff doesn't need to be spoken. It's shown."

"Well, I guess we'd better get to bed. Five a.m. is going to come fast." Lucas stood. "Thanks, Mrs. Crown. Good night."

"Good night." Penny smiled, then reached for her book.

"He's been a very lucky person, having you in his life."

Nick. "The feeling is mutual."

He walked across the room and sat down beside her. "I didn't mean to listen in, but I found your discussion fascinating. I wouldn't have known what to tell him other than suck it up and do what you need to do."

"I never doubted he would do what he needs to do," Penny said. "He wouldn't be Lucas."

"Stefan."

"Yes." She smiled. "After all these years, I'm going to have to adjust to that."

"You'll rise to it, I am sure." Nick smiled. "Jay Voigt will be here before I leave in the morning. I wanted him with Lucas and Kyle to help you watch over them. The guards will be outside, but I don't personally know them."

Penny knew a warning when Nick uttered one. "We'll be extra vigilant."

"You'll find a weapon under your pillow. A backup, just in case you need it."

She nodded.

"If anything goes wrong tomorrow—"

"Nothing will."

"If it does, get them to Secretary Dawson right away," Nick dropped his voice. "Use my plane. The pilot has been alerted."

Another warning shone so clear in his eyes. Was Nick just being cautious or expecting something? "I will." She set the book aside. "Do you know where you're to meet?"

"I'll be told in the morning."

Wise. Even burner phones or secure lines couldn't be trusted these days. "I would feel better if you had backup."

"Gregor's orders are to go alone."

"But if there is trouble—"

"I'll have backup. Stop worrying, Mrs. Crown."

"That's like telling me to stop breathing."

"It does sound like a ridiculous request, I agree. But between us, we have the situation in hand."

Penny searched his face for any sign he was paying her lip service and found none. "Nick, thank you for everything."

He smiled. "Working with you is a privilege and a pleasure, Mrs. Crown."

"For me, too."

"I expect so, but only because you hate working divorce cases. I hope you've realized now your talents are being wasted there."

"I'm paying my dues, as all new detectives do."

"You are far too gifted, and your instincts are too honed to spend your time paying dues."

"I pay my bills spending my time as I do, but one day…"

"One day." He smiled. "Good night, Mrs. Crown."

"Be careful in the morning. I still don't like you going out alone."

"I won't be." He winked.

Still, he offered nothing more, and she knew better than to ask. "Good night, Nick."

June 16th @ 0445

The next morning, Jay arrived at 4:45.

Nick left immediately thereafter to get to the Hoff residence for the contact.

At 5:10 Penny received a text from Nick. She read it, then repeated it aloud to Lucas, Kyle, John William, and Jay. "At exactly 5:00, a lone man dressed as a postal worker made contact and required a biometric signature. Must be transmitted and confirmed before the parcel can be released. In process now."

Jay grunted. "That man doesn't have the parcel."

Penny didn't think so either. They wouldn't risk delivery until after Nick's biometrics had been verified. Too, it seemed odd that they would deliver to the Hoff home. It was a known location, which made it vulnerable. They do all their intricate advance planning and then make this delivery rookie mistake? Highly unlikely. "Nick will be in touch again soon."

Jay sipped from his coffee. "We should be there watching his back."

"They would pick up on us, Jay," Penny said. "His instructions were to come alone."

"I hate this." Lucas dropped a fisted hand to his chair arm.

"It's necessary," Kyle said. "After all that has been done, they dare not risk something like this delivery destroying it all. Have faith."

They sat and waited, drank coffee and tea and more coffee and tea, and still waited. An hour passed, then nearly another.

Finally, just after 7:00, a new text came through to Penny.

Lucas jumped to his feet. "What does it say?"

"Bayside Park. Forked oak. Sniper took out one of ours. Tires shot out on my car. Area now secure. Need Lucas here now."

"We're all going," Kyle said.

"No, we are not." Penny stood up. "If things go badly, Kyle, you'll be needed to expose the entire story. Your institutional memory will be invaluable. Jay will stay to protect you."

Lucas jutted his jaw. "Mrs. Crown, you cannot go with me."

"You don't have a new car yet, Lucas. I must drive you."

"I can drive your car. It isn't safe. He said nothing about capturing the sniper."

"He didn't." She looked Lucas right in the eye. "Which is exactly why I must go. Nick needs backup. My guess is after events there, he isn't sure who to trust. He trusts me."

Lucas opened his mouth to object, but Kyle stood and clasped his arm. "She's right, son. Nicholas has risked himself for us repeatedly. He needs Mrs. Crown now, and if she's willing, then it is she who must go."

"She'll protect me, too," Lucas said. "Putting herself in jeopardy again. And you know it."

"I know she's kept you alive thus far, and I trust she will do all she can to help you and Nicholas. Think, Lucas."

Penny gave him her most stern and unbending mom look. "Are you ready?"

Finally, his defiance fell, and Lucas relented.

When they were in the car, Penny started the engine. As she backed down the driveway, she reminded Lucas that Nick might need help, but he wouldn't bring Lucas into a situation that would harm him. He's far too seasoned and protective to do that.

"He did say the scene was secure."

He had. But he hadn't said the sniper had been arrested or neutralized. "Just in case, look in my purse and retrieve a weapon."

"You want me to carry a gun?"

"I want you able to defend yourself, should the need arise." Heading toward the park, she spared Lucas a glance. "I know for a fact Mark trained you and Lisa both, Lucas."

"It was a secret."

"Not from me, though neither you nor Lisa ever said a word."

"Mr. Crown told you?"

"Of course. We discussed it before he mentioned shooting to you or Lisa. We thought it wise you two learned properly instead of in the woods." That revealed their knowledge of the secret training going on out there to any kid who wanted it. "Better you learn from a professional."

"How did you or Mr. Crown find out about that?" Lucas sat stunned.

"Mark made it his business to find out what you two were trying to hide. As did I."

Lucas chose the .45. "I'll use this one."

"Check it out first."

"I know." He inspected it thoroughly, then put the safety back on. "Satisfactory?"

"Yes." Penny turned into the park and headed for the parking lot. "And timely."

"There are no cars, and no one in sight." Lucas continued scanning.

"Give him a second."

"Who?"

"Nick."

Moments later, Nick appeared from around a thicket of spiny bushes. He ran over to the car, then paused at Penny's window. She lowered the glass. "Good, you're here, Mrs. Crown. I wasn't sure you would get from the text to come."

"I did."

"Both of you, come with me." Nick looked at Lucas. "I'm sorry about this, but you're going to have to go back to the forked oak."

"I thought I might, as soon as I heard to come to the park." He turned his gaze to Penny. "Don't worry. It's fine."

It wasn't fine, but he would deal with it. He had no choice.

Using the islands of bushes as cover, they made their way to the small clearing of lush lawn leading to the forked oak. "Move quickly through the clearing," Nick told Lucas and Penny."

They did without incident and stopped near the tree. "There's no one here," Lucas said.

"Weapons down. They're here," Nick assured him. "Just give them a minute to react to seeing you. They've waited a very long time."

Two men in dark suits dropped out of the tree. Both wore stern expressions and seemed strained.

"Gentlemen." Nick greeted them. "The scanner, please."

"We are to do it personally," the taller of the two said.

"Fine." Nick didn't hesitate. "But touch him and you die."

A cold chill rippled through Penny. Nick meant what he'd said. No one with eyes or ears could doubt it.

The shorter of the two men stepped closer to Lucas. "Please press your right thumb and forefinger against the sensor."

Lucas looked to Nick. When he nodded, Lucas did as the man asked.

The man stepped back and pressed in a series of numbers. A long sequence that Penny assumed was encrypted code. Still, she kept her hand inside her handbag, her hand circling the grip of her .32.

Nick whispered to Penny. "We're waiting for an authorization to come in from Switzerland to release the parcel."

"Has the sniper been secured?" Penny asked.

"Yes." The taller man told her. "Just before Prince Stefan arrived."

At least one of them already believed Lucas was Stefan. Taking that as a good sign, Penny smiled.

The call came through. "Confirmation number?" The shorter man noted it, and quickly made another call. He repeated the number, then disconnected.

An armored truck drove across the park to the tree. A man exited with a box about a foot wide and two feet long. He walked directly toward Lucas.

"Stop," Nick warned him, stepping between them. "I'll check it first. Then you can give it to him."

The man didn't argue. He opened the box, allowed Nick to examine the contents, then closed it again.

"Give it to him," Nick said, waving the man to move on.

He walked the distance to Lucas and bowed. "Prince Stefan, the contents of this parcel were prepared for you by your father. They are critical to your future."

Another ally.

Lucas took the box. "Thank you."

The man returned to his truck, and the tall and short man went with him. The armored truck left the park.

"We're done here." Nick blew out a sharp breath. "Wait until we're back at the safe-house to open that, Lucas."

Fifteen minutes later, they had returned to the safe-house and were seated around the kitchen table.

"No incidents while we were there or on the way back here," Penny said on spotting the worry in John William's eyes. "The delivery person called Lucas Prince Stefan and released the parcel, so his identity is now confirmed in Lovenia."

Kyle seemed pleased by that, and Jay just a little confused.

Penny expected that. "The trouble occurred before we arrived and was handled efficiently."

Understanding crossed Jay's face.

Lucas didn't sit down. He still held the parcel. Penny sensed his hesitancy, and suggested, "Lucas, why don't you and Kyle open the box in the living room, and then you can share what you like with us."

Relief crossed his face. "Thank you, Mrs. Crown." He nodded at Kyle to come with him.

When they left the room, Nick turned to Penny. "Why did you suggest that?"

"Lucas doesn't know what to expect in that box. He's new to this, Nick. He wants to be sure he isn't revealing anything he shouldn't."

That had Nick leaning back in his seat. "Of course." He rubbed at his neck. "I wasn't thinking."

"You've just been shot at by a sniper," John William said. "Is it any wonder?"

"Shot at? In my park?" Jay demanded an explanation.

Penny's jaw went slack. "You didn't tell me the sniper shot at you."

"No one was hurt," Nick said. "Except a little bark on the forked oak."

Penny frowned at Nick's disclosure, then looked at Jay. "And later, the sniper."

"Is he in custody or dead?" Jay asked.

Nick sighed. "Dead. Federal agents took possession of the body. Matter of national security."

"Of course." Jay looked at Penny. "Thank you, Penny."

"Do you have an identity on the sniper?" Penny asked.

"Working on it," Nick said.

Penny would bet the sniper was Dirk. Of course, Nick couldn't confirm that for her to Jay, and she could be wrong.

She nodded and heard Nick's stomach grumble. "Anyone hungry?"

It seemed everyone was, so she went to the kitchen and got busy. Nick joined her to help.

They walked back to the table with platters of fresh fruit and vegetables with dip, and finger sandwiches.

"Should I get Lucas and Kyle?" Jay asked.

"Don't disturb them." Lucas would need a little time to absorb whatever was in the box. "I forgot the plates."

Nick retrieved them and then placed them on the table. Just as he took his seat, Lucas and Kyle joined them.

"Food." Lucas smiled. "I'm starving." He set the box on an empty seat beside him and filled his plate. "Should we eat first, or tell you about the box now?"

"While we eat," Nick said.

Jay and John William agreed.

Penny staved off a sigh. "Whichever you prefer, Lucas."

He wolfed down a few sandwiches and two strawberries, then reached into the box. "This is a photo of King Alexander and Queen Kerra. That little guy on his knee is me, and the girl on her lap is my sister, Brigit." Lucas smiled.

Penny so hoped that Brigit got out of Lovenia alive. Finding his sister would mean the world to Lucas.

"There's a journal of advice that passed king to king. Obviously, I haven't yet read it."

"It's a Lovenia tradition," Kyle said, "for the king to offer wisdom he's gleaned to his successor."

"Like our president passes on insight to the new president here," Penny said. Curiosity about what, if anything, King Alexander wrote to Berthold nearly overwhelmed her. "What else is in there?"

"Legal documents and a letter from King Alexander to Stefan."

"Your father to you," Nick said.

Lucas nodded. "I'm going to have to get used to that, but yes."

"Did you read the letter?" Penny asked, hoping he would share something from it.

"I did." Lucas looked at Penny. "He speaks of the coup and Berthold's guilt. The advice he left in the king's book was for me, not Berthold. Then he talked about the arrangements he'd made to get me to safety."

Kyle interjected. "And he stated his fervent hope that Stefan would return and rule his country."

"Did he mention the family fortune?" Nick asked.

"He did, and it is secure." Kyle smiled. "Exactly as we planned all those years ago."

"Mrs. Crown, you look disappointed." Lucas studied her.

"No, not at all. I just hoped… never mind. This is all wonderful news."

Lucas's eyes gleamed. "He spoke at length of his and my mother's love for me, Brigit, and Lovenia." He smiled. "Is that better?"

Penny swallowed hard. "Perfect."

Kyle cleared his throat. "There are proofs of Stefan's identity that cannot be disputed and the name of a contact at the State Department who assisted with bringing Stefan, Grace, and me to the United States. This contact will also assist in Stefan's return to Lovenia and in claiming his throne."

Nicholas didn't seem surprised at all. Not even a little. That contact must be responsible for involving Nick, through John William, of course."

Nick confirmed it with a knowing look Penny easily recognized. "He'll be in touch anytime now."

Adam? Secretary Dawson? Someone else? Unsure, Penny held her questions and they finished eating, chatting about the parcel's contents. Later, Penny pulled Lucas aside. "Do you need to talk to Dr. Mason to work through all this? It's a lot to absorb."

"No. I really am fine." He paused, then amended his words. "It's overwhelming, but when I think about it, my parents—Kyle and Grace, I mean—have prepared me for this my whole life."

"They have with their stories, but if you need help sorting it out, I'll be happy to call her."

"I don't need her, Mrs. Crown. I have my dad, you, Lisa, and John William. I always have."

She patted his arm. "You do. But if you change your mind, let me know."

Nick took a phone call. "We've arrested a team of six men that were here to prevent Lucas from discovering he is Stefan."

A hit squad of assassins. Penny looked to Nick. "Berthold?"

"We expect he issued the order," Nick said. "But that has not yet been confirmed." He focused on Lucas. "There's a plane waiting to take you to Washington. I'll be escorting you. The contact your father spoke of in the letter will meet you there. He'll help you reclaim your crown and get you and Kyle back to Lovenia."

Penny frowned. "What about Berthold? He won't welcome Lucas with open arms, Nick."

"He's been arrested. Christopher Gregor is taking care of things until Prince Stefan arrives and can be coronated." Nick smiled, looked at Kyle and Lucas. "We can go whenever you two are ready."

"Lucas." Penny clasped his arm. "Please call Lisa before you go. She will miss you so much."

"I'll do that now," he said, pulling out his phone and stepping away for privacy. He motioned to Penny. "I will miss her, too, and she must go to Oxford."

"Honestly, I can't afford it, but—"

"Don't worry about that. It will work out. Lisa must go to Oxford, Mrs. Crown. It's been her dream for as long as I can remember."

"I know." Penny frowned. "But I have to pay for it, and I just can't. I started to say—"

He put a hand to her arm. "She is receiving a full scholarship. She just hasn't been notified yet." Lucas sent Penny a sheepish smile. "I wanted to see which college she would choose. She was aware of the money issue and told me she was going to the University of Georgia because of it. A philanthropist I know, then stepped in."

"John William?" Penny asked.

"No, though he would have," Lucas said. "Kasper Hoffman."

"Kyle?" Penny paused, not sure what to make of that. "Why?"

"For the same reason you do all you do and worry about me."

Lucas smiled. "He loves Lisa like a daughter. Haven't you noticed that only she has been welcome in our home all these years?"

Of course, Penny had noticed. "Lisa knew all about the fairytales."

He nodded. "She was often there during the telling." Lucas grunted. "I should have listened to her. She warned me early on there was more to them than I was seeing. That we both were being trained. Clearly, she did see, but she refused to tell me a thing. She said I would learn for myself when the timing was right."

"She knew?" Penny's jaw dropped.

"I can't say for sure when, but looking back, I believe she did realize the stories were true."

Penny frowned. "That would have been helpful to know through all this."

"She was protecting me." Lucas smiled again. "It runs in your family." His smile disappeared and he looked her straight in the eye. "You and Nick will be at the airport, right?"

Penny nodded.

"And you and Lisa will come to the coronation. I know that's a lot to ask, but we'll arrange everything, and I really want you both to be there. John William, too, if he wouldn't mind and Dr. Handley says he is okay to travel."

"We will do our best." Beyond Lucas's shoulder, Nick was fidgeting, eager to go. "Call Lisa now. The troops are getting restless."

He spoke to Lisa nearly ten minutes and likely would have talked longer but Nick interrupted. "Stefan, you've a call." Nick lifted his phone. "It's the President."

Lucas spoke to him briefly, and then turned to Nick and said something that had Nick nodding and reaching for the phone. He quickly dialed and barked orders about something, then hung up.

Nick told Lucas, "Tell Mrs. Crown to phone Lisa and let her know her transport will be there in fifteen minutes."

Lucas joined Penny. "Lisa will be here. I promised I wouldn't leave without seeing her."

Penny smiled. "I'll let my parents know."

"You heard Nick then?" Lucas asked.

"Lisa probably heard him without a phone." Penny smiled and made the call.

01700

The reunion took place just outside the plane that would take Stefan and Kasper to Washington. John William stood near Penny and Nick and watched Lucas and Lisa embrace.

"I always thought the two of them would wind up together," John William said. He glanced at Penny. "Didn't you?"

"At times, but then Alana came along, and I knew she was right for him." Penny sighed. "I so wish he could have had the life he wanted with her."

"He'll have a full life, Mrs. Crown." Nick assured her. "So will Lisa."

"He'll be a wonderful king," Penny said with conviction. "He will do his best."

Christopher Gregor exited the plane and walked straight over to Penny, where he passed her an envelope. "Don't open this until after we're gone."

She nodded. "I thought you were in Lovenia taking care of things."

"Stealth visit." Gregor smiled. "I'll return before morning. I just had to—"

"See Prince Stefan and Kasper as themselves?" Penny smiled.

"See you, Mrs. Crown." Gregor's leathery face wrinkled the skin around his eyes. "To tell you in person how deeply we regret Alana's death."

"No one was supposed to die," she repeated what Kyle had told her.

Guilt and regret rippled across his face. "The guilty party will face trial."

"Thank you for telling me," Penny said. "Does Lucas know?" It would help him. Give him closure.

"He will at the appropriate time. That, I promise." Gregor cleared his throat. "On another matter, King Alexander once planned to set up a scholarship fund in Queen Kerra's name at the university. We will do that shortly and, with your permission, make it a joint scholarship, honoring Queen Kerra and Alana."

"That would be wonderful." Lucas would love Alana being honored and remembered along with his mother. "Thank you, Gregor."

"Thank you for being so devoted to Stefan and Kasper on behalf of all of us who diligently serve our country. You and your family's steady hand has enormously influenced the boy and the man." He pointed to the envelope. "That is personal, for you alone. Again, please do not open it until after we've gone."

"All right."

Gregor returned to the plane, nudging Lucas to come. Kyle had said his goodbyes and stepped inside a few minutes earlier.

Lucas and Lisa said their last goodbye and he turned for the plane. Lisa walked back toward Penny but kept on going. As she passed Penny and Nick, she snagged John William's arm. "Come with me. I promised to go to the car and not watch him leave."

"Your daughter is in love with him." Nick whispered to Penny.

"I think she has been her whole life." Penny gave Nick a bittersweet smile. "But I think she's only come to realize it."

They watched in silence as Stefan's plane took off and kept watching until it disappeared.

Nick looked back at Penny, clearly seeing the tears rolling down her cheeks. "I guess you'll be returning to your divorce cases now." His expression softening, he touched her face, silently drying her tears.

"They will be even more boring after all this, but until my dues are paid…"

"So, what is in the envelope?" Nick asked.

A plane she recognized as Nick's moved into position on the private runway. "I don't know."

"Well, open it."

She ripped the envelope and slid out a check, unable to hide her surprise. "For investigative services?"

"Oxford money." Nick grunted. "Lisa will be thrilled."

"She will. Nick, I want you to know that I didn't do anything for Lucas for money."

"I'm aware of that, Mrs. Crown. You've always helped Lucas." He met her gaze. "You've always loved him."

"Thank you for seeing that." She sniffed. "I suppose you'll be returning to…wherever it is you go next."

"Washington first, for a short time."

"For Lucas?"

"That's classified." Nick smiled and winked.

"I can rest easy then."

"We make a good team, Mrs. Crown. I never thought I would like working with a partner, but I have enjoyed working with you."

The pilot appeared at the open door of Nick's plane, signaling they were ready to depart. "Ah, it's time for me to go."

"Goodbye Nick. Thank you for everything." Penny smiled, feeling as if she was losing a small part of herself. Not who she had been, but the woman she had become.

"Goodbye." He walked up the stairs toward the open door, suddenly stopped, turned, and then came back down the stairs.

"What's wrong?" Worry flitted through Penny, and then their gazes locked. Was she hallucinating? Did she dare to believe what she saw in his eyes? Her breath hitched. Perhaps there was life on the other side of Mark Crown.

Nick studied her face, and slowly smiled. "Mrs. Crown, do you have a passport?"

Penny smiled.

A NOTE FROM VICKI

Dear Readers,

First and foremost, I want to thank you for following me in whatever I write. That is the highest honor and one that humbles me. Expressing your trust in me is something I never take for granted, and I so appreciate your willingness to come along with me on the journey through whatever story comes next.

This matters a great deal to me. When I started writing, I promised myself two things: One, I would share what I could about writing with other writers. That was a pay-it-forward promise to never forget all who shared their wisdom with me.

The second promise was to never publish a book I didn't love. I've done my best to never write one I didn't love. But it has been your willingness to step into the unknown with me, between the covers of my books, that has enabled me to keep that promise. For that, I am eternally grateful.

I hope you've enjoyed NO ONE WAS SUPPOSED TO DIE. I plan on writing a second, connected novel, NO ONE WAS SUPPOSED TO KNOW. All I can tell you right now is it is about the search for the truth about Briget. What happened to her the

A NOTE FROM VICKI

night of the coup? Is she dead or alive? If dead, what happened to her? If alive, where is she? What has her life been like?

I'm eager to write this story to find out, and to see what Penny Crown, Lisa, Lucas, Nick and John William get into next. I hope you are eager to read it, too!

If you enjoyed NO ONE WAS SUPPOSED TO DIE, please consider posting a review on it. You have no idea how much difference those make in getting word out, or how much they are appreciated by authors and readers alike.

Until next time, I wish you happy reading and many…

Blessings,
Vicki Hinze

ABOUT THE AUTHOR

VICKI HINZE is the author of nearly sixty novels, nonfiction books and hundreds of articles published in more than sixty-three countries. She and her books have received many prestigious awards and nominations, including her selection for *Who's Who in the World* (as a writer and educator), selection for Trademark's *Women of Distinction-Honors Edition*, nominations for Career Achievement and Reviewer's Choice Awards for Best Series and Suspense Storyteller of the Year, Best Romantic Suspense Storyteller of the Year and Best Romantic Intrigue Novel of the Year.

She co-created an innovative, open-ended continuity series of single-title romance novels, an innovative suspense series, and has helped to establish sub-genres in military women's fiction (suspense and intrigue and action and adventure) and in military romantic-thriller novels. Hinze loves genre-blending and blazing new trails for readers and other authors. She is a former columnist for Social-In Global Network and radio host of *Everyday Woman*.

For early access to new releases and more, subscribe to the monthly newsletter at:

http://mad.ly/signups/82943/join

ALSO BY VICKI HINZE

Penny Crown Files

No One Was Supposed to Die

The Philanthropists

The Guardian

Family Secrets Series

Blood Strangers

StormWatch Series

Deep Freeze

Bringing Home Christmas

S.A.S.S. Unit Series

Black Market Body Double | The Sparks Broker | The Mind Thief | Operation Stealing Christmas | S.A.S.S. Confidential

Breakdown Series

so many secrets | her deepest fear (Short Read)

Down and Dead, Inc. Series

Down and Dead in Dixie | Down and Dead in Even

Down and Dead in Dallas

Shadow Watchers (Crossroads Crisis Center related)

The Marked Star | The Marked Bride | The Marked Witness

Crossroads Crisis Center Series

Forget Me Not | Deadly Ties | Not This Time

The Reunion Collection

Her Perfect Life | Mind Reader | Duplicity |

Lost, Inc.

Survive the Night | Christmas Countdown |

Torn Loyalties

War Games Series

Body Double | Double Vision | Double Dare | Smokescreen: Total Recall | Kill Zone

The Lady Duo

Lady Liberty | Lady Justice

Military

Shades of Gray | Acts of Honor | All Due Respect

Paranormal Romantic Suspense

Legend of the Mist | Maybe This Time

Seascape Novels

Beyond the Misty Shore | Upon a Mystic Tide |

Beside a Dreamswept Sea

Other

Girl Talk: Letters Between Friends | My Imperfect Valentine | Invitation to a Murder | Bulletproof | The Madonna Key (series co-creator) | Before the White Rose | Invidia

Multiple-Author Collections (Limited Time)

Dangerous Desires | My Evil Valentine | Risky Brides | Smart Women and Dangerous Men | Christmas Heroes | Love is Murder | Cast of Characters | A Message from Cupid | Seeing Fireworks

Nonfiction

In Case of Emergency: What You Need to Know When I Can't Tell You | One Way to Write a Novel | Writing in the Fast Lane | All About Writing to Sell |

Mistakes Writers Make and How-To Avoid Them |

Between a Rock & Hard Place, Grief During the Pandemic, Job Loss & Toolbox Gems

For a complete listing visit http://vickihinze.com/books

Made in the USA
Columbia, SC
08 January 2025